THE DARE

ALSO BY NATASHA PRESTON

The Cellar

Awake

The Cabin

You Will Be Mine

The Lost

The Twin

The Lake

The Fear

The Island

The Haunting

THE DARE

NATASHA PRESTON

DELACORTE PRESS

This is a work of fiction. Names, characters, places, and incidents either are the product of the author's imagination or are used fictitiously. Any resemblance to actual persons, living or dead, events, or locales is entirely coincidental.

Text copyright © 2024 by Natasha Preston
Cover photographs copyright © 2024: Silas Manhood/Trevillion Images (woods); Dave Wall/Arcangel (car); Miguel Sobriera/Trevillion Images (rose)

All rights reserved. Published in the United States by Delacorte Press, an imprint of Random House Children's Books, a division of Penguin Random House LLC, New York.

Delacorte Press is a registered trademark and the colophon is a trademark of Penguin Random House LLC.

GetUnderlined.com

Educators and librarians, for a variety of teaching tools, visit us at RHTeachersLibrarians.com

Library of Congress Cataloging-in-Publication Data is available upon request.
ISBN 978-0-593-70406-6 (tr. pbk.) — ISBN 978-0-593-70407-3 (ebook)

The text of this book is set in 11-point Janson MT.
Interior design by Ken Crossland

Printed in the United States of America
6th Printing
First Edition

Random House Children's Books supports the First Amendment and celebrates the right to read.

Penguin Random House LLC supports copyright. Copyright fuels creativity, encourages diverse voices, promotes free speech, and creates a vibrant culture. Thank you for buying an authorized edition of this book and for complying with copyright laws by not reproducing, scanning, or distributing any part in any form without permission. You are supporting writers and allowing Penguin Random House to publish books for every reader.

For everyone who loves to relax by spending days in a state of constant anxiety and stress reading about murder

THE DARE

1

Monday, May 22

Senior pranks are a rite of passage. Sometimes they're fun and sometimes they're killer.

They're the last dumb thing you do in high school before you get to do a whole bunch of dumb things in college.

But if you go to my school, they can stop your college dreams *dead.*

Sophomore year I couldn't wait to participate in senior pranks, but in the last two years the pranks have really escalated. The Wilder brothers—putting their last name to good use—took over. Five of them, all a year apart in age and all headed for prison if it weren't for their parents' money, came up with a way to raise the stakes.

Everett

Emmett

Rhett—*ugh*

Garrett

Truett

Their parents really went with that matching-name theme. No wonder they have issues.

I think I remember a kid ribbing Everett about it once. Only once. There's a rumor that the kid had to move to another country.

The brothers all like to exert their dominance. They assign you a prank. A dare, really. If you're brave enough—or stupid enough—to turn it down, a forfeit is forced upon you.

Arrests, expulsions, not walking at graduation, and even college rejections are what we face now. That is if we accept the dares . . . *or* if we don't. Saying no has consequences too.

I watch Rhett laugh and shove one of his followers as he makes his way into the cafeteria, cutting in the line because he doesn't have to wait like the rest of us.

My best friend, Lucia, twirls her shiny black hair around her finger. "Ignore him," she says, pushing what I think is supposed to be a burrito away from her. She's curled up with her boyfriend, Jesse, so far evading the eyes of any teachers monitoring for PDA.

Jesse throws a scowl in Rhett's direction, still holding a grudge against him for getting starting quarterback at the beginning of the year. Jesse and Atlas are better. Rhett's family is richer.

"The dares are going to start soon," I say, turning my nose up. "Rhett's probably already plotting."

With only three weeks left of school, senior pranks are right around the corner. Don't get me wrong, I'm going to go all out to prank Principal Fuller, but I don't want to get messed up in Rhett's games.

Atlas leans in, kissing my cheek. "Nothing's going to stop you and your big brain from going to UCLA."

Last year Billy Halsten had his place at Ohio State stripped because the fire he set in a trash can spread and gutted a 7-Eleven. It was his dare from the second-born Wilder brother. Not to destroy a building but to keep the fire department busy while someone else stole a CPR mannequin.

Since then, the whole thing has made me want to skip the last few weeks of school altogether. There's no way Rhett is going to listen to Fuller's warnings.

We're to keep it safe. No stupid stuff.

The Wilder brothers only do stupid stuff, and I think Rhett might be the worst one of them all.

And I already know Atlas and Jesse won't back down from a dare.

"Nothing will stop college because I'm not playing," I tell him. "We're sticking with eggs and glitter and balloons. That's enough."

Atlas pouts, and I can feel myself starting to relent. He's ridiculously good-looking—dark skin, full lips, football player's physique. He's been mine for the last three years. "Come on, babe, we'll stick to the boring pranks, I promise. But we can't miss out on this."

The ones we've planned are boring. Kind of. They'll annoy the hell out of Fuller, so it'll still be funny. He'll be cleaning glitter from his office long after we've gone.

"He's right," Luce says, jabbing a finger in my arm as Jesse bites her neck and makes her squeal. She pushes his head. "We're not skipping this just because people have been total idiots in the past."

"So you're going to listen to Rhett?" I ask, eyeing them as if they've been taken over by aliens.

Jesse scoffs, runs a hand through his white-blond hair, and glares at Rhett again. I think he hates him as much as I do. "We're not going to let him threaten us. Their family doesn't have as much power as he thinks. If there's something we don't want to do, we won't."

A burst of noise gets my attention. Ruthie cackles when Rhett pokes her in the hips. They take a seat at the table next to us, and he looks over, smirking at me. His eyes are the darkest blue I've ever seen, looking nearly black against his light skin and sandy-blond locks. He just looks rich, you know. The preppy, perfect hair and expensive clothes. He has a ring on his thumb, as if he belongs to some underground organization.

All the brothers wear them, and no one knows why, but they look ridiculous.

I've lost count of the times he's tried to break Atlas and me up, despite having Ruthie hanging off his every word.

He's a typical bored rich kid who's never had to deal with the consequences of any of his actions. It's why he and his brothers hijacked senior pranks.

And he was once my best friend.

He smiles again and I turn away.

Hate, hate, hate.

Atlas, unlike me, is still staring at him.

"Forget him," I say. "He's not worth it."

"I really wish someone would do something about him," Jesse mutters, his light eyes trying to laser into Rhett's head.

Atlas barks a laugh. "Like what?"

"Yeah, like what?" I ask, genuinely invested now.

"I don't know," Jesse says. "But I think we should figure it out."

"You want to mess with a Wilder?" Luce asks, giving him a look as if she thinks he's lost his mind. Luce is too nice and a total rule follower. She wouldn't even pack a fizzy drink on a field trip if you weren't supposed to.

I want to roll my eyes. Not because I think it's a bad idea—because someone needs to stand up to that family—but because it's a waste of our energy when we'll be going to college in a few months.

We'll be out of here, and Rhett will be at a college in state because he's not allowed to go far. His parents are *big* on control; all the brothers have gone to the same college, and all will get an apartment near their parents after so they can join the family business.

I mean, no wonder they act out. Their whole lives have already been planned, and they don't get a choice in any of it. Sounds suffocating as hell.

I still think they're all assholes, though.

"I'm just saying, I'm sure there's some way we can turn these pranks around on him," Jesse says.

"I'm game," I tell him. "We could paint little pink bunnies on his expensive car."

"Why bunnies?" Jesse asks, chuckling.

"Why not?"

"Fair. He'd hate it."

I smile. "And that's all that matters."

Atlas side-eyes me, tapping his fingers on the table. He knows that Rhett and I were close in elementary and middle school—they all do, but I've never really spoken about it.

Atlas looks like he's about to say something, but we're distracted by screams of laughter. I look up as four guys from the football team walk into the cafeteria wearing cheerleader outfits, complete with pom-poms and paint stripes on their cheeks.

The room erupts with cheers and applause.

"Why didn't you do that too!" I say, playfully hitting Atlas's arm.

Luce laughs. "Yeah, come on, I would've *paid* to see that."

The boys don't have time to answer because the honorary cheerleaders begin to chant and jump around. Max spells out "school is shit" with his arms, and I think I actually see steam coming from Fuller's ears.

"They're good," I say, cheering and throwing a wadded-up napkin at them. Max and Charlie both leap up and attempt the splits in midair. It's a hilarious fail, and they both laugh along with everyone else.

This is the dumb stuff we're supposed to do, not burning down buildings.

Fuller is on his feet as the four boys curtsy, holding their skirts to the side. He smiles as he approaches, but it's easy to see the irritation on his face.

"All right, the fun's over," Fuller says. "Five minutes left, so hurry up."

Luce and I jump up, knowing this is our chance, leaving the boys chatting to some guys on the team.

We make our way to Fuller's office with the supplies in my bag. He always walks around the field for the last few minutes of lunchtime, after checking the cafeteria. It wouldn't surprise me if he sits out on his porch watching his neighbors.

We easily slip past the secretaries as they dash to the staff room for their iced coffee fix.

Luce giggles as I look over my shoulder, palm resting on the handle of Fuller's door.

"Go," I say, pushing the door open and slipping inside.

She closes the door behind us and tugs the zipper of my bag, almost bending me backward. "We need to hurry, I'm already sweating," Luce says. "This stuff always makes me feel like I could vomit."

"Can you not pull me over while we do it?" I say, twisting around and sliding the bag off my shoulder. "And don't stress, we're supposed to do pranks like these."

It doesn't hit the floor, thankfully, because she has hold of it, reaching in to get the water-and-glitter-filled balloons. I could only fit three in there because we've filled them as much as we dared. The latex is stretched to the max, almost making them completely translucent.

I take one out carefully, wincing as it bulges, threatening a heavy dose of karma.

"Where are we putting these?" she asks, gritting her brace-covered teeth.

"One on his chair for sure."

"You think he'll sit on it?"

"He doesn't need to, he just needs to pull the chair out and let it drop. It'll explode all over this fancy rug under his desk," I say, toeing the edge of it.

She laughs. "Okay, where else?"

"That display cabinet. We'll balance it on the edge of a shelf and close the glass door carefully."

"He'll see it."

"Doesn't matter. Use yours. It's darker, so he won't see the glitter."

I place a balloon on the chair and gently roll it back under the desk. Luce puts hers on the shelf and shuts the door, holding her hand out in case she needs to catch it. I don't bother telling her that it'll explode all over her if it drops into her hand, because, frankly, that would be hilarious.

For the last one, I balance it on top of the bulb in his tall lamp. It's right beside his desk, so if it bursts while he's sitting, he'll get wet and glittery. The balloon rests on the bulb inside the shade.

Then, because I don't want to kill anyone, I pull the plug out of the wall so he can't turn it on without noticing there's a balloon up there.

"Bit dangerous, Marley," Luce says.

I hold up the plug in my hand, and then let it drop to the floor. "I've got it covered."

She nods. "Okay, because that was almost a dumbass Rhett dare."

I point at her, then grab my bag. "Rude. Let's go, lunch is almost over."

She opens the door and we sneak out, leaving behind three glittery bombs and the promise of a bad day for Fuller.

"Think he'll find it funny?" she asks as I close the door.

"Absolutely not."

I look back over my shoulder just as Mrs. Bell and Miss Romero return to their desks, holding oversized tumblers.

We split up in the hallway. I head to math, usually absolute hell, but it's the end of the school year and we're playing an escape room game.

Our town is huge on memories, and the school does way more for the end of senior year, so we don't finish as early as other schools in the state. I could be home for summer break by now. Unfair.

Up ahead, Rhett leans against the wall, blocking the door I need to go through. As if he gets to decide where I go.

"You need to move," I say.

He lifts a brow, a cocky smirk on his lips. "Do I?"

I go to push past him, but he sidesteps so I can't get by.

"Rhett, just go away."

"I know your parents wouldn't be happy with how rude you're being."

"And I know your parents wouldn't be happy with you being a jackass."

I meet his smug smile with my own, mirroring his contempt. He's the one who ended our friendship, so I don't know why he insists on messing with me. What's the point? I'm so over his crap.

"Everything okay?" Fuller asks, walking the hallways like a security guard. As someone who loves order, he's going to hate the next three weeks.

"Fine," Rhett says, stepping back. "Just chatting with my oldest friend."

I scoff, wanting to disagree, but I also want Fuller to go to his office and Rhett to go away.

Fuller nods and continues on his way. I press my lips together to stop myself from laughing as I watch him head to his office.

"What did you do?" Rhett asks, following my gaze.

"Shhh."

I can't see from here—Fuller's office is too far away—but if things go to plan, I'll definitely hear.

"Come on, what prank did you pull?" he asks, trying to sound bored. If he didn't care about knowing, he would've left.

"Water-and-glitter bombs."

He rolls his eyes. "Are you seven?"

I don't have time to think of a witty retort because Fuller shouts out, his booming voice carrying all the way to the end of the hall.

"How many are in there?" Rhett asks, trying not to smile.

"Two more. I wish I knew which one that was."

"Go take a look."

"I'm not stupid. He'll know it was me."

There's another shout. Rhett and I jump back just as Fuller walks out of the room. I only catch a glimpse, but he's wet and sparkly. Ha.

Rhett rubs his mouth, his way of pretending that he's got an itch and he's not amused. It's a classic Rhett move and one he should know I can see through.

I open the door to math, but before I disappear into the classroom, Rhett says, "Things are about to get very interesting for you and your friends."

"Whatever," I mutter, not giving him the satisfaction of seeing how nervous that makes me. I'm still on the high of Fuller and the water balloons, so I'm not really thinking about what my nemesis has planned.

He can bring it.

What's the worst that could happen?

2

After school I leave the building with Luce. Hanging over the gate to the vegetable garden near the science block is Fuller's rug.

Luce and I both laugh at the wet patch and the shine that makes it look like it's from the Cullens' house in *Twilight.*

"He has a different shirt on," Luce says.

"Yep. Mission accomplished."

"I wish we'd planted a camera in there."

"Next time," I reply.

We walk along the riverside, the lush trees stretching what feels like miles above my head, keeping the path in the shade.

"What do you think my prank will be?" Luce asks.

"Who knows," I reply, my mind drifting back to what Rhett said outside math. Things are about to get interesting for me *and* my friends. I don't want to worry Luce, because she will totally stress if she thinks that Rhett is going to give us the worst dares. Besides, he'll likely only give the worst ones to me.

"We're not doing the dumb stuff, remember. Replacing the

photos in Fuller's office with ones of Taylor Swift, that's the kind of thing we'll stick to."

I cut her a look. "Why does everyone seem to have such a short memory? You do remember how these dares have gone wrong both years?"

Nudging me, she replies, "No one's forgotten, Marley. We all remember and we're ready this year. You let Rhett get to you too often, and before you say anything, I know he winds you up."

"He gets on every single one of my seven trillion nerves."

She laughs, nudging me. "It's his superpower. But we have the last three weeks of school coming up, and I'm going to miss you guys *so* much. Can we try extra hard to ignore Rhett and have the best time? *Please?*"

As the only one with a bad feeling about this, I start to wonder if I'm just being dramatic. I mean, every school does senior pranks, right? Ours is the first I've heard of that *really* went wrong.

Sighing, I relent and say, "I'll try to lighten up."

"Try hard. Like, *hard,* or you're going to regret it after graduation. Look, the door to Creepy Arthur's creepy house is wide-open. What do you think he's doing?"

I look across to the mountain in the distance, where "Creepy Arthur" lives. The river curls around his property, avoiding it as if it knows there's something wrong with it. Set on about twenty acres of land, his huge decaying house is both stunning and, as Luce said, creepy.

Arthur is in his sixties and a total loner. No one visits him, except for his grandson, George, once a year, and he only comes into town to get supplies. He rattles around in that house, letting it slowly fall apart around him. He's had tons of offers on it, from developers to locals wanting to renovate. He always says no . . . yet continues to do nothing with it.

I'd take the money and run. It's worth a *fortune.*

The Wilders have offered him millions, apparently. I'm not sure what it's worth or why they'd want it, since their house is bigger and, you know, not crumbling. But it could all be a rumor.

Most things around here are.

"Do you think he's okay?" I ask, straining to see from this distance. But the only thing visible from here is the house. We have no chance of seeing through the door or any of the windows, two of which have been boarded up for the last year.

A couple of times, Arthur has "disappeared." Last year it was the mailman who let the cops know because he hadn't collected a package from his porch in two days. But it turned out that he'd just been hiking and fishing down the mountain.

"I'm not going in there, so don't even suggest it! His house is haunted," Luce says with a straight face.

I stop dead in my tracks, staring at my science-minded best friend and trying to figure out who's taken over her body. "Tell me you don't actually believe that."

She throws her hands up. "Well, I don't know, do I? Things have happened there that can't be explained."

"Such as?"

"How many people have gone in there and felt that weird vibe? Like something isn't quite right."

"That *not quite right* thing, Luce, is breaking and entering. You let yourself into someone's house and you start to feel a bit paranoid. Come on, you know it's not haunted."

A shudder visibly ripples across her body. "Fine, but you have to admit the house is spooky and Arthur's weird."

"I'll give you that. I've only been in there twice, once with George. He told me his grandad doesn't care about it anymore, thinks he's only staying to piss the Wilders off for wanting to buy him out. What do you think is going on? I've never seen the door left open like that."

"Pass. He's probably doing some work outside," she says, taking her phone out of her pocket at the same time we both get an alert.

Groaning, I open the group message, titled SENIOR DARES, my heart in my mouth.

Rhett:

It's time seniors! Creek 9pm. U know what happens if ur not there.

We don't, in fact, know what will happen, because he hasn't laid out any forfeits to scare us into following through with the stupid dares. None of us want to find out, though.

"Looks like it's starting," Luce says, her tanned skin turning rather pale. She's now stripped of her earlier confidence and enthusiasm, her dark eyes full to the brim with worry. With a place at Vanderbilt in the fall, she also has a lot to lose.

Why risk your future for some dumbass dare a juvenile delinquent has given you?

This was always coming, and since it's Monday and we only have three weeks left, it makes sense to kick it off now.

"Do you think any of the pranks Rhett has in mind are also on Fuller's authorized list?" I ask, laughing.

The sound is hollow, and I wince at how nervous I sound, unease growing in my gut like black mold.

My gut is rarely wrong.

"Not a chance," she replies, shoving the phone back into her pocket. "Are you going?"

We start walking again, the open door to Arthur's house forgotten. "I don't want to . . . but I kind of do. Do you think he actually has something on us?"

"It's not like we've killed a person, Marley. What could he have?"

She makes a solid point. The worst thing I've done is forgotten to reply to messages or call people back. Hardly a crime and not something I think any college would care about.

Still, we look at each other, both thinking the same thing. "We should go . . . just to observe," she says.

And that is exactly how people get pulled into the game.

The Wilders have raised the stakes with the pranks, and that's fine, it's a laugh, but there is no risk to them, not with all their money. But without risk is it even fun?

Luce and I could've been caught in Fuller's office earlier. It was part of the thrill. I can still feel the rush I got from sneaking in and out.

"Yeah, we'll observe," I agree. "Atlas and Jesse will want to go. I think Jesse is hoping for something that he can use to mess with Rhett."

"Like what?"

"No clue. Maybe he'll dare us to spray-paint cars. That way we really could turn it around on him."

"Paint those bunnies on his flashy car. I'd do it with my key," she adds, laughing and linking her arm through mine, though we're practically at her house now.

"See you tonight, I guess," she says, dropping my arm.

"Love ya," I reply, and walk on.

• • •

The sun set a little while ago but it's not that dark out. The sky sparkles with thousands of stars that stretch as far as I can see; it looks like someone dropped a bag of diamonds on navy silk. Or like Fuller's rug, post glitter bomb.

It's so pretty here, but after weeks of unrelenting sun, everything that was green is slowly turning yellow and crusty. The singed grass barely holding in there.

I make a left and walk down the valley to the creek, Arthur's house looming in the distance. I do a double take and realize that his door is now closed, and that makes me feel a whole lot better about being out here alone.

Arthur Nelson has never done anything wrong, other than hate the Wilder family, and that hardly makes him a bad person, but the mystery surrounding him and his lack of human interaction makes people talk.

Gossip is an occupation in our town.

I don't know what to believe. He could be a kingpin or a serial killer or a man who just wants to be left alone. Can we really blame him for not being involved in the town? A town he cofounded with Samuel Wilder, Rhett's grandad, before he was left behind?

I take the shortcut, my calf muscles burning as I carefully walk down the steep incline. Up ahead I can hear muffled voices, like they're speaking to me through a door. Trees loom over my head, and as I move deeper, they swallow me whole.

The brittle sticks and leaves beneath my feet crunch and snap, announcing my arrival.

There's a strict NO OPEN FLAME warning posted.

Note to self: don't accept any dares if matches are involved. The whole mountain would go up in smoke.

I leap over the stream that links the creek and river together and dart back into the forest in front of it. The hovering trees watch down over me like giants tracking my path. They're easily over two hundred feet tall in this part and so dense that the branches look like they're holding hands. Even during the day, they block out all sunlight, preventing much else besides moss from growing.

Two years ago, Rhett's older brother dared his classmates Bryany and Elizabeth to camp here overnight. They saw a bear and freaked out, getting lost for an hour before making it out of the woods. There was a search party because they'd managed to make a frantic call to Elizabeth's dad, who didn't know where she was, before losing the signal.

I never understood why Rhett's eldest brother made them do that; it wasn't a prank on the school, but it was the start of the shift.

The high from putting baby powder in the hand dryers and watching someone getting covered in white was no longer enough.

Rhett and I used to do our own version of parkour in the mountains and woods. We'd be out for hours building dens, jumping to rivers from a higher spot on the mountain each time, and making campfires. So yeah, I understand wanting to take risks and chasing that adrenaline rush you can only get from doing something outside your comfort zone. But why force others to do it?

My stomach clenches in the gnarly grip of anxiety as I move deeper. The trees could be the only other thing in the world out here. I should've gone the long way, where I wouldn't be able to freak myself out.

Just keep going.

Rhett's games haven't even started yet, so it's not like someone's first dare is going to be scaring the crap out of me.

The woods are doing a good enough job of that.

I force myself to move deeper into the shadows. The thick trees start to ease up ahead, giving each other personal space and allowing those who pass through to breathe.

I walk the trodden path, a shortcut from the outskirts of town to the creek. The Wilders live closest to the creek, so Rhett basically thinks he owns it. But it's not on their land.

Another few steps and I'm past the dense vegetation. The incline dips sharply and my feet move faster than I intended. I stumble, my arms wheeling, and then I stop at the bottom, the tips of my shoes buried in the muddy sand.

I look up at the sound of laughter. Rhett leaps over the shallow stream, on his way to the creek. He ignores me, other than finding my stumble amusing.

It's on the tip of my tongue to ask why he's walking to the creek from that direction, but he's likely been off somewhere plotting. There's a shack in the woods that we all meet at to party in the summer.

I need to remember to look where I'm walking, watch out for things that might fall when I open doors, and check the toilet. All things last year's seniors did that I don't want to be victim of.

I let him get ahead and then follow. We'd look weird if anyone could see us, ten feet apart and going in the same direction. I bet I look like one of his admirers. Girls fawn over him; it's all the money and the pretty face—not the personality.

He looks over his shoulder and laughs for a second time.

My patience evaporates. "What do you want?"

"Nothing." His smile couldn't be more fake if he tried. Devious twilight eyes sparkle like the stars above us. There's nothing pretty about his—they're all ego and the desire to meddle in other people's lives.

I grit my teeth to the point where they might snap. He gets under my skin, more so since last year when he accused me of cheating from him on a test. It was settled pretty quickly when the teacher saw that our answers were nothing alike, but it still scared me. Accusations like that have a way of following you around.

That was when I realized just how far he was willing to go to ease his boredom. Before that he mostly ignored me. I get whiplash from his mood changes. Friends to nothing to enemies. I wish he would leave me alone.

"Just keep walking, yeah. I'm sure you're dying to tell us what pranks you've thought up to make your life feel less tragic."

He grips his heart, turning to face me. I stop walking, not wanting to be anywhere near him. "I'm rich, Marley, and you're the scholarship queen waiting for handouts to pay your way through college."

I've heard that enough times from him for it to bounce off me now. His words used to cut, but I'm not ashamed to have worked hard for those scholarships.

"I have a scholarship, and you have your mommy and daddy paying your way. What's the difference, really?"

"Whatever, freak."

I snort, knowing that I've won this round. He resorts to petty name-calling when he's been outsmarted. I press on, walking past him.

Rhett follows me to the creek, where half the senior class has gathered. I don't look back or speed up, because I'm not intimidated by him.

Atlas, Jesse, and Luce are already here, sitting on rocks. Luce has her sandals in her hand, feet gently splashing the clear water, while Jesse looks on like she's lost her mind. He's never been a fan of our little town on the mountain and doesn't understand how anyone could find it magical. He's destined for a big city, preferably one near a racetrack to feed his desire to be the next Jimmie Johnson.

Atlas beckons me over with a wave of his hand.

"Hey." I greet my friends as I sit down and turn to Rhett, who's now holding court.

"Idiot," Luce mutters as we watch Rhett call for silence and stand on a rock as if he's stepping up to a podium.

"I'd love to shove him off that rock," Jesse mutters.

"Seniors, are we ready to raise some hell?" Rhett shouts, lifting his arms in the air.

There's a collective cheer, followed by a couple of suggestions. Burn down the school. Put Fuller on Tinder. Steal the cars of the four senior staff and park them in each other's driveways. I do like the last one.

Rhett points to Leon. "The car thing is sick, dude. As you're aware, over the past two years I've been gathering information. Insurance, if you will. To ensure you all play your parts."

"That's not insurance, that's blackmail," Jesse mutters, glaring at Rhett as if he could slice him down.

I don't know what he could possibly have on anyone. We all have our secrets, but enough to force us to participate in dangerous dares? I'm not so sure.

"Why are we all doing this?" I mutter.

But my question is met with silence because we all know why we don't tell Rhett to get lost.

Henrietta Van Buskirk.

She's the reason that last year's seniors didn't say no to Rhett's equally dumb brother.

The next two Wilder brothers will also get zero resistance. Then what? The current freshmen get a clean slate. No more Wilders. They're *so* lucky.

I was a sophomore myself when Henrietta's life unraveled. All because she refused to slash the tires on Fuller's brand-new Jeep.

Everett didn't care for Henrietta's lack of participation. It was the first year of the prank hijack, and he wanted to make a mark. Only he didn't have anything on the straight-A student who kept her head down and never so much as called another person a crappy name.

With no scandal in her life to exploit, he cruelly made up his own tea. Took a couple of rather sketchy pictures of her cello instructor comforting her after a mistake in a recital. The student-teacher relationship rumor spread like wildfire. Despite there being no evidence and them both denying it, her teacher had to take another job somewhere else and she had to leave school early.

So I guess it doesn't matter what Rhett has on me.

And I guess that's why we're here now.

"So without further ado, our first dare is for my favorite group of losers. Marley, Atlas, Lucia, and Jesse. You're going to sneak into Creepy Arthur's dilapidated house of horrors and bring me a watch. A *gold* watch. Chunky, black dials."

I stare at him while the rest of the senior class turns to us, their eyes wide in both alarm and relief. *What?*

"How's that a prank?" Jesse asks.

"I never said anything about pranks, keep up. These are *dares,*" Rhett replies.

"Whatever."

We can't show him that we're scared. I don't even allow myself to acknowledge the churning in my stomach or the dampening of my palms.

No, we can do this. Easy. I'm not letting a damn watch derail my college dreams when we can just think of a way to return it later.

"Well," Rhett says, craning his neck. "What are you waiting for? Time to pay old Arthur a visit."

3

We walk away from the creek and don't look back. Conversation explodes behind us, but we're a bit too far to pick out individual threads. It's probably all relieved chatter because they're not the ones who have to do this.

The four of us are silent until we're out of earshot. I don't know if it's because we're in shock or if we just don't want anyone to hear us.

Sneaking into Arthur's is nothing new. I think he even knows kids do that almost every Halloween, but stealing is another thing entirely. It makes my skin itch like ants are crawling all over me.

"We're not really doing this, right?" Luce asks, wringing her hands. She looks at each one of us to gauge our reactions.

"Do you want the entire school to start gossiping about you and the drama teacher?" Jesse asks.

"Mr. O'Neil?" she squeaks. "Gross, he's, like, eighty!"

"He's fifty," I say.

Jesse nudges me. "Okay, maybe it's you who's seeing him."

"Fuller hung a birthday banner for him in the cafeteria last month. Pay attention," I reply.

"Can we stop talking about crushing on teachers and discuss how we're going to do this?" Atlas asks.

He's fully on board, then.

"What if one of us knocks on the door and keeps him busy talking while the rest of us go looking for the stupid watch?" Jesse suggests.

Luce does a double take, looking at her boyfriend like he's suggested we all move in with Arthur. "Yeah, any volunteers to talk to him? He's *weird*."

Personally, I don't think disliking people makes you weird, but it's not normal how he hides away, watching from his window. Usually, the nosy neighbors are chatty.

"What's plan B?" Jesse asks.

"We find out where he is, using good old-fashioned stalking, then sneak in," Atlas says.

Jesse laughs. "Okay, plan C?"

"Wait until he's asleep. We run the risk of him locking the doors, though. Rhett didn't say we're against the clock, but . . ." Atlas trails off, knowing the answer.

But we will be.

There's always a clock. Sighing, I say, "Plan B it is."

Atlas takes my hand and smiles, a little too excited for the start of prank week, knowing what's at stake here. "Pretend we're in the middle of some covert operation."

"As opposed to petty theft," I say.

"It's a dare, babe. Arthur will get his watch back."

"Does it not seem strange to you?"

He shrugs one shoulder lazily, his smile easy. He's so laid-back it's unreal. Not much fazes Atlas. It's one of the things I love most about him . . . until it drives me crazy.

"Come on. Luce, Jesse, tell me you don't find this just a little bit suspicious? Why a particular gold watch? It's not even a prank."

"Marley, stop. Let's just get this over with and hope Rhett moves his attention to the others and forgets about us," Jesse says, using that authoritative tone he has on the field.

Atlas jabs his thumb toward Jesse. "I'm with him. We're getting off lightly. I mean, he hasn't asked us to set anything on fire."

"Yet!" I snap, throwing my hands in the air. "Something isn't right about this."

"Marley's right," Luce says, backing me. "Why the watch?"

"Why take anything from the house?" Jesse asks.

"Proof that we snuck in," Atlas replies, squeezing my hand—the show of affection an obvious attempt to soften the fact that he's disagreeing with me. He doesn't want it to turn into an argument. Most things have lately. I don't know if it's just the stress of finishing high school and preparing for college or if it's something more.

"But people do that all the time. Why would he need proof?" I ask.

"What's the theory, then, Marley?" Jesse asks. "You obviously think something else is going on here."

But that's where I'm stumped. Arthur isn't a wealthy man, at least not from appearances, so his watches are likely to be cheap. Rhett's family is loaded. His dad wears a different Rolex for every day of the week.

Rhett can't really want Arthur's watch.

So does he really just want proof that we went inside?

"You got nothing?" Atlas asks.

"That doesn't mean he's not up to something."

Atlas gives me a sympathetic smile. "You're right . . . but does it matter if he is? We just need to get the watch, and we're done."

The house is up ahead, the faded red roof just peeking over the valley. We climb the bank, my thighs burning at this point. I'm spurred on by a spike of adrenaline and dread.

We crouch down, hiding behind lone shrubs that grow in random spots out of the ground.

"The house is dark besides that light in the one window, so he's probably in there," Jesse says.

"Do you think?" Atlas's voice is heavy on the sarcasm.

"I don't see you offering any insight!"

"Stop! Both of you." I feel like I'm about to lose my dinner. "We creep up to the house from the side and then along to the back. We shouldn't be in sight of that window at all."

"What happens when we get to the door?" Luce asks.

"We open it."

Atlas and Jesse laugh. Luce scowls but I'm not sure what else she was expecting.

"Do we think he keeps his watches upstairs?" I ask. "If he even has more than one."

"I think he has two," Jesse replies.

I crane my neck to see him past Luce. "I'm sorry?"

"Dude, how do you know that?" Atlas asks.

"I packed his groceries for him when I used to be a bag boy. No idea what brand they are, but they're big and gold. Flashier than I'd expect him to have, and they looked old. Didn't fit, but I've seen the one Rhett described."

"Flashy, like expensive?" Atlas asks.

Jesse rolls his eyes. "Do I look like an antiques dealer?"

"Kind of," he replies.

I ignore them because their bickering isn't helpful. We need to stay in control here, formulate a plan and then execute it. We're in so much trouble if we're caught.

"All right, let's go."

I pull Atlas up with me before he can argue with Jesse again.

"We're going now, okay," he mutters. "Stay low."

We run, crouched like in some horror movie, to the side of the house right in front of us. I keep my eyes on the light in what I think is the living room.

As we approach the house, I think about the last time I was here. I came with my dad, before he took a new job at the same hospital as Mom. He was called to the house after Arthur's estranged wife died. He told me to wait in the car while he went in, but I didn't. I waited until the private ambulance turned up and then tiptoed in after them, knowing my dad would be distracted.

It was the first time I'd seen a dead body. She was sitting up in the floral armchair just like she was sleeping, head tilted sideways. But there was no movement in her chest. She could've been a mannequin.

She hadn't been ill or anything, so she was taken for an autopsy. Heart attack in the night. She'd apparently slept in her own bedroom, so Arthur didn't find her until the next morning.

I look up just as a shooting star trails across the sky. A bright light that's either telling us to go inside now or warning us to go back. I can't be sure which way it's guiding me.

I'm not going to tell the others either. Atlas and Jesse already think my "signs" are creepy witchcraft that would get me burned at the stake if we lived in the seventeenth century.

Well, we don't, and the gut feeling I get when something captures my attention is usually right.

Even so, this time I ignore it.

"Okay," I whisper, my back now dead straight and pressed against the faded, wood-paneled walls. "We need to creep toward the door, but duck down when you pass that window."

"There are no lights on in that window," Jesse says beside me.

"Do you want to risk it?"

"I could take Arthur, Marley."

"Just do it!" Luce angry whispers. If she didn't have to be so quiet, she'd be shouting. Her eyes are tight, jaw set, and hands balled into fists. She's losing her patience and that's never pretty. She goes a bit . . . off the rails.

Jesse gives her one last look and nods. "Go, Atlas."

We shuffle sideways like four little crabs. My back scrapes along the wall. I'm too pumped to notice, but I bet I'll feel a bunch of splinters when I crash. Atlas reaches the window first and ducks down, awkwardly walking on his haunches.

I do the same, lowering myself down and shuffling. I place my hands on the ground to stop me from falling over, and a couple of rocks lodge themselves in my skin.

When I'm past the window, I rise again, wiping my palms on my shorts. "Ready?"

Atlas nods. "I'll go first. Stay behind me."

"We will," Jesse says over my shoulder.

I watch, hyperaware of my thudding pulse as Atlas reaches for the door handle.

He twists and gently pushes the door.

It creeks loudly like an alarm announcing our arrival. I wince, holding my breath. Somewhere in the house I can hear the low murmur of a TV set to some old movie channel.

Atlas looks back and gestures with his hand for us to follow him.

The entryway is huge but sparse. Wood clads every wall on the inside too. Dust particles hit the back of my throat and I have to stifle a cough. Despite the lack of dusting, it's tidy. From what I can see in the significantly reduced light anyway.

I step forward, and the floorboard beneath my feet screams. Literally, that's what it sounds like. Atlas turns around, his teeth showing in a tense wince, as if he thinks I'm trying to make noise.

Mouthing my apologies, I slowly and gently lift my foot, the same noise ringing through the foyer. Quieter this time.

Jesse and Luce step over the board and we start up the stairs. The lack of carpet makes every step sound like thunder, no matter how gently we go.

At the top I turn to the others and whisper, "Let's each check out a room."

"Split up?" Luce asks.

"We're in a house, Luce, not the forest. I've been here before. There are four rooms. There are four of us. We can be out of here in a few minutes if we separate."

I've only been in the guest room where George stays, so I don't know which of the other three doors lead to bedrooms or bathrooms, but it won't take long to figure out.

"Okay, let's do it," Jesse says, reaching for the handle of the door closest to him.

It's at that exact moment we hear footsteps coming from the room across the hall, and my heart stalls.

4

Jesse pushes the door nearest him open, and we burst inside like water overflowing a dam. He closes it quietly and presses his finger to his lips as if he thinks the rest of us are about to break into a freaking song.

I turn around, breathing as shallowly as I can get away with.

Atlas looks at me wide-eyed.

Luce tiptoes closer to the door and presses her ear to the wood. "I can't hear anything," she whispers. "Find the stupid watch and let's go."

I turn back and pad across the room, keeping on the large, threadbare rug as much as I can. This must be Arthur's room. There's a simple metal-framed bed and half-drunk cups of water on the nightstand.

He doesn't have curtains, which makes this easy, the light from the bright moon and stars guiding our way. His dresser is covered in even more dust. An empty packet of socks is strewn on top along with a couple of items of unidentifiable clothing that I so don't want to touch.

I feel a pang of sadness and a heavy dose of guilt as I look at his musty old things. Most of them look forgotten.

"This feels wrong," I murmur.

Atlas throws an arm over my shoulder. "It *is* wrong, babe."

"Come on, you know what I mean. I don't like this. Can we just go?"

"None of us like this but we don't have a choice. We're going to make it right, remember? We'll bring it back."

I nod, pressing my arm to the thick anxiety weighing heavy in my stomach.

"Find the damn watch so we can get out of here!" Jesse says, his voice low and tight. Screw Rhett for making us do this now rather than wait until Arthur wasn't home.

"Well, there's a watch," Atlas says, pointing to a yellow gold watch that looks more brown than anything. It's sitting in a dish on the dresser with some other jewelry that needs a good cleaning.

"Will you three hurry up!" Jesse snaps.

"It has black dials," I say, reaching out and scooping it up. I shove it into the pocket of my hoodie, wincing as the other jewelry in the dish clashes together.

"If you've got it, let's go," Luce says, her voice laced with apprehension. She spins around and flings her hand up, hitting her chest. We're all quiet, so we hear the tiny clink as something hits the wall and falls to the floor.

"What was that?" I ask.

Luce pats her top and gasps. "My pin!"

"What?" I ask.

"The one we bought at the spring fair. It's gone," she says, moving to the wall where we heard the noise. She crouches down, and I follow.

Jesse groans. "Hurry up!"

"Either help or shut up!" Luce snaps, gently patting the floor in front of her.

"Um, I don't think you're going to find it," I say. "Look at that vent."

Just by my feet, in the floor, is a broken vent. Two of the yellowing plastic bars have been snapped off as if someone's stood on it.

"No, no, no," she says, shoving her hand down the hole.

"Brave. You don't know what's down there," Jesse says, standing over us.

I whack his leg with the back of my hand. "Not helpful."

"I can't feel it and I can't reach the bottom."

Atlas pushes between us. "Are you sure it went down there?"

"It's nowhere else!" she says, her brows almost touching in the middle.

"Calm down, Luce. It's not like he's going to look down there, is it? We should leave. We've already been here too long," Atlas says.

Jesse places a hand on Luce's shoulder. "He's right, babe. Arthur isn't going to look down there, look at how messy the place is. It'll never be found. Come on."

Luce takes one last look and then stands. I get up with her. They are right. I don't think Arthur is suddenly going to clean the vents when he doesn't even vacuum the floor or dust the surfaces.

Atlas pulls my hand, getting me to move. "Let's get out of here."

"Who was in that bedroom across the hall?" Jesse asks, his hand hovering over the handle. "Wasn't Arthur downstairs?"

"The TV was on but that doesn't mean he couldn't come up for something. The bathroom maybe," Atlas says.

"Why wouldn't he pee downstairs?" Jesse replies.

"Probably broken. Look at the state of the place—it's a miracle the whole thing hasn't crumbled to the ground."

"Who cares where he pisses, okay? Let's just get the heck out of here!" Luce hisses. "I can't hear anything now, so I think the coast is clear."

Jesse opens the door slowly. It creaks like everything else in this place, protesting over being used. He looks back over his shoulder and mouths, "Come on."

I hold my breath as I step onto the landing, and I'm drawn to the room where we heard the noise. I can't remember what's in there. I was only up here once, and it wasn't for long.

Silence.

We need to get out of here.

Jesse points to the stairs and we move, tiptoeing on the threadbare carpet, the edges a reminder of how bright the red-and-gold patterns used to be.

Luce goes first, and then Atlas pushes me and Jesse in front of him, holding his finger over his lips. Why does everyone think I'm going to shout?

I roll my eyes and take the first step. That's as far as I get because another noise thuds from the same room, like a door being slammed shut.

We all startle and look up.

"Should we just run?" Luce whispers, her eyes so wide they look like they could pop straight out.

"Wait. . . . No, I can't hear anything else. I don't think he's coming out here," Atlas replies. "Keep going. Be *quiet.*"

My heart pounds as I take another step down. I can see the front door from here, and I long to be outside already.

We creep, descending lower until we're all standing on the first floor. I look back, listening to the sound of the TV, laugher drifting through the house from the speakers. There's something not quite right about it, like it's warped.

Luce opens the front door slowly. I turn sideways to slip through the small opening; any farther and the door will creak. Atlas follows me and then we're all outside.

"Crouch down and go back the way we came," I say, lowering myself to my haunches and shuffling along the burnt grass.

Once we reach the tree line, we stand and run. I look over my shoulder, losing my footing on the uneven ground and almost hitting a thick trunk.

I pause, leaning against a tree once the house disappears through the forest.

Atlas stops too, placing his hand on my back. He's not breathing as heavily as I am, but he trains for longer with the football team than I do for volleyball, so he's fitter.

"Are you okay?" he asks.

I nod. "Yes and no. We could've been caught."

"But we weren't," Luce says. "As terrified as I was, I kind of like the rush it's given me."

"Great," I mutter, not wanting to admit that I don't hate the adrenaline spike I'm currently experiencing either. It makes me feel alive, and I finally understand why previous seniors went along with the edgier stuff, even before the blackmail forced them to.

Jesse chuckles, grinning wide. "Yeah, that was a close one. Come on, let's get back to the creek." He tugs Luce behind him, both of them laughing now that we're safe.

Atlas tilts his head and smiles. "It's over now."

"No, it isn't."

"Well, *this* dare is."

"What would've happened if Arthur had walked out of that room?" I ask.

He shrugs as if he hadn't even considered that. I saw his face back in the house—he was as scared as the rest of us. "He didn't."

"Atlas."

"We would've run. Okay? We would've gotten the hell out of there."

"And when he noticed the missing watch, he would've known it was us. Being arrested for breaking and entering and theft isn't going—"

He takes a step closer and says, "Marley, breathe. That didn't happen. Besides, did you see how much dust that stuff was covered in? I don't think he wears any of it. We'll return it and he'll have no idea."

"We should follow the others and give that idiot the watch he wanted so badly," I say.

Atlas laughs and we walk to the creek.

By the time we get there, Jesse and Luce have joined another group, laughing as Jesse recounts our story. He's making it sound like he wasn't scared. I roll my eyes but don't call him out.

"You want to shove that in his face alone, don't you?" Atlas asks, spotting me shooting daggers at Rhett.

I nod and he takes a sharp turn, heading to our friends. That's one of the things I love most about Atlas: he seems to know exactly what I need. He knows that no one will get more satisfaction from shoving this watch at Rhett than I will.

Rhett probably assumed we'd chicken out and that's why he gave us the first dare. I want to throw the watch at his head, but I'm reluctant to do anything that might heighten his already over-inflated ego.

He stops talking to his group when he sees me. Ruthie's face falls as he pushes past her to walk my way. She folds her arms, tilting her nose to the sky.

I bet she tried to convince him to dare me to move out of the country. That's one dare I wouldn't mind doing right now, to be fair.

"How did it go?" he asks, smirking as if I'm about to confirm his assumption. "If you weren't able to do it, I can give your friends something else to do alone. They'll be able to go through with it without you holding them back."

I grit my teeth, reach into the pocket of my hoodie, and hold the watch up in front of his face.

It takes a second, but his eyes leave mine to look at the piece of dirty gold crap in my hand.

"Nice." He smiles as if he's genuinely proud. He takes it from me. "Which one of you grabbed it?"

"Me."

"I'd hoped so," he replies. "Just didn't think you had it in you anymore."

We were little daredevils back in middle school, so I don't know why he thought I wasn't brave enough. I'm not the one who changed.

"Are we done here?" I ask.

"Not yet."

I narrow my eyes, growing impatient with him. "What else do you want?"

"I'm just about to give Ruthie and her friends a dare. You should stick around."

"What're they doing? Robbing a bank? Stealing an old lady's litter of kittens?"

He chuckles, lifting his brows. "You want in on handing these out? Think of what we could do with the contents of a bank's vault and kittens."

I tap my chin. "Let me think. Do I want to ruin people's lives with you? That would be a massive no. You and your dumbass brothers can go to hell, Rhett."

"Feisty tonight, aren't we?"

"Rhett, come on," Ruthie shouts. "Why're you still talking with *her*?"

"Better run along. Your spiteful, jealous girlfriend wants you back."

He doesn't acknowledge her at all. Instead, he shoves his hands in his chinos' pockets, hiding the watch at the same time, and smiles. "She's not my girlfriend."

"Good for her. And I mean that with absolutely no sarcasm whatsoever."

His smile spreads, amusement glowing in his evil eyes. "Atlas also has a jealous streak, I see."

He's looking behind me. I'm not about to do that. "He'll just be worrying that I might catch something being so close to you. He knows he has nothing to worry about, especially with you."

That smug smile tightens, twisting into hate. His eyes move from Atlas back to me. "You guys should get ready for your next dare. I think you're going to enjoy it much more than taking the watch."

"Can't wait," I reply smoothly, though underneath the fake smile, I'm kind of worried. They always escalate.

"Awesome."

"Awesome," I bat back, playing a super-juvenile game of trying to have the last word.

He raises his hand, waving goodbye while standing two feet away from me. I salute, our last-word game morphing into charades.

I hate what I turn into when I'm around him. The arrogance and entitlement roll off him in tsunami-sized waves. He's the product of his environment, but how could anyone be proud to have sons who think they can get away with anything?

His parents must know about the dares. They're probably ready with the checkbook, waiting to bail him out of whatever mess he gets into over the next few weeks.

"Later," I snap, turning around so I can no longer see him.

I get three steps when I hear him reply, "Speak soon, babe."

Atlas laughs as I reach my friends again, and my shoulders lose the tension I held in them. "What's funny?" I ask.

"You look like you want to kill him," he replies, pulling me into a hug that I really need. The adrenaline is wearing off, leaving me feeling a bit flat. Do I want to do something stupid again to get it back, or go home and forget it happened? Even I can't tell.

I lay my head against Atlas's shoulder, feeling his warmth and worrying that it doesn't quite have the same effect on me as it used to. "I just hate who he is."

And, more than anything, I hate who *we* used to be. It makes me miss him. One day he just changed, no longer called and pretended I didn't exist for, like, two months.

He realized what he could be with money, and none of it included being a decent person.

He bought into the hierarchy, and being rich and confident put him right at the top.

It was the summer that Rhett turned into his older brothers, his parents.

I'm just scared of how far he'll take this game to get to me.

5

Tuesday, May 23

I didn't stick around to hear what dare Rhett gave Ruthie and her coven. But that didn't matter because it came through on the group message anyway.

They have to dye the cafeteria mac and cheese blue today.

I had to reread it five times because I couldn't believe how dumb it was. Rhett had the audacity to tell me the balloon prank was childish. He thinks this is sophisticated? Double standards.

It's the kind of prank that we should all be doing for the last three weeks.

For someone who isn't his girlfriend, he sure has gone easy on her.

It doesn't mean that's the only thing she'll have to do, and the dares get progressively worse for everyone as the weeks go on. My next one will probably be breaking into the sheriff's house.

I get ready for school slowly, being as quiet as I can because my mom finished work at the hospital around three a.m. and will desperately need the sleep. Dad will be home a bit later; we just miss each other.

I fill my water bottle, grab my bag, and leave the house, closing the door as quietly as I can. My car is in the driveway, but I like to walk . . . and gas is expensive. The route between my house and school is pretty, and it's not going to be too hot today.

The roads between my house and school are mostly deserted, since I live on the outskirts of town. I look up the mountain and smile, remembering camping trips with my parents up there. Since the bear sighting, we've gone to a nearby national park instead.

As I turn the corner, Arthur's house comes into view. I feel a pang of guilt as I get closer.

Breaking in was such a crazy thing to do.

We're lucky that Arthur didn't catch us.

We're lucky that he's harmless. Though I can't see him being too impressed if he'd found us in his house. The last time someone snuck into his house, he called their parents. Would we have gotten off that easy, or would he have called the police instead?

Though I can imagine I'd get in more trouble from my parents if they received a call at the hospital about me breaking and entering.

I walk past the entrance to Arthur's driveway. It's more like a dirt track, and every year Rhett's dad tries to get him to repave it. Apparently, the dirt creates a lot of dust. Arthur's car hasn't left his carport for years, so I'm not sure who's kicking up all this dust.

"Marley?"

I look up, startled, and see someone jogging toward me from Arthur's house.

It takes me a second to recognize him. "Oh my god, George!"

Arthur's grandson is now about a foot taller than he was the last time I saw him, over a year ago. His shoulders are wider, and all of him has filled out with muscle that he must put a lot of effort into. He's only a year older than me.

"Sorry, didn't mean to scare you. How's it going?" he asks, stopping in front of me. He has light skin and what looks like very soft shiny chestnut hair. He rolls his sleeves up, revealing toned forearms, and smiles, his stormy-gray eyes shining.

Damn. Talk about a glow up.

"Um. I'm good. What about you? When did you get here? You didn't say you were visiting."

He laughs. "Wanted to surprise you. I've just finished up my first year at college and thought I'd visit my grandad . . . and you. I don't think Grandad sees anyone since my nan and mom died."

"Your mom too? Oh my god, George, I'm so sorry," I mutter, having had no idea that she'd passed. We don't talk every day or anything, but we message enough to tell each other stuff like that.

"Thanks," he replies, scratching the back of his neck.

I guess George only has Arthur now. From what I can remember my parents telling me, George's dad, Arthur's only son, died when George was little, and his mom had grown up in foster care. She raised George a couple of states over, so he never saw Arthur much. But other than that, George never spoke much about his family, so I never asked.

"Will you move here?" I ask, not really knowing what to say or how to help.

He shrugs, and I'm having a hard time keeping my eyes on his face and off those muscles. "I'm not sure about that. It's quite . . ."

"Small, in the middle of nowhere, and full of busybodies?" I finish for him, listing all the things I'll be happy to leave behind.

Laughing, he replies, "Yeah, something like that."

"Do you think he'd sell and move away with you?"

George shrugs. "Grandad loves it here. Well, you know the family history."

I nod. "Yeah, I understand that he doesn't want to be pushed out of his home, but maybe it would be good to start over somewhere else."

"I've told him he should move." George sighs, and it sounds like it's a battle he fought and lost. "I think he could pretty much name his price at this point."

I laugh. "If it were me, I'd be such a sellout."

"Me too," he replies, laughing again.

"Well, maybe he'll want to move where you are."

"Who knows," George says. "You still in school?"

"About to finish," I tell him. "Last few weeks. I can't wait to get out, you know?"

George has never lived here but he seems to get it. They could've lived here on that huge property, but his mom never liked it, hated the beef between the families. I actually heard George refer to the families as the Montagues and Capulets once.

It was the first time I met George, when I was about eight. We played at the creek together, Rhett too, and George's mom rolled up, telling him to get in the car because they were out of there. I don't know what'd gone down before that, but I remember his mom looked mad about something.

"Any plans for college? You always wanted to be in California, right?"

I nod. "Well remembered. I got into UCLA, and I can't wait. Though another four years of studying and taking tests kind of sucks."

"Congrats. You can handle college. I'm thinking of transferring, not loving the cold up north, but I've made some good friends. With Mom gone now, I don't know if I want to start over yet again."

"Makes sense. Hey, if you want sunny, come to Cali. You know me and kind of know Atlas," I say, liking the idea of seeing George more often.

He chuckles. "Thanks. I'll figure out where I'm going next while I'm here over the summer."

Wait. Oh crap.

While he's here over the summer. How long has he been back? He didn't say, and if he didn't arrive just this morning, he would've been in the house when we snuck in last night. Oh god, there was someone in the living room *and* upstairs!

My scalp prickles, though the danger has passed. We were *so* stupid. What would we have done if George had caught us?

"I should get going," I say, clearing my throat. "I'm glad you're back. Arthur must've missed you."

"You okay? You've gone pale, even more than usual."

"Yeah, just the heat," I say, though it's not even that hot yet.

"Get to school and hydrate," he replies as he retreats, walking backward up the driveway to the old house.

It'd be weird if the Wilders did buy the land. I don't know why they need it—it's not like they don't have enough. They probably want it as a graduation present for one of their sons.

Some people have all the luck.

I continue toward school, looking down at my phone as I type a message to my friends, my thumb trembling over the keys. They need to know that George is back.

6

Luce runs toward me as I walk into the school building.

"What do you mean 'George is back'?" she asks, holding up her phone so I can see the screen.

"You're showing me the message I sent you. I already know what it says."

"Don't be smart, Marley, I'm freaking out here. There were two of them in there. Arthur could've walked out of that room and found us upstairs."

"George," I say.

"What? How do you know that?"

"I doubt Arthur was the one watching an old movie. Not that it matters which one of them was upstairs with us." But I'm pretty sure now that the noise came from the guest room where George stays.

She pulls me closer, eyeing people passing by as if this is a secret, but most of them weren't there when Rhett gave us the dare. No one's going to say anything, that's not how it's done.

We're sworn to secrecy. Each of us will be doing something we could get into a lot of trouble for. Mutual destruction is what will keep us all quiet.

"What if he finds my pin badge?"

"At the bottom of the vent in Arthur's room?" I ask. "It's not like anyone would know it's yours."

Her eyes widen. "Marley, there are tons of photos of me wearing that!"

"There are tons of photos of me wearing mine too. If it'll stop you stressing, I won't wear mine anymore. Okay?"

"I don't want you to get into trouble either."

"You're overthinking this. What's going on with you?"

She blows out a long breath and leans back against the wall. "I'm the first person in my family to go to college. I can't do anything to get my acceptance withdrawn, you know that. This means everything to my parents and grandparents."

"Nothing is going to stop you from going to college. Arthur isn't even going to realize anything is missing. We'll return the watch when we know he and George are out, and no one will ever find the badge. Breathe."

It's not like this is something I can afford to screw up either. Everyone in my family has gone to college. They're all doctors, X-ray techs, nurses, and dentists. My two older cousins are in med school. I understand her panic.

She takes a deep breath, and I can feel the tension ebbing from her shoulders.

"Maybe we can buy a new badge," I say, trying to be helpful when I know that's kind of a long shot. We both bought the same one handmade from a stall at the spring fair. There were only two of them. I don't remember the lady's name, and I don't think she's the sort of person to have social media accounts.

"Maybe," she replies, coming to the same conclusion as me. I don't think it's a big deal, though. No one's going to look in a freaking vent. Whoever buys the property next is just going to rip it down, if it hasn't crumbled to the ground before that.

Luce and I have most of the same classes, so I'm able to keep an eye on her throughout the day. We don't see Jesse and Atlas until lunch, but she's back to normal by then anyway.

I pick up a tray and get in line.

"Can you see anything yet?" I ask, wondering if Ruthie's completed her dare and dyed the mac and cheese.

Luce opens her mouth but it's at that moment that someone screams in the line. I look over and see Martha, Ruthie's second-in-command, lying on the floor, gripping her stomach.

I roll my eyes at Luce, spotting Rhett across the room, smirking.

This is the distraction.

The two cafeteria staff run out from behind the counter. I watch Ruthie slip through the door, a bottle of food coloring badly hidden in her fist.

Seniors stand in front of the counter, blocking the way as Ruthie dumps the whole bottle into the deep tray of mac and cheese. She stirs it, laughing silently as the cheese sauce turns a slimy green-blue.

Martha sits up, rubbing her belly. "I'm fine. That cramp just came out of nowhere."

"I want you to go to the nurse," one of the staff says.

She shakes her head, glancing up just as Ruthie joins us back out in the cafeteria. "I'm fine. They're bad sometimes. I'm sorry I scared you."

With a miraculous recovery, she gets to her feet and begins to walk toward the exit. "I'm fine, really, going to grab my water bottle. I'm sure I have Tylenol in my bag."

She turns and runs, no longer holding her stomach that hurt so much five seconds ago.

I watch as the staff return to the kitchen and one of them bursts out laughing when they discover the discolored mac and cheese. The other one scowls.

"All right, all right, very funny," she says, shaking her head as the cafeteria erupts.

Luce nudges me, laughing along with everyone else.

"To be fair, it doesn't look that bad," I say.

"I'm getting some."

The happier of the two takes the tray away. "Sorry, no mac and cheese now. We can't serve something that's been tampered with." A chorus of protests erupts in the line. "Don't fret, the salad is really good today," she adds with a wink.

Rhett walks over, stopping by Luce and me. "You couldn't have dared her to dye the lettuce instead?" I say.

He laughs. "Next time."

"Next time you need to give her something better than that. Our dare was a felony," I remind him.

Actually, I'm not sure that tampering with food isn't, but it wasn't poison and no one's going to eat it. My point is her dare was crap.

"I agree with Marley," Luce says.

"Of course you do," he mutters. "I'm not taking requests, but thanks for the feedback."

"You were taking requests last night."

The line moves but the three of us don't, no one wanting to be the first to back down.

Rhett smirks. His signature expression.

"Hey, can you guys move?" Tony says behind us.

Rhett's head snaps in Tony's direction and Tony cowers back, looking away, his shoulders hunched to make himself small, cheeks blazing.

"Don't be an asshole," I say. "Come on, Luce, I'm hungry."

He walks away before we can move, always needing to be the one in charge.

"I hate that guy," she says.

"Ditto."

I grab a chicken wrap and a bottle of water and sit with Luce. Atlas and Jesse find us a few minutes later. I look up when a few phones beep around the room. I take mine out of my pocket. It's the senior dare group.

Rhett:

next up is Tony. Jacks will be waiting for you outside the science block. Principal's car needs a lift.

"Tony's dare," Luce says.

I shake my head. Poor Tony. After snapping at Rhett in the line, Rhett is trying to teach him a lesson. He's such a bully.

"What happened?" Jesse asks.

"Tony had the audacity to tell Rhett to hurry up. What a crime," I reply. "When do you think we can get that watch back? Shotgun not asking Rhett for it!"

"You can't shotgun that," Jesse says.

"I just did."

"I vote Atlas asks him," Luce says with a devilish smile.

"We all know it needs to be Marley," he replies, narrowing his eyes. "Your shotgun is invalid. We need to return that watch."

Luce nods. "We return that, and he'll never have to report a break-in. The badge will never be found, and I'll go to college."

She's being super dramatic, but it's not like I have a choice. We need to return the watch and not just to save our asses.

"Fine."

"Anyone else still finding it weird that he wanted a watch?" Luce asks.

"Definitely feels like there was an ulterior motive," I say.

"But what?" she asks.

I shrug. "Yeah, that I don't know . . . yet."

Atlas groans. "Don't get involved, babe."

"Aren't you curious? Maybe if we can dig up some dirt on him, we can get him to leave us alone. Think about it, that watch was really old, and his family has a history with Arthur's."

"Might be worth something," Jesse says. "Maybe Rhett's grandad gave it to Arthur when they were friends."

I nod, gently whacking Jesse's arm. "Right, that makes sense."

Luce watches me skeptically, but she nods, hoping that I'm onto something and we can fix the watch issue and stay out of the rest of the pranks.

My phone dings again. Another message in the dare group.

Tony:

leave me out of this

"Uh-oh," Jesse says.

I look across the cafeteria at Tony. He shoves his phone in his pocket and stands up, leaving the room.

"What do you think Rhett's going to do?" Luce asks.

"I think we're about to find out," I reply, watching Rhett whisper to one of his friends and hold his phone to his ear.

Jesse scoffs. "I really hope only bad things happen for that guy."

I grab my tray, finished eating, and leave the cafeteria.

For the rest of the day, I'm on edge. Tony doesn't seem fazed, and I admire that in him. After Henrietta, the rest of us are too scared to push back.

But Luce is breaking down over that badge. We need to put a stop to our prank involvement.

The final bell rings and I shove my pen and notebook in my bag.

Atlas and his team are staying late to play football today, and Luce is going to her grandparents' house, so I start to walk home.

I get to the bridge when Rhett's car flies past me. His rear lights flash as he brakes hard.

Great.

I keep walking and he winds down the passenger window. "Need a ride?"

"No thanks," I reply, not stopping.

The car crawls forward. "Get in."

"I'm not stupid."

"What do you think I'm going to do? Murder you and bury you in the woods?"

I scoff. "Wouldn't shock me. What are you doing with Tony?"

"I'm not going to kill him."

I keep moving and so does he. It certainly looks like he's about to kidnap me. "What do you have planned? I know there will be something. You should just leave him out of it. He doesn't want to play."

"He was at the creek. He's in. Those are the rules."

"You made the rules, you can change them." I fold my arms over my chest, fists tight as I try to refrain from punching his car. I'd do it if it wouldn't hurt. There are no redeeming qualities about Rhett Wilder.

"Why do you care so much about Tony?"

"Because I'm not an asshole!"

"He knew what he was getting into."

"Did he? Do any of us?" I stop and glare at him. He hits the brakes again. "We have no clue what hateful action you're going to take if we don't do these ridiculous dares. Do you have any idea what we risked breaking into Arthur's? If we'd been caught, it could have affected college!"

"You're being dramatic."

"No, I'm not! God, you're so sheltered by your parents' money. You never used to be like that."

Heat explodes in my cheeks. I wasn't supposed to say that. After he ditched me I didn't ever want to show him that I cared or that he'd hurt me so deeply.

"Still think about us splashing in the creek, do you?"

More than I want to.

I ignore him. "Where's the watch and what are you doing to Tony?"

He tilts his head to the side. It takes him a second to reply, as if he's not sure whether to tell the truth or a lie. "The watch is safe."

"Why do you want it?"

"Because it was a dare."

"I call BS. I need it back."

He laughs. "You won't get much for it."

"Not to sell it, you idiot! I need to return it."

Rhett's nose scrunches up like he cannot comprehend why you can't keep someone else's stuff. "No."

"What's does that watch mean to you?"

"Nothing. It's junk."

I hold out my hand, palm facing the overcast sky. Of course it's about to pour on me. "Then hand it over."

"Not going to happen."

"Rhett, I need to take it back."

"He'll never know, stop stressing."

This is getting me nowhere. He loves an argument, and I'm only feeding into that.

I sigh. "Looks like it might rain. That ride a genuine offer?"

"Yeah," he replies, his tone full of suspicion.

Before he has a chance to question me, I open the door and get in. I shove my bag between my feet and turn to him, having absolutely no clue what to say but knowing I need to find a way to get that watch.

"What do you see in Ruthie?"

"Jealous?"

Okay, that I can work with. It feels a tad too manipulative to use it, but I'm desperate here . . . and it's not like he's a good person.

"Answer the question," I say.

He shrugs. "She's all right."

"Are we talking about the same person?"

That makes him laugh. He looks over and grins, and for a second, we could be in middle school again.

But we're not. *Focus.*

"Will you tell me what your plans are for Tony? Oh, I have a better question. Why do you need to blackmail people into doing the dares? What's wrong with normal senior pranks?"

"That was more than one question."

"I want to know why."

"It would be boring if everyone backed out of dares that went beyond Saran Wrap on toilet seats."

I turn my nose up. "That's gross. Don't do that."

He laughs again and slows down as we approach my street. "I know the fire was bad, Marley, I'm not going to dare anyone to burn down a building."

"Billy wasn't dared to do that either."

"The fire spread because Billy was dumb. It's entirely possible to light a small, controlled fire."

I roll my eyes and grab the handle of my bag as my house comes into view, desperate to get away from him. “Please don’t do anything to Tony.”

“Marley, chill. Nothing bad is going to happen to him.”

“Is that because you think he’ll agree to the dare before you can take things too far?”

He stops outside my house. “See you tomorrow.”

“Rhett!”

“Calm down, no one’s going to die. Yet.”

7

Wednesday, May 24

I shovel the last of my pasta in my mouth, the bowl resting on my legs. One move and I'll have mascarpone sauce on my bedsheets. My phone is beside me as I check in with my friends after school, something I promised my parents that I would stop doing. Bad for your health, apparently. Neither one of them told me exactly how, though.

The fan above my bed rattles, wobbling as it spins.

My notifications are going off. What the hell . . .

I open a message from Atlas first.

Atlas:

WTF! Have u seen this?

I look at the screenshot he's sent me. It's a photo of Tony's latest Insta. Or rather the comments on it. Loads from friends of his girlfriend, Jen, calling him an asshole and other not-so-friendly names.

Marley:

What happened?

His reply is a string of five more screenshots. I could just go to Tony's feed, but okay. I look at each one and my mouth drops open. There's a picture that has been posted from a fake account, which we know is Rhett, of Tony kissing Jen's sister.

Her *sister.* Poor Jen. From the comments it looks like she found out the same way the rest of us have.

As I'm reading through the thread, I get another message.

Luce:

Omgomgomgomg it's going down!

I can hear Jen and Ella screaming at each other from across the street!

Marley:

Be cool. Don't film it!

Luce:

Ur no fun.

Marley:

What's happening?

Luce:

Their mom was yelling, Jen's driven off and Ella's crying.

Marley:
Poor Jen. Rhett is such an asshole for embarrassing her like that

Luce:
How did he even know?

I have a theory. He's everywhere in town. Always watching, his younger brothers too . . . and the older ones when they're home. Could they really be *that* bored, though? Who spends all their free time spying on their classmates just so they can blackmail them later?

Not that it surprises me. Rhett's an ass.

Marley:
Stalking

Luce:
Ur kidding?

Marley:
Haven't u noticed that he's always around?

Luce:
I guess. He's a creep!

Marley:
See u at the creek in thirty

The weather is supposed to be super hot again, with rainstorms coming in a couple of days. I can't wait. The air needs to be cleared; it's stuffy and choking. I thought it was going to rain yesterday, but the clouds passed quickly and then it went back to baking hot again.

The house is silent, and if I didn't know that Dad was asleep, I would think I was alone. I've gotten used to my parents' antisocial working hours over the last seven months. It's always easier when they're on the same shifts, though.

I take my bowl downstairs, grab a water, and sit down at the kitchen island to scroll through Tony's Insta. Some comments call him a dog and others are full of praise. People are gross. I can't see a reply from him, and there's nothing new posted, so I guess he's taking a social media break.

I would too if I'd been caught kissing my girlfriend's sister.

Talk about lines you don't cross.

I check out Jen's page next, and there are a lot of sympathetic comments. All the hate is directed at her sister and boyfriend.

Rhett is deplorable. Anger surges through my veins. Who the hell does he think he is? I hate people like him. He thinks nothing of tearing someone's life apart, of hurting them. I dial, too irritated to think logically.

"Marley, not who I expected," he says.

His smug voice makes me want to throw my phone.

"What's wrong with you? What is *actually* wrong with you? Did you not stop and think about Jen for a second?"

"You do like those quick-fire questions, don't you."

"Why did you do it like that? Jen is probably humiliated. Her sister!"

"You don't think she deserved to know?"

"Of course she did! But not like that!"

I wince as my voice bounces off the walls. If I keep this up, I'm going to wake my dad.

I take a breath and place my palm on the cool granite countertop. "Please tell me you understand how insensitive that was. You should've gone to her privately. It still would've broken them up. You still would've gotten your little revenge on Tony for not playing a game with you."

"If you have a problem with the way I do things, you shouldn't have agreed to join in."

"Clearly that was a mistake. I gave you too much credit, believing that after your idiot brothers, you might do things differently. I think you might be the worst one of all."

"Screw you, Marley," he snaps, and the line goes dead.

Okay, I've never known him to be the first to bail out of an argument. It feels *fantastic*. My chances of getting him to hand the watch over have been obliterated, but I can think of another way to get it. Apparently, I'm quite good at breaking and entering and theft. That's not exactly something to be proud of, but it would be so satisfying to take from Rhett the very thing he made me steal.

The world is tinted purple from my sunglasses as I take the shortcut to the creek, killing my quads as I try not to fall down the valley. Everything beneath my feet is sun-scorched yellow. The moss that covers the trees is crusty and crumbling.

It'll all be slimy and green again after the rain comes.

When I get to the creek, it's rammed with most of the senior class.

Great.

Tony and Jen aren't here. Not a surprise—I guess neither of them is up for it.

I find Luce paddling and kick off my tennis shoes. My toes sink beneath the warm water, but as I move deeper the water gets cool. "Hey," I say, wading until the water just kisses the bottom of my shorts. "You see anything else while you were spying on Jen?"

She looks up and smirks. "I was *observing,* and no, nothing else. It was quite disappointing, really. I don't know where Jen went, but I hope it was to kick Tony's ass."

"Imagine being their mom and having to referee that fight. Carnage."

She laughs. "I wish I knew more. Were they seeing each other behind her back, or was it just a kiss?"

"Does it matter?"

"Just curious."

"I have no doubt that we'll find out soon. Oh, great, Rhett's here. I had a fight with him a little while ago . . . and I won," I tell her, tying my long hair up.

Her head snaps in my direction so fast it'll be a miracle if she doesn't get whiplash. "Why didn't you open with that? What happened?"

"Not much, I just called him out for publicly exposing Tony. He didn't like it and hung up on me." I smile proudly.

"Good for you," she replies, patting my shoulder like I'm a dog. "I mean, he's going to get you back, but good for you."

I roll my eyes. "I've never kissed Atlas's brother."

"Glad to hear it," Atlas says, laughing as he throws his arm over my shoulder. "What're we talking about?"

Luce fills him in on my argument with Rhett, and he turns to me.

"*Why* are you getting involved?"

Scowling, I reply, "Because no one else was going to say anything! Jen didn't deserve that. Why do we all stand by and let him do whatever he wants? It's insane!"

I'm not close to Jen, but we have a couple of classes together and she's cool. And also, I can't say the things I really want to say to Rhett, so I pick at everything else.

But I'm not admitting that to anyone, because then they'll know that I miss my old friendship with Rhett. I miss who he used to be.

It's like there are two versions of him. For a long time I wanted to find a way to bring back the version of him I knew. Now I just think he can go to hell.

Atlas raises his palms, dark brows lifting along with them. "It was just a question. You don't have to take him on alone. I've got your back."

"What could he have on us?" I ask, moving closer to him again. "I'm not asking for your secrets here, but is it enough that you can't back out of the pranks and challenge him?" Of course, Rhett could just make stuff up, but we can fight a lie easier than the truth.

Both Luce and Atlas look away from me, waiting for the other to go first.

Wait. . . .

Their silence makes my heart drop. It probably shouldn't—

doesn't everyone have at least one thing they keep to themselves? But I can't ignore how uneasy it makes me feel.

I thought I knew everything about them.

I thought they would tell me I'm silly and that we should go after Rhett. That they don't have anything they wouldn't mind me knowing. Why isn't Atlas telling me I know everything and that he has no secrets?

The strained atmosphere seems to take physical form, pinging between us like a ball.

Jesse nudges Luce as he joins us, smiling at her like she's a prize. They're too cute. Atlas blows out a long breath, relieved to be rescued. From what? Discussing our issues and finding a resolution.

"Who's asking about secrets? Should we be worried? Did Marley piss Rhett off again?" Jesse asks as Luce wraps her arms around his waist. He looks at Atlas and Luce with suspicion in those dark eyes. He witnessed their silence at my question and knows they're hiding something.

I want him to press the issue and ask why they're not sharing with us.

"Marley," Atlas says, tilting his head toward Jesse, prompting me to reply to his questions.

I narrow my eyes. "Yes, I've annoyed him but that's not the point. I was standing up for Jen."

"Marley wants to boycott the pranks," Luce says, glancing back my way nervously as if I've just suggested we commit murder and hop the border.

"Bad idea. We can handle whatever he throws at us. Breaking

into Arthur's was crazy, but we did it." Jesse bounces on his feet, his lips stretched in a wide smile that puts me on edge a little.

He's enjoying this a bit too much.

It's all fun and games until you're caught. I don't want us to run out of luck. Honestly, I want to forget everything to do with the pranks. So I need to drop the secrets thing. . . . I was rocked from the lack of openness in my friend group, but I have to remind myself that I'm not entitled to know every aspect of their lives.

Still, it stings to find out that we don't know each other as well as I thought. I mean, Luce is queen of the no-secrets club.

She knows everything about me . . . even the embarrassing stuff that I would probably have rather taken to the grave.

I kind of feel stupid too. I didn't need to be so open.

But I'm dropping that. . . .

Waving my hand, I reply, "Yeah, forget Rhett. We'll just stick together."

Atlas can barely meet my eyes, but our attention is pulled again by Rhett stepping up on a massive rock that he's using as his platform, ready to hold court again. Idiot.

I sneak another glance Atlas's way before giving Rhett my attention.

"Seniors!" he shouts, holding his hands out as if he's addressing his people. I want to throw rocks at him.

Atlas scoffs and slings an arm around my shoulders, still not quite able to look at me. What does he not want me to find out? It wouldn't bother me if we weren't going through this weird phase.

"We have three dares today. One tomorrow."

There's a cheer from everyone around me, and I find myself smiling. It's easy to get caught up in the hype, the thrill of doing something minorly inconvenient to others in the name of fun.

"The first two we're all involved in, and we need to go now." He shoves his hand into his pocket and produces a key. "We're moving Fuller's office to the great hall. Everything is going. I want pictures first so everything can go in its correct place."

I laugh along with the rest of my classmates. Okay, that one does sound pretty fun.

"Second dare we'll do on the way out. Egging houses. No rain for a few days, so they'll really smell. Third is for Leon. We all know your dad's a duck farmer." Rhett grins and points to him. "I want fifty of them in the school pool by the end of the night."

Leon's eyes widen. "Fifty! How am I going to get fifty?"

"How do you get them to slaughter? Use a truck," Rhett replies as if it's simple.

"I can't drive a truck that big!"

"No, you don't have a license to drive a truck that big," Rhett corrects. "Get it done."

Leon opens his mouth to argue but then snaps it shut. What's he realized? That his secret is twenty-four hours from being exposed if he doesn't do whatever Rhett wants him to? His boyfriend's brother is in his twenties and living in Texas, so I don't think he's been kissing him.

"What's tomorrow's prank?" Ruthie asks, swaying from side to side and looking up at Rhett like he's a prophet. She's part of the problem here. If more people looked at him like the douche he is, he wouldn't have this much power.

“That’s for Marley, Luce, Jesse, and Atlas.” His eyes dart to us, full of contempt. “You’re going blind driving, no headlights, around danger alley.”

My jaw drops.

Oh crap.

8

Thursday, May 25

After the worst night of broken sleep sponsored by anxiety, I arrive at school early in the hope that I can speak to Rhett without a massive audience.

I can't even get too excited about Fuller's reaction to finding his entire office has been relocated to the hall or the ducks in the pool.

Rhett's dare completely ruined the joy of moving all of Fuller's furniture and egging houses. It should've been fun, but I was so distracted. Atlas and Jesse waved it off, telling me and Luce that we'd find a way out and, if not, Jesse could "totally" do it because of his experience behind the wheel.

It's too hot to walk today, so I drove in, and I'm grateful I have somewhere to sit while I wait to kick Rhett's ass. I watch him roll up and narrow my eyes.

Ruthie is in the passenger seat of Rhett's car, and they get out at the same time. I'm in no mood today. "Ruthie, I need to talk to Rhett. Alone," I say, getting out of my car.

She puts her hands on her hips theatrically. "Excuse me?"

"Get lost," I say with even more conviction.

"If you think I'm following orders from a loser—"

I grab Rhett's arm, already frustrated with her hanging around. "Come with me."

He laughs and lets me lead him away from Ruthie. Neither of us looks back, not even as she scoffs and mutters something offensive about me.

"Do you want me to die?" I ask, tugging on his arm and making him turn to face me.

"Hm. I think I would rather you didn't. Why?"

I let go of him and throw my hands up. "The dare, idiot! You know how dangerous blind driving is on a normal road. And you want us to do it fast on danger alley. Are you *out of your mind*?"

"I'm sure your boyfriend will keep you safe."

Anger bubbles inside me. "Rhett, what are you doing? This isn't you! This rich asshole thing has never been you!"

He lifts a brow. "Getting to the root cause of the problem now, aren't we?"

"Change the dare," I demand, just stopping short of stomping my foot.

"No."

"What are you hoping to achieve? No one will even see us! Unless there's a really old watch you just have to have at the end of the road, I don't understand the point."

He chuckles. "Marley, there doesn't have to be a reason behind everything. Sometimes you can do things just for *fun.* You do remember what fun is, right? Or is Atlas too boring?"

He's right, we are getting to the root cause of years of his bullshit.

"Is it fun playing in the creek together? Movie marathons in your cinema room? Length races in your pool? Water fights in my yard? Ice-skating in winter? Camping trips with my dad? Those your definition of fun?"

My plan has worked. His smirk fades and is replaced with tension that rolls from his shoulders. He takes a step closer. I hold my ground, daring him to invade my space. We're standing an inch apart, but I'm not going to be the one to back down, not when I'm right.

He tried to turn this around on me, but I've hit it straight back to him.

This grudge he has is all about me being with Atlas and us not being friends anymore. Something that *he* chose.

"Why are Jesse and Luce even involved in this? I'm guessing you think that if you chuck them in on the dare, it won't be obvious that you're jealous."

"You're really—"

I wave my hands. "We should get all of this out." I'm on a roll cutting people off and getting my point across today. "Are you mad that I didn't try to chase you when you started ghosting me? I can't see why, because you do know me better than that."

I'm surprised that I've gotten this far without him butting in or walking away. We've never had this conversation before. In the past, he walked away, and I let him.

He runs a hand over his perfect, preppy hair. "You've thought about this way too much. I don't think about you at all."

My eye roll is so epic, I practically see my brain. "Sure you don't. Look, we can either talk about this, or you can back off and leave me alone. You can't have both."

"I can have *whatever* I want."

"Oh, but that's not true, is it?"

"Careful, Marley."

"Hey, what the hell is going on?" Atlas yells, jogging our way. "Back off."

Rhett's jaw clenches. "Boyfriend to rescue you."

"I don't need rescuing."

Atlas pushes between us, shoving Rhett back. "Stay the hell away from her."

"She doesn't need you to rescue her, dude. Isn't that right, Marley?"

"I'm fine, Atlas. Rhett and I were just talking about old times and dead grudges."

Rhett scoffs. "You wish. See you at the creek at midnight."

When he's gone, Atlas turns to me, scowling. "What was that about?"

Oh, now he wants to chat? Double standards.

I walk away from him, so freaking irritated that he interrupted. "I can handle him myself."

"Whoa, what have I done wrong?" he asks, catching up with me.

"Why did you rush over?"

He jogs alongside me, both of us moving too fast for a normal conversation. We must look totally weird. I move through the crowd, hearing the roar of laughter.

Yesterday's pranks.

I don't care. I just want to get through today and get the dare over with safely.

• • •

I make my way to the creek, earlier than instructed because Rhett is sometimes first and I need a second try at stopping this. Appealing to his kinder side didn't work this morning, but maybe that was because I went in hard and called him out.

Another approach might work. It's something I have to try because I can't stop the gnawing feeling in my stomach. A sense of dread I get when I'm watching a horror movie and someone's about to get it.

All day the churning anxiety in my gut has been getting worse, to the point where I could barely eat at lunch and dinner.

I walk past Arthur's property, and rather than going around, I cut through. I'm technically on his land but only just. It'll save me five minutes and Arthur has never cared about us walking here. There's even a trodden-down path, the grass trampled so often that it gave up growing.

It's eleven-forty-five and dark but still ungodly hot.

I look up at the trees in front of me and shudder at how the world disappears beyond them, the dense woods like a black hole.

"Marley?"

Startled, I jump back and spin around.

George raises his hand and jogs over.

"Where were you?" I ask, scanning the area. There's a shed close to him, but it's barely standing, the rotten panels being held together by a few rusty nails. He could've been in there, but why? It'd take a miracle to repair that.

"Sorry, didn't mean to scare you. I was just seeing if I can fix a few things while I'm here." He takes a quick look back at the house and sighs like he has the weight of the world on his shoulders. I want to ask what's going on. How he really is after losing his mom. But I don't. "Not sure I can do much to turn this place around. I wish he'd just move closer to me."

"Have you said that to him?" I nudge him. "I mean not just suggest he moves but actually ask him to."

George shrugs. "Sure. He hasn't been feeling well, so I don't want to stress him out with a move just yet. Says he's not in pain, but he doesn't always move comfortably. He's also gotten a bit confused recently. Nothing major but he's talking about the past a lot, almost exclusively. I think the Wilders have offered to buy the property again. Can't see him ever selling to *them*."

"I didn't know they'd offered again," I say, wondering if the watch theft has anything to do with that. But why? It's not like it was treasured by Arthur or anything.

"I'm not certain, but he doesn't usually talk about them. Last time was a couple of years ago when they hand delivered an offer, as far as I know."

George shakes his head, running his hand over his shoulder and along his arm, massaging as he goes. I feel for him. He has a lot to take on and he's only nineteen.

"Right," I say, my mind still trying to fit the puzzle together, but I feel like I have dozens of missing pieces. I get the impression that George doesn't want to let anyone in.

The watch can't be relevant to the property. It has to be personal. Maybe Rhett is just trying to make Arthur feel unsafe.

"Where are you going anyway? It's late."

"Just meeting Atlas at the creek."

"It's almost midnight."

I shrug. "My parents wouldn't let him stay over this late."

He nods stiffly. "So you're sneaking out."

"Yeah." The lies roll off my tongue as if I've practiced them. I don't really know why I'm not telling George the truth. It's not like he wouldn't have played pranks in high school. But there's something about the one I'm trying to get out of that makes me want to hide.

He nods again. "I remember doing that in high school."

"I can't wait for college. No more sneaking around."

"You want me to walk you there? Just until you see Atlas?"

"Thanks, but I'm okay."

"Not your first time sneaking out, I get it. We should do something soon, though. I've missed hanging out with the one normal person in this town."

"That's almost a compliment, but it's a low bar," I joke, making him laugh.

My eyes drift to a window, where I find Arthur watching us.

"I think he might want you," I say, nodding to the house.

George glances over his shoulder. "Right."

"Is he okay? It's pretty late."

He sighs again and turns back to me. "I don't know. I hope so."

"Can you get him to see a doctor?"

"I've tried. He says he can deal with it. Whatever that means."

Arthur has never been a weak old man. I get the impression that he stopped caring about the farm because most of the town sided with the Wilders, not because he couldn't handle it.

"Do you and Arthur need some help? My parents both work at the hospital."

He looks over his shoulder and back again. "Thanks, Marley, I'll ask if he'll let them help, but I have a feeling it's going to be a no. Everything is a no."

"Are *you* okay? You should come out sometime," I say, adding the invitation so that he can easily ignore my question if he doesn't want to open up. Forcing a laugh, I continue, "I know this town is lame, but staying on the farm twenty-four seven isn't good."

Why am I being so awkward?

George laughs. "I'm good, no need to worry that I'll turn into my grandad."

"I'm not, I just . . ."

Have no idea how to help you, if you even want it.

"I'm messing with you. Thanks for the offer, we'll definitely catch up soon. You should probably go meet Atlas, though."

"Okay. Bye, George."

He nods and then turns away, walking back toward the house. Somehow leaving him feels wrong. A nervous feeling in my gut tells me George isn't doing so well. I mean, his mom died recently, and his grandad is . . . his grandad. I make a mental note to check in more regularly.

I take one last look at Arthur through the window, just standing there, and then I continue to the creek.

Rhett is sitting on his rock when I arrive. He looks up as I approach, and for a heartbeat, he smiles. He recovers quickly and scowls.

"The answer is no."

Sighing, I step closer, knowing it's pointless to try changing his mind and that I was stupid for thinking I could. "Do you ever wish things had turned out differently?"

"You're doing the dare."

I throw my hands up. "Forget the dares!"

"Everyone will be here in a minute."

"Will you not care at all if we get hurt doing this?"

"Marley, come on. Jesse can do this. It's not like this is his first time racing or blind driving."

"On that road it is!"

"You'll be fine, don't stress."

I open my mouth to argue my point further, but he stands, dismissing me.

"Here he is!" Rhett says, holding out his arms.

Jesse, Luce, and Atlas walk toward us. It's then I notice other seniors approaching from different directions. I didn't have enough time to try to reason with Rhett, but a lifetime probably wouldn't be enough.

"Let's roll!" Jesse calls. "My truck's on the road. Luce and Marley, we can drop you before the fork and circle back after if you want."

Luce holds his hand, looking up at him like she's praying his confidence is justified. Jesse's a good driver—he's been go-karting since he was four and dreams of NASCAR but thinks it's already too late without a team or sponsorship.

He's good enough but he hasn't had the opportunities or parental support.

You don't usually have three passengers at night in NASCAR.

No one pays much attention to us as we walk off because Rhett starts to address his people again. I don't hear what he says, but I know I don't care.

"This is a terrible idea," I say, buckling myself into the back of Jesse's truck.

"It'll be fine," Atlas says, taking the passenger seat.

Luce is beside me, her eyes big and burning a hole in the back of Jesse's head. "Marley's right. You can't do it without your lights on, it's too dark."

"I know these roads, Luce. I could do this with my eyes closed too," Jesse replies, starting the engine.

Atlas looks over his shoulder. "He's got this."

"Do *not* close your eyes," I tell him. "Rhett said you have to do that stretch with the lights out, so keep them on until we hit the fork."

The fork is the junction that splits into three directions, one heading around the mountain, one toward town, and the other toward the freeway.

We're going straight on, around the mountain, where you really don't want to take any risks. And we're doing that without lights.

Stupid.

"I think I'm going to throw up," Luce mutters as we pick up speed long before we need to.

"Seriously, you and Marley can get out if you want," Jesse says.

"I'm not leaving you to die alone," Luce says, and I don't know if she's joking or not.

Jesse laughs and presses harder on the gas. "No one's dying."

"How's mission 'stop Rhett' going?" Luce asks, gripping the side of the seat near her knees. "Because I would very much like you to find some dirt on him before we reach the fork."

"I wonder if he'd stop if Marley asked him *really* nicely," Jesse teases, laughing at his own crap joke.

Atlas punches his arm.

If it would work, I would totally flirt with Rhett to stop the dare levels increasing. I'd just need to bathe in bleach after.

"There's the fork," Atlas says, leaning between the driver and passenger seats.

Jesse doesn't stop at the sign. Instead he turns his lights off, and we're plunged into darkness. I gasp as my eyes adjust. All I can see is a faint glow from the dash reflecting onto Atlas and Jesse. Beyond that is *nothing.* Jesse tightens his hands around the steering wheel and puts his foot down.

"Jesse, slow down," Luce says, her voice trembling.

He makes the bend, going too fast. Somewhere on the other side of the road is a drop. It's not a huge one, maybe the height of a one-story building, but it's still considerable when you're in a car that could flip.

"Okay, dude, you're going a bit too fast," Atlas says, putting his hands on the dash. "Seriously, I can't see three feet in front of me. They can't even see us now. Slow the hell down."

The side of the mountain flashes past in a dark blur, barely visible beside me.

"It's fine. I told you I know what I'm doing! Besides, don't you want to get this over with?" Jesse bites back.

I close my eyes and take a shallow breath, trying to calm the nausea before I vomit all over the interior. "Jesse, please! Rhett never said anything about driving this fast. They won't know."

My body shifts as we follow the road around a bend. I look up and strain my eyes to see through the windshield. I can still only make out the side of the mountain beside me and that's it.

I think I know where we are—the road widens ahead, the mountain giving way to the edge of the forest. *It's going to be okay.*

"Jesse!" Atlas bellows.

My heart free-falls at the terror in his voice before I hear the thud. The truck jolts and Jesse slams the brakes, tires screaming until we slide to a stop on the muddy road.

"Oh my god, what was that?" I cry. "What was that?"

"What did we hit?" Luce adds.

Jesse turns the lights on, and the road ahead bursts into view, dust flying around us. I hold on to the headrest in front of me, staring out the window as the dust begins to settle. We're in the middle of the road, almost sideways.

"It must've been a deer," Jesse finally says, looking back. "Is everyone okay?"

"It was bigger than a deer," Atlas mutters, his voice like steel.

Luce and I look at each other. "What does that mean?" I ask. "What was it?"

"A bear?" Jesse asks. "They've been getting closer. Hit harder than a deer would."

I reach across for the door handle, my trembling hands missing twice, and the interior lights come on.

"No, stay in the car, Marley!" Atlas snaps. "I'll go. Wait here."

"Whatever it was could be injured," I say.

Jesse opens his door, swearing under his breath. "I'm checking my hood. My dad's going to kill me if I've dented the truck. It's only just come back from the shop."

Screw this. I unbuckle and get out.

Atlas does a double take as he spots me gaining on him. "Really? Stay behind me in case it is a bear," he says, taking my hand.

I squeeze his hand, my heart still thumping from the shock. "Do you think it'll be alive?"

"It was hit hard but who knows what it can survive." He looks at me. "I don't like you being out here."

I look back to see that Luce is also out of the car, but she's gone to Jesse as he checks what damage has been done. He's just had a massive bull bar put on the front of it after crashing into a post last month. I can't see there being anything wrong with the truck.

Whatever we hit didn't go over the top, or it would've hit the windshield.

Jesse looks up at the sky. It's hard to know what he's thinking. Hitting anything will bruise his ego because he's supposed to be able to avoid accidents.

"Did you see where it went?" I ask, moving closer to Atlas. He doesn't let me get beside him; his arm snakes around his back to hold me in position. "Atlas, I'm fine. You don't need to be a hero."

We walk slowly. Atlas uses the flashlight on his phone to light the way. I can see the tire marks in the mud on the road, but I don't think Jesse's left much rubber thanks to the dirt.

"Which way do you think it would go?" I ask. If it was injured it would run for safety, right?

"Well, if it didn't go toward the trees, it'll be down there." He points the flashlight toward the drop-off and beyond into the forest.

"It might've run away to die in the woods," I suggest.

"Maybe," he mutters, distracted as he searches.

"How big was it?"

"I can't be sure. It was taller than a deer, stood upright."

Upright. I lick my dry lips as the hot evening air prickles my skin. "Atlas, bears walk on all fours."

"They can stand on two."

"Not for an evening stroll! What did we hit?" The panic in my voice makes Atlas's eyes widen.

"Shhh, don't," he says. The stony fear in his voice tells me that he's considered another possibility too.

"Who would be out here at midnight?" I ask.

"Marley, look for the bear!" he snaps, and squeezes my hand in lieu of an apology. I can't blame him. I don't want to believe that we could've hit a person either.

But I'm right, who would be out here? It doesn't make sense to be in the middle of nowhere on a dark road without even a flashlight or reflective gear.

"There," I say, spotting something lying in the ditch.

Atlas points the light and we both breathe sighs of relief.

On the ground, surrounded by scorched grass and huge bottle flies, is the carcass of a deer.

He blows out a long breath. "Thank god for that. I thought—"

"Atlas," I say, cutting him off because something isn't right. "It's been dead a while. I don't think the flies would've swarmed that fast."

"I can't see anything else," he replies. "Damn it! All right, let's walk on a bit, it could've rolled."

I take another step and grip Atlas's arm tighter. "I'm scared," I whisper.

"Why?"

He knows exactly why. He'll convince himself that everything's fine until the very second it's not. I wish I could do that rather than always thinking the worst.

He shines the light along the shoulder, shadows from long grass dancing in the soft breeze. The heat is stifling and my scalp stings with anticipation.

"Bear . . . ," he says, the end of the word dying on his lips. He lifts the flashlight and that's when I see why he's stopped talking. The dark legs he's stumbled upon don't belong to a bear . . . they belong to a man.

9

A scream rips past my lips and I slap my hand over my mouth to stifle it, but the sound escapes through my fingers and echoes across the mountain.

Atlas shouts, jumping back and almost knocking both of us to the ground.

"No, no, no!" I chant as he holds me so tight my ribs ache. The pain a reminder that I'm not dreaming. "Atlas! Who is . . . Who is that?"

"I—I . . . ," he stammers, his voice fading into the night.

Move. Do something! Help!

Gasping, I push away from Atlas, retching as I turn back to the person on the ground. "Is he dead?"

"Marley!" Atlas says, grabbing my hand.

"We have to help!" I snap, pulling my hand away.

"What the hell are you two doing?" Jesse calls, laughing. "Just kick whatever it is onto the shoulder and let's go."

"Yeah, hurry up," Luce adds, echoing everything Jesse says, as always.

Bile hits the back of my throat. I shuffle closer and step onto the grass, my body turning ice-cold. "Atlas, we need to call for help. My cell's in the car. I—I think." I mean, it must be.

He doesn't reply, but he falls in line with me, stretching his arm out in front of my stomach as if he thinks the guy is going to jump up.

His flashlight reveals the torso of the person, dressed in a dark, long-sleeve sweater. It's a stupid observation, but I can't help but think he's picked an odd wardrobe choice for summer.

"What's going on?" Luce shouts. "Stop freaking Marley out, and let's beat it."

Atlas shines the flashlight higher, and we reach his face. I gasp, my hand flying to my mouth, stifling another scream.

No, no, no.

"What did we do?" Atlas mutters, gagging. "Oh my god."

Staring back at us are the wide dead eyes of Arthur Nelson.

I want to look away, but I'm unable to, my body frozen and forcing me to look at what we've done. All I can do is stare at Arthur's lifeless body. His limbs splayed out in the dirt like he's a rag doll that's been discarded. His head . . . not right.

Atlas wraps his arms around my stomach and lifts me, turning us around so I can no longer see Arthur. It's useless; his face is lasered on the inside of my eyelids. I'll *never* forget.

"Is he dead?" I ask as we lean heavily against each other. I'm not sure which one of us is holding the other up. "Is he dead, Atlas? We need to check!"

"Is who dead?" Luce asks. She and Jesse make their way over to us, no longer messing around.

"What's going on?" Jesse asks. "What are you two talking—" He gasps and spins around, his hands gripping his hair. "Oh my god."

Luce screams and it's at least ten times louder than mine. "No!" She doubles over and gags. "No! Oh no! Please no, please, please. Tell me we didn't . . ."

Atlas still has a hold of me, but I break free again, stumbling as I try to take my own weight. "We have to do something," I say, swallowing my horror and walking back to Arthur. "We have to do something!"

"Don't touch him!" Jesse snaps, running to stand in front of me, blocking my way. He shakes his head. "He's dead, Marley, look at him. He's gone. Look at his head. God, look at it."

I don't want to do that ever again, but I comply. This time I see a few more details and realize why his head looks strange. It's now an odd shape, a large dip in the side of it hiding his ear. He must've landed hard, his head taking the brunt of the impact on the asphalt.

Yeah, he's dead. There's no way he could've survived that. His head is caved in. I press my lips together and breathe through my nose, smelling the stuffy, dry night air.

"What're we going to do?" Luce asks.

"Call for help!" I say. "Atlas!"

"Calm down and think for a second," Jesse orders. "He's already gone. We can't save him, Marley. He's dead. We need to think about what this means for *us*."

"What? We have to try. What are you talking about?"

"What happens after we call for help? This was our fault," Jesse says, his voice rough, like he thinks this is all my fault. He drags his hands down his cheeks. "What do we tell the cops?"

"That it was an *accident.* He just walked out into the road in the middle of the night. We didn't see him. Jesse, come on."

He throws his arms up. "We didn't see him because my *lights were off.*"

"The cops don't know that. We won't tell them."

"Do you really think no one at the creek is going to speak up and tell the cops the truth? Think, Marley."

I shake my head at his words, not quite able to figure out exactly what he's saying or what he wants to do. "I don't know all of the details, but we can't just leave him here."

"No, we can't. Everyone knows what stretch of road we were on. When Arthur is found, they'll come for us."

"Jesse," Luce whispers, stumbling closer to him, her legs moving robotically as if she's forgotten how to function. "What are you suggesting?"

"What I'm *saying* is we have to get rid of the body."

"What the hell, man?" Atlas snaps.

I take a step back, almost falling down the slope. "No! Come on, we can't do that."

Luce takes Jesse's hand, moving in front of him, and I notice that she's trembling. "Jesse, you're scared, and I get that. I am too, but we *can't* do that to him. We can't take his body somewhere else."

"No, we don't *want* to. We can and we have to. Think about the consequences, Luce."

"Like Marley said, it was an *accident.*"

"Like that's going to stand up. We were all in that car. We all got in knowing the lights were going out. What do you think's going to happen when our colleges find out? Think about that for a second, all of you. Do you really want your whole future flushed because of an accident?"

Jesse's using the soft voice, the one that makes her turn to mush.

"It's Arthur," I say, cutting in. "We know him. He's a person."

"I'm sorry, Marley. I'm so damn sorry that this happened. But he walked into the middle of the road at night. He could hear the car even if he couldn't see it."

"This isn't Arthur's fault," I say.

"It isn't anyone's!" Jesse snaps. "We can't lose our heads, Marley. We need to be smart here."

"Covering up a murder isn't smart."

"Going to jail isn't smart!"

Atlas steps between us, pushing Jesse's chest. "Calm down, dude. We need to breathe. We need to take a second to think about what we should do."

My jaw falls open. "Tell me you don't agree with him."

"I don't want to, babe. Look, we're *all* responsible for this."

"So we cover this up?" Luce asks, her voice high as a kite. It's nice to know that she hasn't jumped straight on board with what Jesse is suggesting.

Jesse cuts her a look. "What other choice do we have? We took a dangerous dare, and this is what happened. We fess up and we're done."

She opens her mouth, about to say something, and then snaps

her teeth shut. "College. I can't lose my chance at college," Luce says, her voice small.

Didn't take her long to change her mind.

I look from Atlas to Luce and then Jesse, unable to recognize any of them. Three strangers on the side of the road, each one deciding way too fast that dumping a body is our best option.

This isn't who we are. How do we cover this up and then fly off to college as if nothing has happened?

I suck in a gulp of warm oxygen, feeling lightheaded. The night refuses to cool, the air so hot and thick it's almost solid, threatening to choke me. I rake in another shallow breath, my lungs like a sieve.

"We can't," I whisper, tears rolling down my cheeks.

"You don't have to do anything but sit in the truck," Jesse tells me. He uses that soft voice again, but it doesn't have the same effect on me . . . and I can see the tightness in his jaw and darkness in his eyes. He wants me to go along with this, and he's irritated that I'm challenging their decision.

"What about George?" I say. "What if this was your grandad?"

"It's not. George isn't even close to Arthur. He sees him, what, once every couple years?" Jesse says as if that makes it okay. "Quit worrying about George and focus on *us*."

Atlas nods. "He's right, Marley. I hate this too, and I don't want to, but we don't have another choice. We'll keep an eye on George. He'll probably be going home soon anyway."

"To who? His mom died! Arthur is all he has . . . had."

Luce hiccups as she tries to hold it together, tears rolling over her unusually pale cheeks. "What are we going to do?"

"Okay. I have gloves in the toolbox in the bed," Jesse says. "No one touch him without wearing them."

"Oh god," I mutter, feeling queasy.

Atlas rubs my back but listens to Jesse, giving him his full attention. I shake his hand away, not wanting anyone near me.

"We take him off trail into the forest and bury him," Jesse says. "No one will find him deep in the mountain. We're in this together, so we stick together. Okay. All of us."

"Agreed. Now . . . how do we get him there?" Atlas asks.

Jesse's face twists. "How do you think? We'll carry him."

"Do you have anything in the truck we can use to dig?" Atlas asks.

Jesse shakes his head. "We'll swing by my house and get shovels. Mom was the only one who gardened, so we haven't used them since she took off."

"Jesse," I whisper. "Listen to what you're saying."

"I'm saving us."

No, he's saving himself. He was the one driving.

How much trouble could the rest of us really get into? But we were all there. And everyone in town gossips.

This is a nightmare.

"So what happens after?" Atlas asks. "Why didn't we go back to the creek?"

"Rhett never told us to. As soon as I drop you off, I want you all to post something from the day. Location on. Make it sound like you've been there a while. Finished homework or watching a show and now posting whatever from wherever," Jesse says.

I have a few photos from the creek. Silly selfies of Luce and me and a candid one of Atlas looking at the water. None of them I want to share, not anymore. I'm not doing that.

I've been railroaded. Atlas and Luce have jumped on board with Jesse's plan of self-preservation and they're not listening to me at all.

"So that's it? Bury him and spend the rest of the night on Insta and TikTok?" I ask.

"I'll post for you," Atlas says as if that's the part I'm struggling with.

"My fingers work. We're talking about burying our neighbor in the woods!"

"So call the cops, Marley. Get your phone and do the right thing. I'm not going to stop you."

"What?" Jesse spits, but Atlas holds his hand up to silence him, giving me the chance to decide.

"No!" Luce snaps. "I want to do the right thing too, but I don't want Jesse to go to prison. I don't want the rest of us to lose college or whatever else will happen. Our families. Come on, Marley, what's going to happen to your mom and dad? You really think the hospital would keep them on board?"

My mom is an emergency room nurse and dad an X-ray tech. They've dedicated their lives to helping people, and I've done the opposite.

I turn away, my stomach burning with an anger that I'm surprised hasn't set the whole town alight. How dare she use my parents as a bargaining chip.

How dare she be right.

Would they lose their jobs? I don't know if the hospital would fire them, but if there was backlash from patients, they wouldn't have a choice but to let them go.

All because I couldn't keep my mouth shut.

It's not like I don't want to protect Jesse too. He's one of my best friends. It's just shocking that they all reached this decision so fast. I haven't had time to catch up, to think every scenario through.

But I can't deny that they have a point. If we want a normal future, the one we've been working so hard for, we have to bury Arthur and pretend that this didn't happen.

I wipe my tears on the back of my hand. "Okay. I don't want my parents to lose everything. I'm with you," I say, hating how quickly I've already thrown Arthur away.

"Get in the car, Marley," Atlas says.

"Yeah, you don't need to do this. Just don't say anything," Jesse adds, as if he's doing me a favor. "I'm going to grab the gloves, and I think I have a blanket."

Jesse jogs back to the car and Luce follows after him.

I'm trying to hold myself together. "I don't understand how you can be okay with this, Atlas."

He slowly lifts a brow and takes a step back. "I don't understand how you can think I'm okay with this."

"We're covering up a murder."

"We didn't mean to do it. It's not murder."

"I don't care what the correct term is, Atlas," I snap, pointing to Arthur on the ground. "He's dead because of us."

"You think I don't know that?" His loud voice carries. If the wind was blowing, everyone in town would probably hear him. "I'm sorry." He sighs. "I'm just trying to make the best of a *very* bad situation here. Everything Jesse said is right. Our futures are over if this gets out."

He moves closer, his gaze dragging me in. "We're not going unpunished. We will have to live with this for the rest of our lives." His movements are slow and premeditated, like he's unsure how to approach me, whether I'll let him get close or lash out.

"I'm scared," I whisper.

"No one is going to find out."

"I'm scared about how this changes all of us."

"Nothing is going to change. I'll make sure of it," he says, taking two brave strides until he's in front of me. I tilt my chin so I look up at him. He adds, "Trust me."

I've always trusted him in the past . . . but we've also never had to survive something like *this* before.

I hate what we're about to do, what we're doing to George, but I know that I'm going to go along with it. That makes me the worst person in the world.

"I have the gloves," Jesse says. "Put these on. Marley, what're you doing?"

I shake my head. "I can't touch him."

"Go back to the car."

"I'll stand back," I say, not wanting to be on my own.

Luce squeezes my shoulder as she passes, following the boys to Arthur on the ground.

I shuffle to the side of the road.

Atlas and Jesse stand beside Arthur. He seems so much smaller and slimmer from this vantage point.

"Get your hands underneath him," Jesse says, using his gloved hands to touch Arthur's back.

"Be careful," Luce adds. "Don't hurt him."

Atlas and Jesse glance her way at the same time, but I get it. Okay, it's not like they can harm him now, but the very least they can do is treat his body respectfully . . . before we bury him in the woods.

I press the back of my palm to my damp forehead and count my breaths, my body too hot. *Do not pass out.*

They heave him up. That was the point of no return, and I turn away. We can no longer change our minds. We've moved the body, not something you would do if you were calling for help.

This is it.

We're covering up a murder.

10

"The road," I say, glancing around and keeping my back to Atlas, Jesse, and *Arthur*. Luce stands near me, watching as they move him.

"What, Marley?" Atlas asks. I can hear the impatience in his voice.

"There are tire marks in the mud. You can see where the car veered." But, thankfully, I can't see any blood from where Arthur hit the ground. He must've rolled onto the shoulder straightaway.

"There always are on this stretch," he replies, his tone now strained. It's not because he's annoyed with me; it's because he's carrying Arthur.

"They don't usually skid. We need to do something about them."

"Yeah, you're right," Jesse replies. "Good thinking. Use your foot to smooth it out. It's supposed to rain soon anyway, but we can't be too careful."

"I'll help," Luce says, nodding as if she's talking to herself. Her wide eyes proof that she's still in shock.

It was supposed to be an animal.

We walk in the middle of the road, and I use my foot to kick mud over the tire marks, the evidence of our accident getting swept away in the dirt.

Luce moves behind me, going over the area where I've been. "Doesn't look like a car was here now," she mutters. "We're going to be okay."

We're not, and the fact that I'm covering up, actively helping, makes me feel more awful. I'm just as much a part of this as Jesse, Luce, and Atlas now. Doesn't matter if I agree we're doing the right thing or not.

We're all in this nightmare together.

Atlas's and Jesse's footsteps shuffle behind me as they struggle with the weight of Arthur.

Luce grabs my hand, looking at me with horror and desperation in her eyes.

"I know," I say. "I can't believe this is happening either."

We should've just called straightaway. The cops wouldn't have been able to prove that Jesse hadn't turned his lights back on. Maybe it could've been okay.

"We'll get through this?" she asks. "Won't we?"

I shrug. "It's a lot to get through. I have no idea how we do it, but I don't see how we have a choice. It's done now, isn't it?"

My question is only half rhetorical because it doesn't have to be done. We could still stop this and do the right thing.

She nods, shining her flashlight at the road. "There's no going back, Marley. This is how it has to be."

I turn from her again but only because she's right. What I wish we could do doesn't matter. The boys are never going to agree to go to the cops. We can't go back now.

Something catches my eye in the distance. *Oh shit!* There are headlights coming toward us. They're tiny now and disappear around the bend, but it won't be long before they're back, and then whoever is driving will be able to see us.

"Car!" I call, spinning around as my heart drops.

"Get the bed open!" Jesse shouts, his eyes darting up and down the road.

Luce sprints toward them, and I follow, the four of us dashing to the car to hide Arthur's body. We have maybe two minutes to get Arthur into the truck and get out of here.

"Luce, start the engine!" Jesse orders as we reach his truck. "Marley, the bed, *now*!"

I run around the back of the truck and tug, my fingers pressing the button at the same time. The door lowers so slowly it's like it's working against us, wanting us to get caught.

"Come on," I say, gasping hot air that lies thick in my lungs.

"Get in," Atlas tells me as he and Jesse gently place Arthur in the back.

I listen to his command, spinning to run around the side of the vehicle. All I can think about is that car approaching. My mind conjuring images of the driver seeing what we're doing. The police coming. My parents turning up at the station. The questioning. Charges. *Prison.*

Luce climbs into the back through the middle and brings her feet up on the seat, wrapping her arms around her legs. She looks just as shattered as I feel. We have a dead body in the bed. We're traveling with him.

What the hell *are we doing?*

I chew on my lip almost hard enough to draw blood and mutter, "Hurry. Please hurry."

"Keep the lights off," Atlas says as he and Jesse pile in the car.

Just hurry.

Jesse nods, accelerating into the dark. I can't see his features properly from back here, but . . . does he look excited?

I turn my head and slump heavily against the door as we speed along the road, trying to keep up with the events . . . and what we have to do next.

"I can't see anyone yet," Atlas says, peering over his shoulder out the back. He gives me a smile, a feeble attempt to make me feel better. I appreciate the effort, but nothing is going to work. "You definitely saw someone, Marley?"

"Yes," I murmur. "I saw headlights."

"They might take another direction at the fork."

"Do you want to risk that?"

He sighs. "I'm not looking for an argument, just asking."

"You did the right thing, Marley," Jesse says. "You did good." He's being oddly nice. Not that he's usually horrible, but it sounds fake nice, as if he feels the need to be on my side and keep me sweet.

He knows I don't want to do this. He was the one driving. Ultimately, it would be him with the harsher sentence. He has the most to lose.

"I'm not saying she didn't do the right thing," Atlas counters.

"Please don't argue," Luce says. "I can't take it on top of everything else. You said we need to stick together, and that has to start right now if we're going to have a chance of getting through this."

"No one's arguing," Jesse says, taking a turn and switching the lights back on.

I breathe easier—a fraction easier—knowing that he can see properly. He pulls off the road onto a hiking trail. From here you can hike the mountain and get down the other side to the creek.

He cuts the lights again and kills the engine.

"What're we doing?" I ask.

"I don't want to risk that car coming up behind us. We'll wait for it to pass," he replies, turning in his seat to look out the back window.

I do the same, and we watch. Arthur is barely a few feet away from where I'm sitting. "What're you going to do about your car?" I ask. "There will be traces of him."

"My dad said he'd get a detail done once the dent was fixed and bull bars were on. So I'm going to do just that."

He's going to let someone else clean up the evidence of a murder.

The thought turns my stomach more than the prospect of us doing it.

"Is that a good idea?" Atlas asks.

"It's already booked, along with his car. It won't look suspicious, don't sweat it."

He's entirely too calm in this situation. I understand that he's scared, but how quickly he was able to plan a murder cover-up is a major freaking red flag.

"I see lights," I say.

Seconds later, a car speeds past. Jesse gasps.

My heart stops.

A goddam *state trooper.*

"You're a legend, babe," Atlas says. "If you hadn't seen them . . ."

Fear trickles down my spine, leaving me breathless. That was a close call, one I don't ever want to encounter again. I know, in this moment, that I'll go along with everything my friends have decided. I hate myself for it.

"If the cops are out this late, are we safe to . . . well, you know?" Luce asks, pressing her hand to her stomach.

Dump the body. Those are the words she's struggling to say, the ones making her sick.

No one speaks as Jesse runs into his house to retrieve the shovels. His dad is away for work until next week, so it takes him just seconds to grab the shovels from his absent mom's old shed. Each of us stuck inside this nightmare. Right now, we're all too scared, four souls changed forever, bound by the worst secret you could ever have to keep. We sit perfectly still like statues, and the only sound is the quiet breaths as we all try to come to terms with what we've done . . . and what we're about to do.

If I could, I would stay here forever.

Eventually, though, Jesse comes back and takes the off-road trail to the edge of the forest.

"All right. We'll pass the trail and walk for about twenty minutes into the forest," Jesse says, getting back into the truck. He stands the shovels in the foot well, the wooden handles sticking up and almost touching the roof of the truck.

"Will that be far enough?" Atlas asks.

"Off trail, yeah," I reply, knowing the forest better than any of them. "No one will be going out there. I know where he means. Dense forest, nothing to navigate with. People don't risk it."

Jesse pulls into a turnout and parks, the car creeping into the woods.

We're betting a lot on people sticking to the trail.

"All right." Atlas gestures for me to get out of the car.

I do so because it's claustrophobic as hell in there, despite the size of it.

"Should we tell Rhett the dare is done?" I ask. "I mean, he'd want to know."

Jesse nods, walking around the truck. "Yeah, Luce should message him. He'll want to keep Marley talking if she does it. Be snarky but make it clear that you're now home."

"Okay," she says, tapping away on her phone. I watch over her shoulder as she types.

Luce:
your dumbass dare is done now leave us alone

Rhett:
where are u?

I take a breath as she replies with a lie.

Luce:

home

Rhett:

why?

"What do I say?" she asks.

I take the phone and do it for her.

Luce:

we've done the dare

and the creek was boring

I don't expect a reply to that one because we're basically saying *he's* boring.

Luce sniffs, pocketing her phone, and turns away, detaching from the moment.

"It's done," I say, walking to the back of the truck, where they're shuffling Arthur's body down.

It's slightly easier to pretend there's not a person in there when I can't see him.

"Okay," Jesse says, holding what I think are Arthur's legs as he shuffles backward.

Atlas takes his shoulders.

"Lead the way, Marley," Jesse says. "You know these woods."

Luce picks up the two shovels and nods at me, disbelief glowing in her dark eyes. Her gloved hand gripping the poles so tight I'm surprised they don't snap.

She's not the only one with gloves. We all have them. . . . I raise my hands as I turn around, looking at the nylon that will protect me from leaving my fingerprints all over the burial site.

We are the worst people in the world.

"This way," I mutter, wanting no part of this but knowing that's not an option.

I briefly let my mind wander as I step off the trail and lead them deeper into the forest, the world around us turning darker with every step. I want to turn us around and go back.

What would they do if I changed my mind?

There's no point in even thinking about it. They've all made it clear what we need to do. I have to follow through, take this to *my* grave.

I walk on, stepping over roots that have erupted from the ground. The woods have always been my safe space. If I need a break or I'm feeling down, I hike. Now I'm making them a crime scene.

"How much longer?" Atlas asks.

He sounds out of breath and kind of annoyed, as if he thinks I'm taking the long route for fun. I look over my shoulder. Both boys are gritting their teeth, and we're only five minutes in.

"Not long," I say, lying. I turn back just in time to see that I'm about to trip over a root. "Watch out for that. Low-lying branches ahead too."

"I still feel queasy," Luce says.

"Same. Let's just get this over with," I say, wiping my brow. It might be the middle of the night, but it's still stuffy as hell. Thick leaves acting like insulation, fueling the torture of tonight. Or maybe that's just what it feels like because we deserve the torture. It's definitely cooler than it was on the road.

Branches poke out from trees as if they're trying to reach each other, to band together and catch us before we get away with what we're about to do. I push them aside, silently pleading with them to keep our secret.

We weave through, the boys awkwardly maneuvering Arthur as they go, both panting, foreheads shiny with sweat. Each step I take is a *monumental* effort, every cell in my body wanting to stop this.

"All right, here's the spot," I say when we reach the area, the words burning my throat like acid. "This good with you, Jesse?"

He nods and they lower Arthur to the ground. Atlas shakes his hands out and crouches down, tucking his head into his chin.

"Luce and I will start," I tell them, my nylon-covered hands trembling.

Atlas and Jesse look beyond exhausted, and they did carry him all this way.

I take one of the shovels and stab it into the ground. Luce does the same, and very slowly we begin to dig, the odd sniff from me and the sound of spades cutting through the earth making the only sounds.

"Take the top layer off, like how you see turf. We need to be able to put it back," I say.

I dig again, tilt the shovel, and take up the top layer of forest floor. I repeat the motions, my mind wandering elsewhere to protect me from what I'm doing.

We put the turf neatly to the side, knowing we'll need it to look as natural as possible, just in case. Neat piles of the top ground that will conceal our crime.

"We can chuck some leaves on top too," Jesse says, hunting around for fallen leaves. There aren't many in summer, but he manages to grab some.

"Does it need to be long?" Luce asks.

I let out an involuntary gasp, unable to hide my horror. "Yes! We're not folding him in half."

The least we can do is bury him properly, not squashed into a hole.

She nods, retching. "Folding. Oh god. Of course we're not. I don't know what I was saying."

"Let me do some," Atlas says, taking the shovel from me. "Sit down, babe."

I'd usually tell him not to treat me like I'm made of glass, but I'm so grateful that he's ready to take over that I squeeze his arm and go sit down on the ground. My legs give out and I fall on a crusty pile of moss.

Jesse takes over for Luce and marks out where the grave needs to end. He and Atlas work in silence, none of us able to talk much.

It takes hours. Or maybe that's just how it feels. We alternate digging, deciding to go even deeper because we can't stand the thought of Arthur being found by animals.

Or humans.

Eventually we have a hole big enough and a mound of mud beside it.

I heave, gasping for breath, and drop the shovel. Every muscle in my body aches, and the dirt covers my arms so thickly that I don't think I'll ever get it all off.

"Let's get him in," Jesse says, bending down.

Atlas and Jesse pant as they shuffle closer with Arthur flopped over their arms.

I brush my hands on my shorts, trying to get the mud off my nylon-covered palms.

Luce crouches down beside me, breathing through her nose as if she's trying to prevent a breakdown.

I look up through the trees and see the stars shining down on us like thousands of eyes witnessing what we're doing. But we're alone here.

"Marley," Luce whispers. "I don't feel good."

"Don't puke!" Jesse says, his voice bouncing off the trees around us.

"She's not going to," I reply, dropping to my knees and rubbing her back. Well, she might, but I don't want him pressuring her. "It's okay, Luce, just breathe. It's going to be okay."

She shakes her head, looking down at her feet. Her hands are splayed on the ground, just as muddy as I am. The smell of mud so potent I can taste it.

Jesse stumbles in front of us, and they all nearly fall over.

"Careful," I say. They manage to keep hold of Arthur, groaning as they right their balance.

If they'd dropped him, I think I would've been the one to throw up.

Luce raises her head, her usual olive-toned skin now a sickly gray.

"Breathe," I say again. The last thing we need is her leaving DNA near the burial site. Would we have to fill the hole in and dig somewhere else?

I can't do that again. My body is *spent.* I don't have the energy to do anything other than shower and fall into bed. I want to sleep and wake up in the morning with no memory of what we've done.

I'd give anything to be able to forget.

"Okay, turn. Yeah, Atlas, walk toward the girls," Jesse says, giving instructions as if he's talking through plays on the field.

Atlas steps sideways, narrowly missing us. Arthur's foot a yard from my face.

"Wait," Luce says, getting to her feet. I rise with her, ready to catch her if she falls or whisk her away if she's about to hurl. "Once we do this, we can't go back. This is our last chance to do the right thing."

"This *is* the right thing, Lucia," Jesse says, using her full name as if she's a misbehaving kid. "There's no other choice. Go back to the car if you're going to screw this up."

"Don't talk to me like that!"

He grits his teeth. "Look, we'll talk in a bit, but I promise you we're doing what we have to."

"Can we just get this over with?" Atlas says, the tips of his fingers white where he's gripping Arthur so hard.

They shuffle a couple more steps and then bend, the two of them in sync as if they do this regularly.

I watch Atlas's knees sink into the moss-covered ground beside the grave.

"And drop," Jesse says.

Drop.

I close my eyes. "Sorry," I whisper, wincing as I hear a loud thud that I'm sure will replay in my head every second of every day until I die.

When I look up again, Atlas pushes back, almost falling into my side. He turns and presses his face against my shoulder. "Don't hate me," he whispers.

"I don't," I reply, wrapping my arms around his waist and crying. "I love you. We're going to be okay."

I say the words and hope he believes them.

"We need to cover him," Jesse says, trying to sound as gentle as possible when we're talking about throwing mud on a man we just killed. His voice doesn't quite sound right, though. "Get to pushing the dirt on him, and then we'll place the turf back. It won't be perfect, but I think it'll grow and knit together with the undisturbed stuff before anyone notices. That is if anyone ever comes this way again."

We're so far off the trails that it's unlikely you would accidentally stumble across it . . . but that doesn't mean no one ever will.

I have to push that thought away or it will drive me crazy.

Atlas moves aside and I crawl up to the grave. Using the palms of my hands, I push the mound of dirt into the grave, sobbing and whispering over and over how sorry I am.

My body is numb, as if I'm someone else doing this. I work on autopilot, but I still feel the tears rolling down my cheeks, a welcome reminder that I'm not dead inside.

11

"Let's get out of here!" Luce says as I gently lay the last of the turf, sniffing as I tuck Arthur in. I press the soil down as tight as I can, willing it to be enough protection to keep him safe from animals.

"Marley, come on!" Atlas snaps.

I don't want to leave him, but I force myself to my feet, my legs like jelly, and walk away with them.

"I'll drop you all home," Jesse tells us.

"We can't pretend we were home earlier," I say as we all climb back into a truck I'd rather burn.

"We have to, Marley," Luce replies. "I've already told Rhett we were home."

"No, I mean we shouldn't. Or rather *I* shouldn't. I have a doorbell that will show I got home later."

"Delete it from the log," Atlas says.

"Usually I would, but wouldn't it look suspicious if on this particular night there's no evidence of me getting back?"

"A lot of things need to happen before that becomes suspicious," Jesse says. "We've just taken care of the body."

"Arthur," I say.

"New plan," Atlas says. "Drop Marley and me off at mine. I'll take her home. It'll look like she went back with me after the dare."

The lies just keep piling up. One on top of the other, ready to bury us. How long before there are too many to keep straight?

"Good plan," Jesse replies.

No plans we've made tonight have been good, but it seems to be the best we can do.

Jesse drops me and Atlas off first, meaning he'll have to circle back to take Luce home.

Atlas drives to mine in absolute silence, both of us trying to wrap our minds around what happened tonight. I feel so cold, but I don't want to turn up the heat because he's still sweating. I grab a packet of hand wipes he keeps in his car and clean mud off my clothes as best I can. The camera is going to see everything.

"You should stop before mine," I tell him, stuffing the used wipes into my pocket. Another thing to destroy to cover my tracks.

"Why?"

"Because I'm the one with a camera on the door. You can pretend you got home earlier . . . but if you're seen dropping me off, it'll incriminate you too."

"Marley . . ."

I watch him frown as he decides if he wants to potentially save himself and let me go down alone. At least, it seems to be a struggle.

"It's fine, Atlas. Just do it."

He puts the brakes on, stopping before the first house on my street.

"Hey, we're not going to get caught," he says with such conviction I almost believe him. "I mean it."

He can't be certain of that. Doesn't the truth have a nasty habit of always coming out?

"Um . . . I'll see you later," I say, ignoring the sting of him leaving me to do this alone. This was my idea. I want to protect him.

He nods. "I'll message you in a bit."

"Yeah."

On autopilot I get out of his car and walk half a block to my house. If this footage is seen, I need to look like everything is fine. So I try not to look as miserable as I feel and unlock the door.

As soon as I'm inside, I start to shake, adrenaline and shock pumping through my body. I lock the door behind me, fumbling with the handle and almost dropping the key onto the mat.

I flick the light on and walk upstairs. I need to shower until I no longer feel so disgusting. If that's even possible.

Soon there will be no evidence left of what we've done.

Of course, a quarter of the senior class, plus George, saw me out late, but my parents aren't going to question any of them.

I reach around the wall in the bathroom and turn the light on before I walk into the room. My nerves are frazzled, tricking me into believing it's possible for Arthur to be standing by the bathtub.

I spin around, closing and bolting the door. My legs wobble and give out, no longer able to hold my weight or the weight of what I've done. The cool tile seeps into my skin and scatters goose bumps along my bare legs.

Arthur is dead.

I lift my hands in front of my face and notice the dirt beneath my nails, which somehow got in despite the gloves. That has to come off.

I need to get the dirt from Arthur's grave off me.

Gasping, I push myself up from the floor and run to the shower. Once I've turned that on as hot as I'll be able to stand, I tear at my clothes. Jesse said to get rid of them. I don't know if that's as simple as just throwing them away or if I should burn them.

That wouldn't be an easy explanation to my parents, though. We're coming up on a summer that's been forecast as the hottest one on record, and I decide to start my own personal bonfire.

I step under the spray and scrub myself until my skin burns and the quicks of my nails bleed.

It takes me a good ten minutes after I'm clean to turn off the shower and step out. I want to stay in there forever and avoid dealing with what I've done.

But I know that I can't. My parents will be home in an hour, and I need to make it appear like I've been asleep for ages. So I wrap a towel around my body, ignoring how rough it feels against my sensitive skin, and wipe down the mirror.

My reflection staring back at me might as well be that of a stranger. I look different. I can't describe how, nothing about my physical appearance has changed, but I'm not the same.

I can see the horror in my bright eyes.

Turning away, I grab a trash bag from the cabinet and shove my clothes and gloves into it. I'm not sure what to do with them yet, so I carry the bag into my room and stuff it in the bottom of my closet behind my hiking backpack. I'll have to come up with a better plan, but that'll do for tonight.

I can't think about one more thing to cover up what we've done, or I'll lose it, and I'm already just hanging on.

One of my bedroom windows faces the street, so I don't turn the light on, but I can see well enough from the one on the landing that I left on earlier. My parents will expect it too. We always leave a light on.

I dry my hair as fast as I can, chuck the towel in the laundry basket, and put some pajamas on. It's only when I climb into bed that I totally break. Big, fat tears roll down my cheeks, soaking the pillow.

I gasp for oxygen but get nothing.

What have we done?

I've watched this happen on TV before. An accidental death and then the aftermath.

It *never* works out.

My lungs flatten and I gasp again, guilt trying to end me.

My phone dinging gives me some sort of normality, a distraction, and I cling to it like it's a raft in the middle of the ocean.

I lift my head and reach out.

Atlas:

love u

For the longest time, I'm utterly unable to move, as if my brain has forgotten how to send a message. I can't bring myself to do it.

I do love him, and it's such a normal thing to say, but we don't deserve any normal moments.

None of us are okay and we never will be again. I lie in the dark and wait as three dancing dots prepare to deliver another message.

I close my eyes and let the phone drop onto the bed, leaving Atlas's message unanswered. Rolling onto my back, I pray that sleep will hurry the hell up because all I can think about is the sound Arthur's body made when it hit the car and the smell of the dirt when we dug his grave.

• • •

Friday, May 26

Groaning, I stretch my arms and arch my back like a cat. I sit up and notice sunlight streaming through my blinds. But it's a beautiful day, so I can't be annoyed.

And then it hits me. Hard.

My breath catches in my throat as the events of last night come flooding back, crashing into my body and physically knocking me back down.

I bounce gently on the mattress and grip the blanket.

Arthur.

The crash, stuffing him into the truck, digging the hole, rolling him in.

My stomach lurches and I bolt out of bed.

Bursting through the bathroom door, I drop in front of the toilet and vomit, my abs contracting. Tears sting the corners of my eyes. When I'm done, I flush the toilet and stand with trembling legs. Perspiration sits on my skin, making me feel gross.

"Marley?" Mom calls. "Are you okay? It sounded like you were throwing up."

Great.

"Um, yeah. It must've been the leftovers I ate yesterday," I say, the lie rolling off my tongue. I'm getting used to doing that.

"Can I come in?"

"One minute," I say, turning the faucet on and rinsing my acidic mouth. I splash water on my face and neck and press my trembling hands to my cheeks.

I open the door and smile. At least I think I'm smiling, but she looks at me like I'm on my deathbed.

She places her cool palm on my forehead. "Goodness, you're very pale. Get back into bed, you can't go to school like this. It's Friday anyway."

Her soft smile almost makes me double over. Mom has preached and demonstrated kindness every day of my life. She will be so devastated and disappointed if she ever finds out what I've done.

How are we going to keep this a secret for the rest of our lives? Right now, I don't think I can keep it in for one more second.

I clear my throat. "Okay."

She follows me to my room and watches as I climb into bed. My dirty grave-digging clothes are in the closet opposite me.

I take a breath.

"Do you need anything?"

"No, I already have water," I tell her. It's from yesterday so I don't want to drink it, but I do want her to leave me alone.

I press my face into the pillow. "Going to sleep," I mutter. Her softness and concern only make me feel worse.

"All right. I'm going to do the same, but I'm here if you need me, okay? I'm never too tired for you."

Please just go!

I nod and she backs away, leaving my door open. When I hear her go back into her room, I send a message to Atlas. I don't have the energy for the group chat.

Marley:

not coming to school, been throwing up.

Atlas:

what can I do?

Marley:

nothing. See u tomorrow

Atlas:

I'll come by later

I roll over in bed, still feeling as sick as when I first threw up. How am I supposed to keep this secret in? I can't do this. I can't spend the rest of my life pretending that I don't know exactly what happened to Arthur and where he is. George deserves better.

I spend the day in bed, my parents checking in on me a lot. I manage to avoid talking to them by pretending that I'm asleep. But by late afternoon, they "wake" me to check if I'm well enough for them to go into work.

Of course I say yes, because I don't want to be near anyone.

That was a good plan, until they open the door to leave, and I hear them calling up the stairs, telling me Atlas is here and they're heading out.

"Send him up," I shout back, trying to sound like seeing him is something I want to do. They'll be suspicious if I tell them to send him away. I've never done that.

I sit up in bed and run my fingers through my hair, trying in vain to make myself look a little more like myself.

"Hey," he says from the doorway, not quite managing to smile. His dark eyes are full of regret.

"Hi."

"You feeling better?"

"I don't think I'm going to throw up again, if that's what you're asking. How are you? How was school?"

He sits down on the bed, scoots closer, and wraps me in a hug. I take that as school sucked as much as I assumed it would.

I fold into his embrace, wishing I could disappear. Atlas sucks in a breath that sounds like he's struggling to hold it together too. This used to be my safe space, but I don't feel anything right now.

He rubs the back of his neck and sighs as I sit back up. I can see the faint lines of stress around his eyes and the shadows underneath that show a terrible night's sleep.

"Sorry. I'm trying so damn hard to forget it but . . ."

"It's impossible," I say, finishing his sentence.

"Yeah. What did you tell your parents?"

"They heard me throwing up, so I told them I must've eaten something off."

"You were really sick?"

Nodding, I tell him, "I keep replaying the moment the car hit him in my mind."

Atlas groans and lies down beside me. "I'm so sorry, Marley. What can I do?"

"We made the wrong choice."

"I'm not disagreeing."

I sit up and he pushes himself onto his elbow. "You're not?"

"Of course. I'm not a monster! What can we do about it now, though? He's dead and fessing up isn't going to change that. I'd do it if it would."

"George will never know what happened to his grandad."

"We'll lose *everything* if we do . . . the right thing." He groans again, throwing his hand over his eyes. "I'm so conflicted. Jesse and Luce are sure we're doing what we need to do."

I shake my head, anger burning, hating all of us.

"Stuff like this always comes out, Atlas. How long before Arthur is reported missing? It's not like he's home alone anymore."

"I'm on your side," he says, moving his hand and rubbing my leg. "Can we not argue? This is hard enough, and I really need you."

"Okay," I whisper, dialing back on the attitude. I lie down, and we look at each other, the same fear and regret mirrored. "What are we going to do?"

"I'm not sure. But whatever it is, we stick together. *Me* and *you*."

"Why do you say it like that?" I ask, taking his hand, trying to cling on to sanity. "Why not the four of us?" Yesterday Jesse told us we *all* had to stick together. Today Atlas is dividing us.

He shrugs one shoulder. "You're my girl."

No way am I buying that. I can tell when he's omitting something. Or straight up lying.

"Atlas . . ."

"You didn't see Jesse today. Luce too, kind of. He was acting as if nothing happened. I know that's what we agreed to, but he's too good at it. I could barely eat, and I'm not sure I took anything in today. Thank god finals are over."

"Hold on. He was really okay?"

"You'd never know anything was wrong. For me every second was a battle."

I shudder, my body turning cold. "No. That doesn't mean he's not feeling it."

"No."

His reply is hollow, telling me what he thinks I want to hear. The worry etched into his face tells me something entirely different.

It's too easy for Jesse to forget and pretend.

He's scared of losing his future.

But so are we and neither of us is doing great.

"Atlas, what are you saying *exactly*?"

"Nothing. I'm being judgmental."

"You're giving me whiplash here."

He brushes a stray tendril of hair out of my face. "I just mean that I think he should behave the way I am, or there must be something wrong. But he could be struggling as much as us, right?"

"He must be, Atlas. He's one of our best friends. We've known him for years."

I want to see how Luce is doing. She's always gone along with whatever Jesse says or does, the two of them like a little gang within our group.

"Are you coming back to school on Monday?"

"I have to, or they'll get suspicious."

"Your parents will get suspicious?"

"Them and everyone else. It's the final two weeks. Were there any pranks today?"

He nods and closes his eyes. "Rhett's been wandering the halls like he owns the place. God, I *hate* him, Marley. He ruins people's lives and walks away. No remorse."

"He doesn't know what happened last night . . . does he?" I whisper.

He recoils like I've just said the most ridiculous thing he's ever heard. "No. We have a pact. The secret dies with us."

"The secret might be what kills us."

"Don't say that." His hand tightens around mine.

My phone dings with a message. Atlas and I both look at the screen, seeing Rhett's name. It's not the group chat this time.

"What does he want?" Atlas sneers.

I pick it up and read. My mouth drops, and I turn the screen so Atlas can see it.

Rhett:

Your individual dare is to spend the night in the forest.

It's a recycled dare, and not one I have any intention of following through on. I'm done, beyond done, with the stupid dares.

We killed a man.

I toss my phone onto the mattress. "Looks like I have another dare," I tell him. "So, I'm guessing he wants me to sneak out after dark and back in before my parents wake up."

"What? This is insane. You're not going to do it, are you?"

"No way!"

"Good."

"Yeah? I thought you'd try to talk me into it."

"I don't want you to have anything to do with that asshole. I knew the dares would ramp up. Rhett needs to go bigger than Everett and Emmett did." He rolls his eyes, fingers so tight around mine that my knuckles crunch together. It's not an unpleasant feeling; it's keeping my mind from wandering.

"He didn't ask us to kill anyone. He wasn't behind the wheel, and he didn't pick up a shovel."

Atlas's eyes cut to me as if he thinks I'm defending Rhett. I'm not. It's just the truth. We can't blame anyone else for what we did.

"Doesn't matter what he asked us to do. He's dangerous. Who gives that kind of dare anyway? You'll stay away from him, right? He's still got a massive thing for you."

It's not the first time I've heard that, but it is the first time that it physically makes me ill. My stomach heaves. Thankfully there's nothing left inside me to bring up, so I swallow the urge to retch and snuggle closer to Atlas.

"When do you think he'll want you to do the dare?"

"No idea," I reply, covering a yawn with the back of my hand.

With Atlas here, I suddenly feel exhausted and like I could sleep for a whole year, but my conscience is only letting me get a few minutes at a time.

I don't want to do any more of Rhett's dares, but getting lost in the woods doesn't sound too bad right now.

12

Monday, May 29

School feels bigger and darker today, like the building grew over the weekend. It's blistering hot and humid, but the sun is hidden behind thick gray clouds. I wish it would rain, wash away the layer of sweat that already sits on my skin.

Wash away the horror of the last four nights too.

I managed to have a quiet weekend, avoiding almost everyone. It was a necessity. I felt like my guilt was etched into my forehead and anyone would be able to see. Atlas came over for a bit, but he mostly wanted to be alone too.

As soon as I pull into the lot, I'm greeted by Luce, who runs to my car and opens my door. "I'm so happy to see you, Marley," she says, pulling on my wrist so I get out faster. Her dark hair is tied in an intentionally messy bun, and her face is glowing.

"Yeah," I reply, unable to meet her eye. Why doesn't she look a mess like me? I spent more time on my appearance than usual, but I still think I look like I haven't slept in a month.

"Are you okay?" she asks, and I finally hear the apprehension in her voice.

"Are you?"

She dips her chin and kicks a stray rock on the ground. "Obviously not. I can tell what you're thinking, and I'm not fine. People are around and we can't let anyone know something's up, can we?"

I'm not sure if that's rhetorical. I wish she was genuinely asking because I really need to know that she's struggling with this decision too.

Arthur was dead when we found him, and it took us, like, five minutes to turn into criminals. I don't think there was any chance that he could've been revived even if we knew what we were doing . . . but we still should've called for help and tried.

Now we're just killers.

That's what we'll be before anything else for the rest of our lives.

Cold. Calculated. Killers.

I look over my shoulder in case anyone's coming near us. "We could let someone know what's up, but the decision to lie has already been made."

She steps closer, head whipping in both directions. For someone who doesn't want anything to look out of the ordinary, she's doing a shockingly good job of looking suspicious.

"I hate this too, Marley," she whispers, her voice wobbly like she's about to cry.

I raise my head and finally look at her properly. There are tears in her eyes that she rapidly blinks away. I've never felt so relieved to see raw guilt on my best friend's face before.

"Luce, how are we going to pretend that this never happened? Arthur's body *will* be found. There will be an investigation."

"Shhh. We made a mistake. I hate that he was hurt, but we'll lose everything if this gets out."

"He wasn't hurt, Luce. We *killed* him."

She stumbles back like my words are a physical blow. "He didn't mean to do it."

Her defense of Jesse doesn't surprise me, and she's not wrong. But Arthur is still dead because of him. And he's buried in the forest because of us.

I raise my palms to pacify her. We can't turn this into a fight. I thought returning to school would make things worse, but I see more clearly now. If we're going to figure out what to do long-term, we have to stay calm.

"I was there, Luce. I know it was an accident."

"Good. It's going to be okay. We stick together. Look, I need to meet Jesse, so I'll see you later."

Before I can reply, she spins and jogs off toward the main entrance.

That was kind of weird.

"Why didn't you reply to my message?" a familiar voice calls out from behind me.

Are you kidding me?

I turn to face Rhett as he approaches. This asshole makes me want to throw up, but I'm not letting him get to me.

"Why would I?"

"You have a dare."

"I've done two already. We're the only ones who've done two, and you want me to do a third. Why?"

The anger, the pure, unfiltered anger that I have for him seeps from my every pore. If it wasn't for him and his stupid dares, we wouldn't have been on the road that night. Arthur would be alive.

He's not to blame!

"You think you're so goddam important, Rhett, but you're a small-town boy who I'm not even going to remember next month. No one cares about you or your pathetic games, so grow the hell up and leave me alone."

His pale eyebrows shoot to the top of his head. I might be the first person who's ever said that to him.

I ball my hands into fists and push them into the apprehension in my gut as if I could squish every last part of it into nothing. I wish it made me feel better. Even just a fraction.

"Wow, Marley. I'm impressed."

"I don't care what you are." I go to pass him, but his arm shoots out, blocking my way. "Move!"

"No, I don't think I will. You've been given a dare."

"What about your dares, huh? Or are you too scared to join in yourself? Worried what Mommy and Daddy might say?"

"You think you're baiting me but you're not."

That's a total lie. I can tell by the way his dead eyes fire lasers into me.

"Are you sure?"

"All right . . . we'll camp in the forest together."

I don't mean to laugh, because there's very little humor in my life after Arthur, but I do. I laugh in his face and don't even try to hide it. "I'd rather get eaten by bears."

"You might if you go alone."

"Is that what you're hoping?"

He smirks, and I have no idea what he's thinking. My guess would be "totally."

"I'm done here," I say, shoving his arm aside and walking past him. How can I be frightened of whatever he has planned when I've already committed the worst crime?

I walk into school, and I'm immediately hit with a rotten fish smell that stings my nose and makes me gag.

What the hell kind of prank is this? Pressing my palm to my nose and mouth, I rush through the corridor, watching people look for the source of the smell. It's so bad that I almost vomit. Fuller and two teachers are pacing the corridor, looking up as if they'll magically find the source of the smell on the ceiling.

I make my way to the gym, ignoring the stupid pranks. They're no longer fun.

I have a full morning of sports to get through on the field, but first I need to change. Whoever thought it would be a "treat" to force us into multiple sporting activities for two hours needs firing. At least I'm in the first half of seniors. The other half gets the torture after lunch.

I can think of about a million other things I'd rather do, but I have to appear normal.

Out on the field, I see Jesse.

He's chatting with a couple of guys from the team. He laughs, throwing his head back. Nothing about his demeanor shows that he's struggling. I didn't think his acting was that good—I had drama with him for two years.

He notices me approach, slaps Jake on the back, and jogs toward me.

"Hi," I say.

But I can tell I'm not going to be met with the same greeting by the scowl on his face.

"You can't have another day off, Marley! Think about how that looks. And where the hell were you this weekend? You could've at least shown your face in town."

Did Atlas?

"I'm fine now, thanks. How are you?"

His head tilts and he grits his teeth. "I'm not playing here. You're not screwing this up."

"What the hell, Jesse? I haven't done anything wrong."

Atlas wasn't lying when he said he was different. It's day four and I barely recognize him. What's he's doing?

Stop, he's just panicking.

He steps closer. "I'm sorry if I'm not behaving in the way you want me to, but there's a lot riding on this."

"I understand that!"

We both pause as a couple of people walk past us.

As soon as they pass, I say, "How is it going to look if you suddenly stop talking to me?"

"Who said I'm not talking to you? And you're the one who went MIA."

"I just needed time. I was off on Friday, so it doesn't look weird that I wasn't in town over the weekend. It looks like I'm getting over a bug. If you keep arguing with me, it'll look weird."

"I didn't come over to argue. I just wanted to know what you're thinking." He looks over my shoulder, checking that we're alone, paranoia hitting hard.

"I just needed a few days. My mom heard me throwing up and wouldn't let me come to school."

"Don't let it happen again."

"You can't control when you puke, Jesse! Stop acting like we're freaking enemies. I have enough of that with Rhett."

He pinches the bridge of his nose. "I can't deal with your drama right now, just keep it together. The rest of us aren't going down because you can't hold your own."

I open my mouth to tell him he's way off, I'm not the weak link here, I don't want to break my parents' hearts or throw away my future, but he walks past me.

His teammates frown as he walks back over to them. I don't know if he thought about how icing me out would look. After Rhett it shouldn't hurt, but it does.

He might not be trying to ditch me, but how he's acting triggers something in me, and I hate the thought of someone else I care about walking away like I mean nothing.

After a few games of dodgeball, we go to lunch. Fuller walks through the cafeteria with a face like thunder. He shakes his head, muttering something about shrimp and locks on the refrigerators.

"The smell was shrimp?" I ask Luce. She's sitting opposite me, leaning against Jesse.

Atlas takes a seat next to me and kisses my cheek. "Yep. Shrimp in the air vents. You've been outside all morning, but there were people here searching for it."

Luce laughs. "You should've seen how mad Fuller was. He's seriously over senior pranks."

"I wonder how much money these pranks cost the school," Jesse mutters around a mouthful of hamburger. There's nothing wrong with his appetite.

"Ew, don't talk," chides Luce.

I turn to Atlas while they bicker and whisper, "Is Jesse acting weird with you?"

"No, he's been fine. Why?"

Great, so it *is* just me. "We had a bit of an argument. He walked off and didn't speak to me for the rest of the morning, took off as soon as the games were over."

He rolls his eyes. "He's just as stressed as the rest of us, Marley. I mean, he was driving, right?"

I glance up, but Jesse and Luce are still oblivious that other people exist. "I can give him some space."

It's understandable that he's struggling, but I'm annoyed that he's instantly written me off as the one who's going to crack.

"What're you talking about?" Jesse asks, his attention now on us.

I sit up straight. "Nothing. Everything's cool."

His brows rise. "Are you sure?"

"Why are you only asking me?"

Atlas puts his hand on my back as if he believes I'm the one causing this friction.

"You weren't here Friday. I already checked in with Luce and Atlas."

Okay, fine . . . but we have had a similar conversation already. I feel like he's checking up on me.

"Sorry, I'm just . . . devastated."

"Yeah, I get it," he replies. "Marley, we all are, and it's only a matter of time before George reports him missing."

I drop my fork back on the plate, no longer hungry. George must be going out of his mind worrying. We're already on the fourth day. Arthur does go off on trips sometimes, but it's not common for him to be gone that long.

"Did you destroy the clothes and gloves?" I whisper.

He nods, pushing fries around on his plate. Looks like his appetite is gone too. "It's taken care of. The shovels are at Luce's, stored in her uncle's shed with the rest of his gardening equipment."

Luce's uncle lives with Luce and her parents and owns a garden maintenance company that my dad uses. I've seen the shed. It's absolutely massive and full of everything you could possibly need for gardening.

"There are so many shovels and rakes, I don't think he'd notice two more," Luce adds.

"Is that a good idea, though?"

"We'll think of something to do with them," Jesse says. "They've been cleaned for now. I can't burn them because of the metal parts. I might be able to take them to the landfill."

"You should definitely do that," Atlas says.

Jesse glances over at me, and the way he looks is as if he's scrutinizing everything I say and do. I wonder what he's thinking about me.

When he doesn't look away, I ask, "We okay, Jesse?"

He stares into my eyes in a way that makes me feel . . . odd.

Atlas waves a hand in his direction. "She hasn't done anything wrong, dude."

He finally nods. "Yeah, we're good."

For the first time, I don't believe him. He's done nothing but shut me out and lie to me today. His gaze follows me a little too hard.

"Fuller's going out of his mind," Jesse says, laughing and changing the subject. "Not impressed with today's pranks."

Luce playfully whacks him. "I don't know what Fuller is so worked up about, it took them twenty minutes tops to clean things up."

"Are we really talking about pranks?" I ask, my eyes flitting between my two friends.

Jesse scowls. "Don't start."

"Drop it," Atlas says, and for a second, I think he's talking to Jesse.

But he's looking at me, and his stare is a warning. What the hell?

I turn away, my insides burning. We have to act normal, sure, but we don't need to discuss dares or pranks.

13

The summer fair is another thing I was excited for. It's held on the school field every year because there isn't another space big enough—that isn't taken up by tons of trees anyway.

It's the perfect afternoon too, warm but overcast so we don't all burn under the sun. One of the reasons it's held after work and school.

I pass traditional fairground games like Skee-Ball, Whac-A-Mole, and horseshoes, searching for Atlas. He was helping to set up earlier.

I'm still annoyed at him for the thing in the cafeteria today. I'm not trying to constantly remind him of what we've done, but I also can't just zap back to being completely normal. It's like Jesse isn't even pretending. When we're alone, I don't think we should joke about pranks.

Fuller is about, along with a few teachers, but it's mostly residents who make today possible. He's only here because some of the school is unlocked so people can use the restrooms. He doesn't trust anyone else.

I walk around the giant ring toss and almost slam into Rhett. His brows lift and he tilts his head like a villain. "Hey, Marley."

"Have you seen Atlas?"

"Many times, unfortunately."

That was my bad—I shouldn't have assumed he'd tell me if he had.

"Never mind," I say, walking around him.

I don't get far because he grabs my wrist. "What's going on with you? You've been acting weird."

Out of everyone in the whole school, he is the last person I expect to notice. All he's done since he cut ties with me is act like I'm a constant irritation.

"What?" I ask, flustered.

"You were off Friday, which is weird in itself—you never miss school. You looked like a zombie this morning. What gives?"

I force a smile on my lips, not too genuine-looking, or he'll know. "Rhett. It's the end of the year, there's lots going on, and lots to do to prepare for college. Now, if you don't mind, I'm bored of you."

That was just bitchy enough for him to believe that I'm a bit tired and it's still me under there. He scoffs, stepping to let me by and muttering, "Loser."

He's off his game too.

I wonder what his reason is.

I don't get two steps before my next shock. He turns, and the air leaves my lungs as if he's punched me in the chest.

"George," I mutter, my heart aching at the sight of him. No news about Arthur has spread, but that's not exactly a surprise.

"Got a crush on him, have you?" Rhett asks, still not leaving me the hell alone.

George lifts his hand as he makes his way over.

I do a double take and scowl at Rhett. "What are you still doing here? Go find Ruthie."

I walk away from him, knowing his little comments aren't going to help when I have to face George . . . which will be in about three seconds because his long legs take big strides.

"Hey, I was hoping I'd run into you," he says. "I have a question."

My skin itches all over at talking to him, but I manage a reply. "Shoot."

"I know he's pretty reclusive, but I don't suppose you've seen my grandad?"

"What?" I ask, looking around with anxiety gnawing in my stomach.

This was always going to happen. Breathe. Act.

He laughs. "No, not here."

I know he's not here—I'm looking for help. Even Rhett will do. I was wrong: it's so much worse talking to George alone, especially when he brings Arthur up. George is worried.

"Oh. No, sorry. Why?"

"I know you pass the house to get from home to school, so I just wondered."

"Are you looking for him here?"

"No. I volunteered for this. Grandad's suggestion, believe me. Wanted something to keep me busy," he says, leaning in. "Look, I haven't seen him since Thursday night. The cops aren't worried."

My heart skips a beat. He's been searching for him. Of course he has. I don't know what I expected; this was always going to happen.

I wring my hands together to stop myself scratching at the itch along my arms. "Another hike or fishing trip, maybe."

"No." He huffs and rubs his shoulder. "At least, I don't think so. All of his supplies are still at the house, and besides, he hasn't gone out to fish in years."

I frown. "He does go into the mountain a lot. Your shoulder okay?"

"Huh? Oh, yeah, just aches from holding a flashlight all night while I searched the forest. No one else seems to think it's strange for him to take off. I've known him to go for a day or two, that's it."

"I mean, there are times when we don't see him at all for weeks. He doesn't come out a lot. I think he does still fish, I've seen him with rods."

This isn't strictly true, and I hate myself for planting a seed of hope in George's mind, but what other choice do I have?

"Where in the mountains?"

"I'm not sure exactly. But he's not always home, George. It is strange that it's happened when you're in town, but he does disappear. I take it he doesn't have a phone?"

He shakes his head. "Only the landline, and I'm not sure that even works anymore."

"How do you keep in contact with him?"

"He used to write letters to my mom." Dipping his head, he adds, "I haven't kept in touch as much as I should've."

That's really sad. They're both lonely. Or George is lonely and Arthur was.

I almost reach out for George but stop myself. Comforting him would also be comforting myself, and I don't deserve it. "Don't beat yourself up over that. He knows you care."

"I don't know what to do now. There's no sign of him."

His words are like a mace hitting me over and over. *There's no sign of him.* We made sure of that. The tire marks are gone. The blanket and gloves are gone. Arthur is gone.

"Did he know you were coming?"

"No, I surprised him."

I touch his arm. "Then he might've had it planned. It's not like he's used to factoring someone else in when he makes plans. It could've slipped his mind to tell you."

"Maybe. His car's gone but none of his clothes are. Or I don't think they are."

I jolt at his words. Arthur's car is gone? We didn't do that.

Well, *I* didn't do that.

"Would you know if all of his clothes were there?" I mutter, blindsided by the missing car. I don't know when they did that or why they didn't tell me.

George frowns. "Okay, maybe not. But if you were going on a trip, you'd pack a few things. His drawers are full."

The urge to get him to shut up is overwhelming. I lick my lips. "H-he'll come back soon, George, I'm sure. Try not to worry."

"I should get to my stall," he says, smiling sadly. "Thanks for listening, Marley."

"Wait. Let me know if I can do anything or if you just want to chat. You have my number."

"Thanks."

I watch him retreat, heading to the cotton candy stall. I'll be skipping that one today.

How long before the cops start searching?

Will they just assume he's dead when they can't find him? That's what we're waiting for.

"I've been looking for you," Atlas says, throwing his arm over my shoulder and holding me a little too tight. He's worried. "Was that George?"

"Yes," I whisper.

"And?"

"He's gone to the cops about Arthur being missing, but they're not worried yet."

"We knew this was coming," he says, robotically kissing the side of my head. "It's not a surprise."

"Doesn't mean I'm not freaking out. George is worried. Arthur has someone who worries about him."

He wraps me in his arms. To everyone else we look loved up, but I know he's trying to stop anyone from seeing my expression or meltdown. His embrace feels forced. Why didn't he tell me about the car?

Cold dread pumps through my veins. This is going to unravel.

No. I'm not going to let it get that far. I won't fall apart and be the reason we all lose out on college and end up in prison.

We just have to get through this initial phase.

I can't believe I'm wishing for a time when everyone gives up on Arthur.

"I'm fine, but Jesse isn't. Did you know that Arthur's car is missing?"

He holds me tighter. "I can feel your heart racing."

I pull back and scowl at him. "Atlas, did you know that Arthur's car is missing?"

"Not here," he says, smiling and almost making me laugh at how his expression and tone are polar opposites. But I'm not laughing, because he knows.

"Not here? You have to be kidding! Why are you lying to me?"

He doesn't let go, and his expression never changes, but I can feel the tension rolling from his body. "Jesse took care of it. He had to. We need it to appear like he went away."

"Why didn't you tell me?"

"Because you were struggling. You took a day off. We couldn't risk your reaction."

"My reaction. My reaction to stealing the car from the guy we'd just—"

"Stop," he hushes.

No one around us is paying any attention whatsoever. I narrow my eyes, wanting nothing more than to shove him away. His hands feel like ice around my back.

"Don't tell me to stop! I can't believe you all did this and kept it quiet."

"What choice did we have? You were physically sick, babe, and we didn't want to make it worse."

"Now you're making it seem like you were doing me a favor. You're with them, aren't you? Thinking I'm going to crack like an egg and drop us all in prison. I don't want to spend the rest of my life in a cell either. And I don't want to hurt my parents!"

"All right, all right. I'm sorry. I don't know how to do this, Marley. I'm trying to figure out what's best as I go. God, I'm not good at this."

"I don't want you to keep things from me."

He drops his gaze for half a second before looking at me again. "Okay."

"Where's the car?"

"Jesse wouldn't say. Just told us that it's taken care of."

"What about Luce?"

"She knows but she didn't go with him."

Of course she knows.

"Right."

Well, at least it's only Jesse's DNA in it.

"Can we have some fun this afternoon?" he asks, pulling me closer. "Please?"

"Sure," I reply, though I feel like doing anything else. "Come on."

Playing innocent is the hardest task I have taken on. Everything changes when you've committed a crime as horrific as what we've done. You start to look at things differently, wonder if people are looking at you because they know. Did George ask me because I pass the house or because he suspects me?

Has Rhett found out somehow?

Do I look like a killer?

I hold Atlas's hand tight and we walk around the fair, doing a lap to see what we can stomach pretending is fun. I'm hyperaware of George at the cotton candy stall. He hasn't searched for me again, as far as I'm aware, but that doesn't stop my heart from dropping every time I see a tall blond guy walking in my direction.

"What do you want to do?" Atlas asks.

I'm about to argue when I see the fear in his eyes. He might not be outwardly struggling, but he's as shattered as I am. No need to make this harder.

Clearing my throat, I reply, "What about if you try to win me a two-dollar teddy by knocking down coconuts? It'll only cost you thirty bucks."

The teddies are probably worth about thirty cents, but it makes him laugh and makes me feel like maybe one day I can be normal again.

"You got it."

We reach the stall, and Rhett is throwing a wooden ball, Ruthie beside him giggling as if Rhett has ever made a decent joke in his life.

"Let's come back later," I say.

"What? No, Marley. He's not getting the satisfaction."

"I don't want to be anywhere near him . . . not after the dares."

Not after Arthur.

"That's exactly why we're staying. Everything's fine."

Ruthie looks over her shoulder, and her pointy face turns into one big scowl. "Oh great, the trash is out to play."

Rhett does a double take and smirks as he spots us. "Want a turn, Atlas?"

"I'll wait."

"I don't mind sharing. Here," he says, holding out a ball.

If it wasn't for you and those stupid dares . . .

I narrow my eyes at Rhett, hate pouring into my bloodstream.

"Just finish up and move on, Rhett. You're exhausting," I say.

"Hey, I insist. Atlas needs to do something to cheer you up."

Atlas's hand tightens around mine, but his face doesn't display any hint of alarm. He just looks like he wants to hit Rhett.

"Marley's got nothing to do with you."

"Um. Hello!" Ruthie snaps, seething as Rhett pays more attention to us than her.

I don't know why she stays with him. Absolutely no self-respect. She turns her gaze, and a shudder rocks through my body at the smirk on her face and dark glint in her eye. It's a look like she knows something that I don't. It's smug and makes her ugly.

"Come on, this is boring anyway," Rhett says, taking Ruthie's hand and dragging her away.

"Did you see the way she just looked at me?" I ask Atlas.

"She hates you because he likes you."

"No." I have no time for that drama. "I'm not talking about her asshole boyfriend. It was . . . It put me on edge. Like the way a serial killer looks right before the final blow."

"You think she wants to kill you?" He arches his brow like he thinks I'm losing it. That's absolutely how I feel, but this isn't about Ruthie.

"No," I sigh. "I'm saying . . ."

He waits, running his hands up and down my arms as if I'm cold. "What are you saying?"

Honestly, I don't know. There's just something about her that's put me on edge. More than usual.

"Ignore me. You're probably right, she's never been a fan."

"You sure you're okay?"

"Def. Have you noticed that Luce and Jesse are keeping their distance?" I ask, spotting Luce look over and quickly away again.

"They're just doing their own thing."

"Since when?"

He shrugs. "Stop reading into everything. Are you bored with me?"

"Of course not, I just think it's weird they're not with us."

I look around for Jesse and find him quickly. His eyes pinned on me, watching like I'm his prey. He's jolted by Theo, another member of the team, and it takes Jesse a second to greet him.

"They have other friends too," Atlas says, noticing where I'm looking.

Good. He's been nothing but crappy to me since that night. I don't really want Jesse with us . . . but Luce is my best friend. I hate that she's keeping her distance.

With an uneasy gnawing in my stomach, I ask, "Are you going to win me a tiny teddy, then?"

Atlas laughs and flexes his muscles. He has a good arm—that's what got him on the football team. I follow him to the front, and he picks up one of the three wooden balls.

My attention is pulled away after he's thrown the first ball, eyes drifting to George's stand. The hairs on the back of my neck stand as I notice George staring back at me. Then he quickly turns to Jesse and Luce.

I gasp quietly. They've gone over to him. Why would they voluntarily talk to him?

George hands over two sticks of cotton candy, and they all laugh at something Jesse just said.

My stomach rolls, bile hitting the back of my throat. I feel like the world is spinning. I want them away from George.

"I just need the bathroom, be back in a minute," I tell Atlas. He barely acknowledges me, too distracted, and I jog to the building.

The doors are open but thankfully the bathroom is deserted.

I grip the edges of the sink and look in the mirror. Atlas is right, I'm struggling. Big-time. How the hell am I going to get through the last few weeks of school?

Breathing deeply, I wait until I don't feel like I might pass out and then turn the faucet on to splash some cold water on my face.

Water drips down my wrists, soaking into the sleeves bunched at my elbows.

"Get it together," I whisper to my ghostly reflection, the horror of what I've done stripping the electric blue from my eyes.

I walk out of the bathroom and almost jolt. George is moving toward me.

"You okay?" I ask, managing to keep my voice level, when inside I'm freaking out.

Has he figured it out?

Frowning, he asks, "Are you?"

"Yeah, why?"

"Nothing, you just look a bit jumpy. Pale."

I force a laugh. "Sorry, didn't expect anyone to be there. Halls are quiet. I'm always pale. I was thinking, have you tried the green lake?"

"The what?"

"Right, you're not from around here. Um, it's the lake right at the bottom of the mountain, surrounded by so much moss all you can see is green. I've only been there a few times because it's so far away, but I'm thinking that wouldn't be an issue for Arthur."

"Thanks, I'll tell the cops. Sounds like I'd get lost if I tried finding it."

I nod. "For sure you would."

"I just wish he'd let me know he's okay."

"He probably forgot. Doesn't usually have to tell anyone he's taking off."

George scratches his jaw. "Yeah, you're—"

"Marley."

George and I both startle and turn to find Jesse.

"I'll see you around," George says, walking off toward the bathrooms. I want to go after him and figure out what's going on.

Where is Luce? She was right with Jesse.

"What?" I say as he approaches, trying to act casual. The scowl on his face and his rigid shoulders make me nervous. He wants to intimidate me.

Mission accomplished.

"Why are you talking to him again?"

It takes every ounce of courage I have not to step back. "He came up to me, Jesse. What would you like me to do, ignore him?"

"Yeah."

I tilt my head. "Because that would look totally normal. Stop focusing on me and start thinking about yourself. Is there CCTV anywhere you drove Arthur's car?"

He narrows his eyes, jaw twitching at being challenged. "That's not for you to worry about."

"How can you say that? I'm not the one leaving DNA in Arthur's freaking car."

"There is no DNA left, and I'm not the one getting cozy with his grandson."

No DNA left. So maybe he burned it or drove it into a river.

"Grow up, we were just talking. I'm done here, you need to cool off," I say, moving past him.

He doesn't call me back or say anything else, but I also don't hear his footsteps. I can feel his gaze burning the back of my head.

14

Tuesday, May 30

I watch out my window as rain pelts the ground, bouncing back up as if it's trying to get home to the clouds. The drains outside my house are already overflowing, water drifting along the road, ripples reflecting in the streetlight.

The rain was needed. It was too hot and dry for such a long time. It comes down so heavy I can barely see beyond it. I wish it would wash away my guilt.

I ignore another message from Jesse, but I see it flash up on my screen.

Jesse:

don't talk to anyone

The previous two read "I'm keeping an eye on u" and "this goes to our grave." He sounds nothing like the friend he used to be. I can't get my head around how fast he's changing.

All I can think about is how he kept watching me and then cornered me at the fair. It was intense with George and Jesse. Even Luce, with her avoidance.

I feel like we're all slowly falling apart. Will we have a two-way split soon? Me and Atlas. Jesse and Luce. College is coming up so fast, it would be easy to drift apart. That's what's coming anyway, right?

That's what probably should happen. I don't see how we can find a way to go back to how things were before Arthur. Half of me wants us to all go our separate ways, and the other half thinks that would only add to the tragedy.

Only Atlas and I will be in the same state. It's a six-hour drive between UCLA and Berkeley, but still close enough to spend weekends together. He's even planned the fastest route.

He will be over soon, but I asked him not to mention it to the others. After the way Jesse is treating me, I don't want him in my house. I mean, he thought what yesterday? That I was going to confess everything to George outside the restrooms at school?

I open my closet and look at the bag of clothes at the back, neatly hidden behind my hiking bag and a pile of blankets. I know the others have gotten rid of their clothes, but I can't light a fire without my parents getting suspicious. Throwing them away seems careless.

So I'm holding on to them, which seems worse, but I think I have an idea.

I hear the rumble of Atlas's car as he pulls into my driveway. I step back and close the closet door. He would help me dispose of the clothes if I asked him. I don't know why I don't.

I glance out the window and watch him sprint from his car to the house. He lets himself in as always.

"I'm upstairs," I shout as I hear the door open and close.

His footsteps thud up to my room. He's brushing off his damp hair when he walks in. "Hey," he says, coming to the window to sit on the window seat with me. "What're you doing?"

"Watching the rain. Did you tell the others?"

"No, you said not to. I think Jesse is going to Luce's anyway. They seem in their own world even more lately. I guess they're making the most of the time before they're in different states."

Yeah, I suppose we can pretend that's true, and that Arthur hasn't changed everything.

"I've had three messages from Jesse today. He keeps checking in on me."

"He's worried."

"I understand but it's not helpful. He's . . . different."

"You don't think we all are?" He clears his throat, rubs his jaw, and then looks up at me. "We'll never be the same again, Marley."

"Well aware of that. He's different with *me*."

Why can't Atlas see that?

He smiles and sits back against the wall, looking out to the rain. He doesn't believe me. Or he just thinks I'm being stupid and dramatic. Of course we're not all going to have the same relationship.

We share a horrible secret, one that we could all ruin each other with. But we'd destroy ourselves in the process.

My phone dings, making me jump. Atlas laughs and nudges my leg. Not funny. It doesn't take much to spook me now.

Unknown:

heavy rain is killer for the mud

I suck in a ragged breath. *What?*

As I go for a reread, the message disappears, and my eyes widen.

"Oh my god."

"What?" Atlas asks, his voice sounding far away. "Hey, what's wrong?"

"I just got a text, but it's gone. It said 'heavy rain is killer for the mud.'"

"What? Are you sure?" He takes my phone but there's nothing there now.

"I'm *really* sure."

Killer for the mud. Arthur's grave.

"Who the hell was it from?"

I finally blink as my eyes start to sting. It snaps me out of my trance. "Unknown number and I can't see now. Atlas, someone knows!"

"Just calm down a second, we don't know that."

"What else can that mean? We have to go back!" I press my fingers to my temples, massaging a headache away. Doesn't work. "W-we need to know."

"It could be a trap, Marley. Let's just take a minute."

"What do you suggest, then?" I snap. "We can't ignore this. What if the grave has been disturbed? If it has, animals could get to him."

There's something about Arthur being eaten by wildlife that makes my heart break.

Atlas pinches the bridge of his nose. "Okay, let's think. We need to find out, I'm with you there. But if this person does know, we have to be careful."

"It wouldn't be Jesse, would it?"

"Why would it be Jesse?"

"I don't know. Maybe he wants to scare me. He's freaking out because he thinks I'm going to crack and tell someone. I'm not."

"I know," he replies, staring at the screen. "He wouldn't do this. Think about it. Why push you when he knows you're struggling?"

I shrug. He's right, it wouldn't make sense for Jesse to do this. He wants to keep me quiet.

"Who else could it be?" I ask.

"Do you remember seeing anyone else on the road that night?"

I try to think back, but it's not a memory I want to relive. I've worked *really* hard to block it all out. "Only that cop car, but we took care of that. It drove straight past us. This is going to come out, Atlas," I say, nibbling the skin around my nails. "We're going to be caught, and it'll be worse because we tried to hide it."

"You're getting ahead of yourself. Stop panicking and we'll figure it out. We have to tell the others about this, you know that, right? We need to get them here."

"I don't want them here."

"Marley!"

"All right!" I say, looking back out the window. "Call them."

Atlas sighs and makes a call.

"You're taking this personally," he says, once he hangs up. "We're all scared and trying to figure this out. I've argued with them too. They've snapped at me."

"Is Jesse constantly checking up on you? Is your best friend ghosting you?"

"Just give them time to get their heads around this, okay?"

Neither of us says anything else, because we keep going around in circles. It's exhausting and a total downward spiral. I can't keep a level head, so I'm going to wait for the others and see how they handle it. At this point, I'm happy to follow their lead, because I have no clue what we should do.

It takes ten minutes, but they turn up in Jesse's truck. The last couple of days, they've arrived at school in Luce's car. They're both here to sort out my latest drama. At least, that's probably how Jesse is going to see it.

Why was the message only sent to me?

I've been going over that, and honestly, I have nothing.

I wasn't the one driving the car. Why wasn't the text sent to Jesse?

"What the hell is this?" Jesse asks, bursting into my room with Luce trailing behind.

Luce is the only one who looks scared. Jesse looks *angry*.

I hold my phone up, and he snatches it from my fingers.

"There's no way of finding out who this is?" he asks.

"I don't see how," I reply.

"Maybe we should ask who it is," Luce suggests.

Jesse turns to her. "I'm sure they'll tell us."

"Will you stop?" she snaps. "We're all fed up, Jesse. Quit acting like you're in charge."

I'd applaud if I wasn't so terrified about the text. She doesn't often stand up to him like that. I'm proud.

Jesse straightens his back. No one says anything for a full minute, all waiting to see how he'll react. He's never usually like this. He doesn't yell at us or treat us like crap.

"All right. I'm sorry." He looks at each one of us. "I don't mean to be an asshole, Luce, okay? I'm just trying to hold this together. We'll be off to college soon, and everything will be fine. We just need to hold on a bit longer, and this message is seriously screwing with that."

"Rhett?" I offer. "It was his dare, so it'd make sense for him to watch it through."

"Would he wait around, though? The accident happened after Jesse reached the fork," Atlas says.

"No, she's onto something," Jesse says. "He hates all of us, and this is exactly something that he'd use. Think about it—anyone else would've called the cops, right? Rhett is the kind of rotten-to-the-core person who would use this to get something he wants."

If Rhett is rotten to the core for messing with us rather than going to the cops, what does that make us? I don't ask Jesse because it's unhelpful right now . . . and I also know the answer.

We are way worse than Rhett, or whoever this person is.

"How do we expose him?" Luce asks. "What does he want?"

"First thing we need to do is find out if Arthur's grave really is caving in," Jesse says.

"Now?" Atlas asks. "Because I'm not sure I can swing that. I'm meant to be home in an hour, spending time with my dad."

"And there is no way I can see that grave again without throwing up," Luce says, pressing her hand into her stomach.

Jesse sighs. "Marley, you have anywhere to be?"

“No.”

“Your stomach okay?”

No.

“Yeah.”

He nods. “Then let’s go for a hike.”

15

Jesse drives, his wipers snapping back and forth, swishing water from the windshield only for it to be replaced the next second. Rain drops from the sky like a giant waterfall.

"It's getting worse," I say.

"We'll be fine."

I side-eye him, noticing how tense his shoulders are and how hard he's gripping the steering wheel. He's no longer relaxed behind the wheel . . . or with me.

That makes two of us.

"Jesse, you know I'm not going to mess this up, don't you?"

"No, I don't. You wanted to go to the cops right away."

Isn't that a normal instinct?

"I wasn't thinking," I tell him. "I know this is what we have to do, and I'm in. Forever."

The words don't quite feel right to me because this isn't what I intend to do for the rest of my life, but I realize, with fear trickling down my spine, that I'm saying it because I'm scared of Jesse.

"Good," he replies as he parks where he did the night we buried Arthur.

I zip up my waterproof coat and pull the hood over my head. Jesse does the same, preparing for a very soggy hike.

"Jesse, what if whoever sent the message is watching us?"

"Have you seen anyone?"

"No."

"Neither have I, and I've been looking."

"We didn't notice anyone that night. Besides the cop."

He holds a hand up. "Let's not go there. We were preoccupied. There's no point speculating, we have to deal with what's happening now. Okay?"

"Okay. Let's go."

We get out of the car, and rain pelts at me, bouncing off my waterproof jacket. It won't be long until I'm soaked through if it keeps up like this.

Jesse and I jog along the trail and then break off, moving into the trees the way we did that night. Only it's much easier this time. Physically, anyway.

I remember our route as if the map is tattooed onto my brain. I remember every single detail about that day.

"How much farther?" Jesse asks.

"Not far."

"When I find out who's behind this . . ."

His razor-sharp voice sends a shiver down my spine.

"Jesse," I say, not really certain how to handle this. He's never seemed so . . . volatile before.

He cuts me a look, eyes stony. "Don't start. Someone's messing with us, and if they really do know, which—let's face it—they do, then we're in serious trouble. I'm not letting *anyone* expose us."

I want to ask how he plans to silence them, because it's not like he has Rhett's money and influence, but I'm terrified of the answer.

An accident is one thing, to kill in cold blood is another. Would he go that far?

"Where is it?" he asks.

It?

I clear my throat. "Not far."

He's never been that in love with the mountain, never hiked or camped anywhere, always preferring to be on the road. I might be able to take him to another spot and convince him it was there, but I think even he would notice the undisturbed ground.

And right now, I'm scared of what he's capable of. He changed *so* quickly, like a switch was flipped. I didn't see it coming.

We weave between trees. I step over roots and my feet sink into wet moss. The rain is still coming down hard, nosily hitting leaves above us, but it's so dense in here that we're sheltered from the worst of it.

I push my hood down and point. "There."

Up ahead is the disturbed ground of Arthur's grave.

"It doesn't look like it's caved in," Jesse says.

No, but we're still too far away to be certain and we can't take any chances.

"Come on, we have to be sure."

I move closer, my stomach tying knots and threatening to eject my dinner.

"Why're you slowing down?" Jesse asks, moving past me as if we're just off to see a friend.

I watch him as I shuffle forward. Shoulders relaxed, long strides toward the man we killed like it's a deer down there.

I stop a few feet away from Jesse and look at the ground.

"No," I say, taking a sharp breath.

The grave has sunk about an inch. Arthur is still covered, but the caved rectangle frames his grave.

"What do we do?" I ask.

Jesse scratches his head. "If no one knew, I'd say leave him. Take the top layer up and chuck more mud in there before replacing it. But we can't do that." He turns to me. "We've got to dig him up and move him."

I know that. I mean, what else can we do to hide what we've done if someone knows the grave's location? But it still hits me like a sledgehammer to the chest, crushing my bones.

Digging him up again is a new low, and I don't know how much further we can sink before we're lost forever.

"We can't do that alone. And having your car detailed again will make it obvious."

"How far is the river from here?" he asks.

I open my mouth, but nothing comes out, the shock of his words stealing mine.

Jesse wants to chuck him in the freaking river!

"Marley?" he prompts, already out of patience.

"Um . . . like, what, twenty minutes north? But we can't do that."

"We have no choice. I'll call the others, we're going to need help," he says, holding his phone up and walking to get a signal.

I close my eyes and crouch down. “I’m sorry,” I whisper to Arthur, hoping that wherever he is, he can forgive me.

Jesse walks back a minute later, wiping water from his eyes. “They’re moaning but they’re on their way.”

I jolt, my eyes fly open, and I stand. “What?”

Jesse rolls his eyes. “They’re whining about shit they have to do today as if it’s more important than this. But they’re coming. We’ll have to be fast because they can’t be out long.”

“Okay,” I reply weakly.

He pulls something from his pocket and holds up nylon-coated gloves.

I reach out and take a pair, realizing that he’d always come here with the intention of moving Arthur. I’m unsure what I thought this was about. What were we going to do, just leave him so this stalker could go to the cops?

Jesse pulls the gloves on and crouches down. I watch him as I get ready. He carefully lifts the top soil with the moss and grass. It’s soaking wet and caves in, breaking in two as soon as he moves it.

“Damn it!” he says.

“Don’t worry about that, we don’t have time. They’ll be here in, what, thirty minutes? We can disturb the rest of the ground around it, make a giant circle and put rocks in the middle, make it look like it was used for a campfire.”

He throws the moss lump beside him and looks up. “Brilliant idea. Should we actually light the fire?”

“Everything’s too wet. We could come back another time, but that’s risky. No one will question it if they even find it because the rain would've washed away any embers. I don't know if forensics would be able to tell someone has been under there, but we should move the soil directly around him and replace it from another area."

Jesse watches me with pride in his eyes. It creates a fresh wave of guilt and a heavy dose of shame. I want to change my name and move to another country so I will never see him again. I'm *not* the same as him.

I'm not the same.

I kneel beside him, my knees sinking into the damp moss and tears blurring my vision. Using my gloved hands, I begin to dig.

It doesn't take long because we're no longer being careful. I scrape the mud and my fingertips brush something hard. I swallow bile that hits the back of my throat and brush dirt from Arthur's leg.

The stench stings my nose. I turn my head to breathe fresh air, gagging.

"Don't stop, Marley, we're nearly there," Jesse says. "Think I can see the head."

The head.

Depersonalizing him, turning him into a piece of meat.

"Go careful, he's still a person," I say, recoiling in horror.

"I know what he is. Hurry up."

"What the hell, guys," Atlas says.

I turn to see him and Luce, drenched and jogging toward us.

"I don't want to do this again," Luce says, pushing her hair away from her face.

I didn't want to do it the first time. We're always going to be one step behind, wondering what we need to do next to cover up our crime.

They're all drenched, but it's better under the trees where we are.

"Save the theatrics, Luce," Jesse snaps. "We've almost got him out. We're taking him to the river. Come on."

Atlas looks to me, wide-eyed. "Marley?"

I shake my head, stopping him from coming closer. "Don't. Just help us so we can get this over with."

I'm boiling hot, sweating under this waterproof jacket, and again covered in dirt. This is what we're doing, so we just need to do it.

"Who sent the message?" Luce asks.

"Arthur didn't say," Jesse replies sarcastically. "Help, Luce! Dig!"

She sobs but drops to her knees, leaning over and scraping mud away from Arthur. With the four of us working together, we uncover him quickly. Soon we'll throw him in the water.

The river flows fast, the current heading toward the sea. It'll take a long time because we're not exactly near the coast, but that'll be where Arthur will head.

"All right, let's get him out," Atlas says.

Atlas and Jesse get into the grave to hoist him out and lay him on the edge. They lift themselves out, Atlas caving in one side of the grave. Loose, wet soil tumbles in place of Arthur.

"Please get him before that side goes," I say, my heart lurching.

Atlas scowls at me but I ignore it. He and Jesse pick up either end, same as before.

"Lead the way, Marley," Jesse says. "Luce, you stay behind, move dirt and make a circle. Build a campfire, no wood."

I take a minute then to properly explain the aim of that, and she nods, I think grateful to do this part rather than dumping Arthur.

"Where are we going?" Atlas asks. "Because isn't the river the other way?"

"We need to go where it's deeper," I say. "Everyone swims near the creek. We'll go near where the bridge is, because it's too dangerous to swim or sail there."

"It's farther and he's heavy," Atlas says.

"Man up, dude!" Jesse snaps. "This is the only way to ensure he's gone for good."

Atlas doesn't reply to that. What's there to say? Jesse might be heartless but he's not wrong. We need this to end.

"What if we're seen from the bridge?" Atlas finally asks.

"I'll be lookout," I say. "The edge of the forest is near the riverbank. It won't take long to . . . you get it."

To throw him in.

"How far is the hike?" he asks. "Don't look at me like that, Jesse, it's only a question! Twenty minutes?"

"Yeah, about that," I reply, deciding not to tell him that it'll probably be longer due to the fact that Arthur is slowing us down.

I wipe rainwater from my face as drops make it down through the trees, not bothering with my hood anymore. My hands are sweaty and still covered by the gloves. I'm too paranoid to take them off yet.

I check my phone as we walk. No new message from the stalker, no threat, nothing. It must be someone from the creek, a senior. They were the only ones who knew we were out there, and that road can't be seen from anywhere in town. The only other car was the cop, and I think they'd take a different approach if they saw.

Rhett would definitely use something like this, but I don't think he'd do it anonymously. Unless he was trying to drive us crazy before he revealed himself and whatever he wants in return for his silence.

Who else would choose this rather than running straight to the cops?

I can't think of anyone.

"Here we are," I say as we reach the edge of the forest. "Wait here, don't put him down. I'll check the road."

The river stretches for miles, and the only way across is the bridge that cuts straight through to the road on either side of the water.

Rain hammers down when I leave the cover of the trees. I use my hand as a shield so the rain doesn't get in my eyes and look up at the bridge. I can't hear much over the rain hitting the river, but the bridge is clear. That road is a bit sketchy in the rain, so I think most people would avoid it.

I can't count on it, though, so I wait another minute and then say, "Now. Hurry!"

The boys emerge from the forest, struggling as they move quickly toward the riverbank. It's a sheer drop, about ten feet from where we're standing down into the river.

Rain bounces noisily off the surface of the river. I keep my eyes on the bridge, only just able to make it out through the storm, my heart in my mouth as I wait for them to do it.

"Ready?" Atlas asks.

"Throw," Jesse says.

My stomach churns. Then, a second later, I hear the splash.

I turn in time to watch Arthur sink and then float off. The river is wide and the current particularly strong today. It's the perfect place to keep your secrets. It gobbles them up and hides them forever.

Arthur's gone in seconds.

"B-back into the woods," I say, watching the river with tears in my eyes and water streaming down my face.

There's no sign of him now. He's gone.

16

Wednesday, May 31

By morning, the rainstorm has passed, and it's time for school. I spent far too long in the shower last night, trying to wash away the events of that evening. I was frozen to the bone, my clothes soaked through and stuck to my skin.

We all have our clothes and gloves to dispose of again.

Luce was sitting in the middle of the circle, crying, when we got back to her. She'd made an authentic campfire, using a couple of logs around the outside to make it look like someone had been sitting there.

I don't know if it'll stand up if this stalker decides to tell the cops where the grave was, but if there's no evidence Arthur was there and no body, I don't see how the cops could take it seriously.

I walk today, needing the fresh air and outdoors. It's something I'm having to force myself to do, because I will pass Arthur's. But I can't give my friends another excuse to push me away or write me off.

As I approach Arthur's, I spot George in the yard, holding a toolbox. He looks up and waves.

"Hi," I say, my voice almost cracking. "Any news?"

He jogs over to the sidewalk and shakes his head. "It's been six days and nothing."

"What have the cops said?"

"He goes off a lot." He shrugs. "They said this isn't the first time someone's come forward about him. It's just . . ." He lets out a resigned sigh. "That's basically it for now. They've done a quick sweep, but they're not putting many hours into it yet."

"I'm sorry. I think the forest is good for him, you know. He's not exactly made to feel welcome here by everyone, and the mountain is his place to forget it all. I get that, do it myself."

"You hike alone a lot?"

"No, I go with my dad or friends. I'm just saying, I understand why he needs to go off for a while."

"Cops said sometimes he's gone a week or more too."

"He's definitely had mail left for longer than a week. Mailman was telling my dad last year that he had to stack it all in an empty food cooler on his porch in case it rained."

That's kind of the truth. It happened, but it was only, like, five days.

I *hate* lying to him. His life has been nothing but loss. He doesn't deserve what we're doing to him. I wish there was something I could do to make this better, but it feels like the more I try, the worse things get.

"So I have around four days left before I should really worry?"

I shrug. "I'd say so. We've worried before and he's just turned up back in town, mucky as hell, grabbing beers and beef jerky before heading back home."

George chuckles. "He has a thing about beef jerky. There are packets of the stuff in the cupboard."

We're quiet for a moment. "You ready for graduation and summer . . . then college?" George asks, breaking the silence.

"Yeah, I can't wait," I say. I can't wait to leave, that is. This nightmare needs to be over. Or at least continue in another place.

I wish I could go to California now. Atlas and I could just go, put all of this behind us with each mile we travel.

"So senior pranks are in full swing?"

He asks the question so casually, but a bolt of dread ripples through my body. Where did that suddenly come from?

"Um. Yeah."

"Get up to anything stupid? I heard the Wilder assholes do dumb stuff."

"No," I say, clearing my throat. "Just the usual."

He smiles, nodding once, but his inquisitive eyes hold mine for a long time. What's he thinking? I wish I could read his mind because I'm freaking out.

Does he know?

No.

He can't. Arthur's his grandad. He wouldn't be sending messages, he'd be running to the cops.

You're paranoid.

"Right," he finally says. "What've you been doing, then?"

"Oh. Ducks in the pool, chickens in the quad, glitter bombs in Fuller's office. That kind of thing."

He nods, stuffing his free hand in his pocket.

"What're you doing with the tools?" I ask.

"Attempting some DIY. Figured I'd keep busy until he gets home and repair a few things for him."

I nod. "I'm sure he'll appreciate that. Anyway, I should go."

"Yeah, go," he says, stepping backward. It takes him another second, but then he breaks eye contact and retreats.

What the hell was that?

My panic free-falls, a bolt of anxiety telling me something is very off here. It could just be my paranoia, though.

I press on, power walking because I need to talk to my friends right freaking now.

But what if I'm not only paranoid? I mean, it did kind of sound like George was suspicious. He randomly asked about pranks. I move faster, needing to tell my friends because this is going to play on my mind all day.

I find Atlas, Jesse, and Luce chatting by Jesse's locker and head over. Jesse mutters something and they all look up at the same time.

My cheeks heat at their lack of subtlety. They were talking about me.

"Hey," I say, frowning. "Everything okay?"

"Yeah," Atlas says, kissing me. "You good?"

The tension is palpable, like a physical being standing between us.

"Um, I just saw George," I tell them, looking at each one. None of them quite meet my eye. "What's going on?"

"Nothing, we were just talking," Jess says.

"About me?"

Atlas laughs. "No."

"You made us realize anyone could walk up," Jesse says, and I don't believe either of them. "What happened with George?"

"Okay, I . . . I think he could be the one who messaged me."

"Shut up! What . . . are you sure?" Jesse asks, stepping closer, getting into my personal space as if he's ready to fight me.

"No. I'm not sure!"

"Why would George have sent the message?"

"I don't know."

He throws his hands up. "Then why suggest it?"

"Back up and tell us why you think that," Atlas orders.

"I just walked past his place and he came over. He was just asking questions about the pranks, if we've done anything stupid that Rhett ordered. I mean, it can't be him. His grandad was killed. If he knew, he'd hardly be sending us messages."

Atlas nods. "That's true. Who wouldn't go to the cops if they knew the person responsible for the death of their relative?"

"We thought it might be Rhett," Jesse says, and he makes it sound like there's been a second discussion that I wasn't part of.

I frown and say, "Yeah. It still might."

"But why would George suddenly ask about the pranks?" Atlas wraps an arm around me. "He didn't mention those to you before, did he?"

"Nope. He's asked about school and stuff before Arthur was . . . you know, but not the pranks. It just seemed a weird time to bring it up. I mean, why not ask that on the other occasions I saw him, particularly the one where we were on school grounds?"

"So why now?" Luce says, almost to herself.

Jesse grits his teeth. "It must be him. We'd expect Rhett to be more . . . smug if he knew?"

"Yeah," I reply. I definitely think he'd throw it in our faces more, making comments like in the text. But he could be playing the long game.

Atlas groans. "I think it's George. I mean, he stopped looking for Arthur real quick, didn't he? Anyone else seen him around town?"

"Not recently, and he said today the cops told him about Arthur's hiking trips. I backed it up, said he's sometimes gone for a week or more."

"Don't get too involved, Marley," Jesse says.

"I'm not, it was a passing comment because George brought it up. It'd look weirder if I ignored it."

"Of course it would," Atlas says.

My pulse quickens as I stand with my friends but feel like an outsider. I try to get Luce to look at me, but she focuses on Jesse.

"Why wouldn't he go to the cops?" Luce asks.

Jesse runs his hand over his hair. "Who do you think inherits the property, Luce?"

I stand straighter. The four of us are silent for a moment as we digest that little nugget of information. He's right. With Arthur's son dead and no other family, George will get *everything.*

"Okay, but if he does inherit everything, why message us? Why not just keep quiet?" Luce asks.

"Because without a body, he won't inherit for a long time," I say. "He needs Arthur to be found."

"Yeah, well, we need him to not be," Jesse says, stating the absolute obvious.

"I think I should meet whoever this is," I say. "They're watching me, right, so maybe I can get a message to them."

Atlas wastes no time in objecting. "No way! Terrible idea, what the hell?"

"We need to know, Atlas. Whoever it is, they only contacted me. That has to mean something."

I'm the one Rhett has the biggest issue with.

I'm the one George speaks to in our group.

"She's right," Jesse says.

"Shut up, dude. We're not letting her go meet the person blackmailing us."

"They're not blackmailing us," I say, kind of pathetically. I haven't been asked to do anything in return for his silence, but there must be a reason for the message. It's only a matter of time until it's revealed.

"We can't just ignore them," Luce says.

Jesse nods. "Right, and it's not like Marley will be alone. She gets a message to them, arranges to meet, and we'll be hiding out there."

"Okay," I say, not waiting for Atlas to agree. "I'll try to spend more time with George and Rhett, see whether they say anything else suspicious."

Three pairs of eyes watch me, all with identical fear-filled stares.

"I can't believe this is our life," Luce mutters.

"It won't be for much longer," Jesse says. "We've come this far. I'm not going to let anyone screw this up. Marley, don't get this wrong."

"I won't!"

The bell rings, and we all have different activities this morning.

My first one being graduation practice, you know, just in case some of us can't figure out how to walk across the stage.

After school we all go back to my house and discuss the whole thing until we've convinced ourselves that it's George. So much so that Jesse is pacing and trying to figure out what we're going to do.

"Hey," Jesse says, jumping back from the window in my living room. He grabs Atlas, who's closest to him, and shoves him back out of view.

"What the hell was that?" Atlas asks.

"George is walking past . . . the day he questioned you about senior pranks. It's *him*!"

"What?" I say, peering around the side of the window in time to see George just move past the neighbor's house, heading back toward his place.

"What was he doing out here?" Luce asks.

I'm on the outskirts with three other houses. As far as I know, he's not friends with any of my three neighbors. I've never seen him come out this way before.

"Checking in on you," Jesse says. "My truck is in the driveway, that's probably why he left."

"You think he was going to knock?" I ask, my eyes wide. "I don't want him in my house."

"Keep the door locked and the alarm on," Atlas says.

I don't think George is dangerous, but I have no clue what he wants from me, what the message meant, or why he's not dropping an anonymous tip to the cops if he wants Arthur found.

Is he messing with me first? Getting a bit of revenge in before he drops us all in it.

"Do you want me to stay?" Atlas asks. "I can make something up for my parents."

"No, I'm fine. You guys go. I'll lock up."

I kind of hope he comes back when they leave. The stress and anxiety are eating me from the inside out. It's all I can think about. I just want to have a conversation with George. I want to apologize and ask what he wants, why he hasn't gone to the cops.

Atlas kisses me and follows the others out of my house.

I lock the door and lean back against it.

What the hell am I going to do?

17

I'm about to get into bed, having stayed up until just after one in the morning in the living room, half watching a new series on Netflix and half listening for George outside. I've mostly been watching the front door on the home security app.

Nothing.

As I close my bedroom door, I hear sirens. Opening my blinds, I peer out to see what's going on and gasp. In the distance I can see smoke billowing out of . . . no, that can't be right.

I open the window and lean out, and I'm just about able to see Arthur's house.

On *fire.*

My hands shake as I dial George's number.

It goes to voicemail. Twice.

Oh god, he's probably inside.

Without a second thought, I throw on my hoodie and run. My keys are by the front door. I snatch them from the side table and run to my car, my heart beating loudly in my ears.

Earlier, Jesse was talking about "taking care" of George, and now this happens.

But he wouldn't. He couldn't do this. Arthur was one thing, that was an accident, but to plan and execute a murder . . . No, this *has* to be an accident.

We had a plan.

I start the car and shove it into drive.

I fly down the road, taking the twists and turns slowly and speeding whenever there is a stretch of straight road. The more direct route to Arthur's is via the road where we ran him over, and I've been avoiding taking it.

It only takes me an extra two minutes to arrive outside their property, though. Two fire engines and a couple of cop cars are on the scene. I park out of the way, passing an ambulance that stops on the road.

I get out and run toward the firefighters. "Where's George?" I shout.

One of them turns, a tall man with a thick mustache. He steps toward me, holding his arm out as if he thinks I'm about to run into that burning house.

"Where's George?" I repeat.

"Stay back, we're searching for him now. Do you have his phone number?"

"Yeah. I've tried calling it, but he's not picking up. He's in there! You have to get him out."

"We'll find him," he says. "Please step back."

I back up and look at the house, the heat reaching us from all the way on the road. Red-hot flames crack windows, burning out the rotting wooden frames. Smoke pours from the house like a faucet.

I tilt my head and watch the smoke steal the stars, stretching out across the sky.

If George is in there . . .

What chance does he have?

I try his phone again but get his voicemail.

"George, please," I whisper, tightly gripping my phone.

He was out earlier, but I don't think he really does anything around town. I've even tried inviting him out, but he just stays there with Arthur. *Used* to stay with Arthur. Now he's just alone.

"Marley?"

I spin. "Rhett. What are you doing here?"

He shuts his car door and walks over. "I just heard. Is George out?"

I shrug. "I don't think so. He's not picking up his phone. They're searching for him, but look, the house is almost gutted. How did you hear?"

Why would he come? He's not friends with George.

"Sirens," he says.

"You heard them from your house?"

"I never said I was at my house."

I glance at him out of the corner of my eye. It's almost one-thirty a.m.

"Why are you here?" he asks.

"Saw from my window," I mutter.

"Where are your parents?"

"Work."

Ruthie's is closer to Arthur's, but I still doubt he'd see it from there, not with the forest in the way.

Shouting distracts me from trying to figure Rhett out. A firefighter runs from the house with George in his arms, limp like he's already dead. The image is almost identical to the boys carrying Arthur.

Rhett's eyes widen and he looks over at me.

"Do you think he's . . . ?" I can't bring myself to finish that sentence. I don't want to think about George dying.

"Marley, you've gone pale."

My heart thumps so hard that my head feels like it's floating. George is whisked off into the back of an ambulance. An oxygen mask is attached to his face before the doors close and the vehicle speeds toward the hospital.

Will Mom and Dad see him when he comes in? Mom probably but Dad only if George needs an X-ray.

"He's alive," I say, my shoulders sagging in relief. I can hear a couple of the firefighters talking, the ones who're working the hose, ensuring water is being continuously pumped through it.

"It's a bad one, man. I don't think there'll be much left," one of the firefighters says.

The house. It doesn't matter about the house. It was falling down anyway.

"The owner's missing. Strange, don't you think?" the other firefighter adds.

"Jimmy doesn't think it was an accident," the first replies. "Smelled gas when he was first on the scene."

"I'm leaving," I say. My world is shrinking, and I don't know what to do or who to trust.

Was this Jesse's way of ensuring George can never speak out? He can't . . . Arthur was an accident, this wasn't.

Now that I know George is safe, I need to find out if it was Jesse who did this.

"Whoa, I don't think you should drive. Seriously, Marley, you look like you're going to hit the floor," Rhett says.

"No, I'm okay. It's just a shock."

I can't let Rhett know that I'm freaking out. We still don't know if the message was from him. . . . And why was he out here in the middle of the night?

"Marley?" he calls as I walk away from him. "Damn it, will you just let me help you?"

"You've done enough," I reply. When I'm safely in my car, I begin to sob.

• • •

Thursday, June 1

I head to the hospital early in the morning because I need to be near George. He deserves someone to care for him. Yeah, my parents still have a couple of hours left of their shift, so it's risky, but I'm confident that I can get in and out without them noticing.

It wouldn't even be that weird if they did see me—they know I'm friendly with George—but I'm paranoid as hell and don't want it to seem like I'm here out of guilt.

I park between two cars despite there being an empty corner. If my car is surrounded, they'll never see it. Not that they get much time to glance out the windows anyway.

Inside, I head to the desk, and smile when I notice that Maude is working today so it should be easier to get past.

She smiles as she spots me. "Marley, hello."

"Hey."

"What can I do for you?"

"I've just come to see George. I know I'm not family or anything, but his parents have both passed away."

She nods and looks over her shoulder. "Go on through, but don't be too long."

"I won't, I promise. Thank you," I say, dashing past her desk and pushing open the door that buzzes after Maude presses a button.

I'm nowhere near the emergency room, thankfully. The smell of sterilizer is almost overpowering. A cleaning team up ahead is mopping the floor.

I walk around the WET FLOOR sign and peer through his window.

"God," I whisper.

George is lying in bed, deathly still, eyes closed, hooked up to a machine. His skin is an alarmingly pale shade of gray. The only evidence of life is the slow rising of his gown-covered chest.

"Are you here to visit?" a nurse asks.

I gasp, startled. "Oh, I was just checking in on him."

"Sorry I scared you. Are you family? We haven't had much luck getting hold of anyone."

"He doesn't really have any. Maude let me in because George has no one here right now. He's my neighbor's grandson. My friend."

"Can you reach his grandparents?"

No, I really can't.

I lick my lips. "His grandad is hiking, apparently."

She places her hand over her heart. "Goodness. He doesn't know about the house or George."

"When he gets better, there will be a lot of people ready to help." The words flow from my mouth smoothly. Lies becoming easier to say but harder to live with.

"He has to wake up," I say, more to myself than anyone.

She squeezes my arm. "Keep faith."

I watch her walk off and wonder what my friends are thinking. They've been quiet since I texted them. They all know what happened, where George is, and not one of them has said more than "Hope he's okay."

He's not okay!

Are they all willing George to wake up, or do they hope he'll die?

This can't be real.

Could Jesse really kill in cold blood to keep this secret from being exposed?

Jesse stole Arthur's car to make it look like he'd taken off. Now *this.* He's a lost cause. I understand that now. I started to see darkness in him almost immediately after Arthur died, and it just keeps growing.

Yet I'm the one being excluded from private chats and treated like a pariah.

"I'll come back. Please hold on," I whisper to George through the window. Then I leave the hospital and head to school.

The whole drive I'm barely aware. My mind on Jesse and what

he's capable of. I want to believe this was an accident. The wiring in that house can't be good, but the firefighter said it was likely lit deliberately.

I park in the lot and head into school, almost freezing when I notice my friends bunched together near my locker. Adrenaline spikes, and I want to take them on, get all of this out and beg George for forgiveness . . . if he makes it.

"What's going on?" I ask. This wouldn't be weird pre-Arthur, but they've barely spent any time with me since.

"Where the hell have you been?" Jesse snaps.

"I'm not late," I say. The warning bell hasn't even rung yet.

"I tried calling," Atlas says.

Clenching my fists, I ask, "Why, what's up?"

"Nothing, we just didn't know where you were," Jesse says, as if he constantly needs to know my location.

I frown, not really following. "Where was I supposed to be?"

We didn't have plans to meet or anything.

"Why didn't you pick up, babe? I was worried."

My eyes drift to Jesse. How can they stand to be around him after he set Arthur's house on fire with George inside?

"My phone's been on silent. I was at the *hospital*," I say, holding Jesse's gaze. "You know, since Arthur's house was burned to the ground with George inside last night. I went to see if he's going to pull through or if Jesse has murdered two people."

"Watch it," he bites through gritted teeth.

He's not denying it. He's not even sorry. He's standing in front of me with folded arms like I'm the problem. His reaction is all I need. This was definitely Jesse.

Atlas and Luce don't seem worried or repulsed.

I narrow my eyes. "Or what, you'll take care of me too?"

"Whoa, calm down," Atlas says, refereeing. "This is not helpful, Marley."

My jaw drops open. "Me? How can you say that after what he's done? George is fighting for his life!"

"I did what was necessary. You should be thanking me because you're standing here right now and not in a prison cell."

"Luce, come on," I say, hoping she will see reason. "You can't be on their side."

Jesse puts his arm around her shoulder, and she shakes her head at me. "I don't like any of this, Marley, but Jesse's done what he needed to. I have to go to college. I have to, so you need to keep your mouth shut. Okay?"

No, that is not okay! I almost say the words aloud, but something stops me. Fear.

Would they all bury me if Jesse decided I was too much of a risk?

Tears well in my eyes, and I will them not to fall. I don't want to cry in front of them.

"So that's it?" I say. "He could've been killed! He still might die."

"George is taken care of," Jesse says as if he's already dead.

There have been no improvements, and he's in a serious condition, but even if he does wake up, I think he'll be too scared to say anything now. Jesse obviously has no problem killing to save himself.

"Right. Well, okay. I guess I'll see you guys later."

"Yeah, whatever," Jesse says, walking away. Luce follows him like the Grim Reaper's pet.

"Do you think I'm the problem, Atlas?"

"I . . . No, but I don't think you're making it easier. Leave George alone and hold it together. We've almost made it out."

He needs me to pretend harder. To throw away every last ounce of humanity I have left inside me.

"See you at lunch," I say.

He nods and walks away first. I turn to watch him go, and that's when I notice Rhett staring at me from the end of the hallway.

He pulls out his phone and holds it up, eyes still piercing through mine.

I stop breathing.

Rhett heads into the classroom nearest me, followed by Ruthie and a couple of her friends.

I turn and run to the bathroom and grip hold of the sink so I don't pass out. Watching my reflection, I count until I'm sure I'm not going to die. It takes until seventy-two, but I start to feel a bit better.

It's short-lived because my phone dings.

Unknown:

u better do the dare

I shake my head, tears welling in my eyes, and I miss the moment the message disappears.

The dare. Camping-in-the-forest dare.

It's him. This is Rhett.

18

I had to think quick, and that meant making a call to Rhett first and then meeting up with my friends at my house after school.

"What do you mean now you think it's Rhett who knows?" Atlas asks. "It was just George! Jesus, Marley. He's in the hospital because of this."

"Are you kidding me? Yeah, George is in the hospital *because of Jesse*! How was I supposed to know that voicing my theory would result in that? He didn't even wait to find any evidence; he just burned his freaking house down."

Jesse takes a step closer, putting himself firmly in my personal space. "All right, Marley, chill. You're all over the place, creating more problems than you're solving."

Luce looks between us but says nothing.

I narrow my eyes, holding my ground. *Nope, you're not intimidating me.* "Excuse me? Why the hell am I getting the blame for all of this?"

"Babe, will you just stop? This isn't helping," Atlas says.

The fact that Atlas directs his warning at me makes me want to scream. I've never felt like he was against me before. He's supposed to have my back.

I don't know why I've gone to them with this. Maybe because I'm scared that Jesse will go back to finish George off, and I know he won't be able to touch Rhett.

Maybe because I'm totally lost, and I can't do this alone.

"The person knows about my latest dare. George wouldn't . . . and he's currently fighting for his life, so I don't think he has time to send a quick text!"

"So your solution is to go camping with Rhett. This is crazy. You're not going," Atlas says.

If he shows up tonight, I'll know it's him. Rhett's the kind of person who would use this information to his advantage, get us to do his dirty work. He'd have total control.

"Whoa, hold on." Luce takes my phone and shoves it in Atlas's face. "We don't have a choice here. Think about what's at stake. If he tells anyone what we've done . . ."

"We're talking about leaving Marley alone all night with him!"

"He's not going to do anything," I say. "Come on, he can threaten and use his money to get what he wants, but at no point ever has he gotten his hands dirty. I have to do this because we have to find out what he knows."

"She's right," Luce says, her big eyes full of guilt and worry. "But will you be okay?"

"I'll be fine." I turn to Atlas, who's huffing. "I have to do this."

"I know," he replies, blowing out a long breath. "I just don't like it."

I'm not exactly looking forward to it either. Spending more than thirty seconds in Rhett's presence makes me want to commit a felony—another one, I guess—so the thought of all night in the woods with him . . . Yeah, not happy.

"When are you doing it?" Jesse asks.

"Tonight."

Atlas's head snaps in my direction. *"What?"*

"Has to be. My mom's off tomorrow, and then she's back on the day shift. Tonight is the only night I'll be alone here, and I can't risk being caught if I have to sneak out. We all need this to be fixed."

Atlas runs his hands through his hair. "What are we doing, guys? How long can we keep this up for?"

"Tell me you're not thinking of doing something stupid," Jesse says. "It's not just me who'll get in trouble. You understand that, right? Your life will be over too. You're—"

"Yeah, yeah." Atlas cuts him off with a glare. "I'm not an idiot and I haven't forgotten. But is there no part of you that thinks we're going to get found out?"

"We can control that," Jesse says.

"Naive."

"He's not naive. We've covered our tracks." Luce lowers her voice, totally Jesse's puppet. "No one is ever going to find out what we've done. We can't throw our lives away now, or what was the point? We can make up for what we've done."

"By going to college, getting married, and having kids? I think Arthur would rather be alive," I say.

Luce's shoulders sag. She looks done in, like she could evaporate into thin air. "Not helpful. This is killing me too, Marley, but we have to get through this."

I wish this conversation could've been a text, but I think Jesse needs the control in-person offers. Not that I can misread a message from him. I'll never think him telling me he's watching is him looking out for me.

"You guys should leave. I'm going to shower and pretend that I'm having an early night so my parents don't try calling me on their first break."

"Are you certain you want to do this?" Atlas asks. "Because all you have to do is say the word, and we'll figure something else out."

I'd be lying if I said I didn't want to take him up on his offer, but this is the easiest way I can think of, and we don't have time to come up with another plan. It's hard to figure out something else when we don't even know what Rhett plans to do with the information.

"I'm sure," I tell him. "Let me figure this out." I don't want Jesse involved.

"Do you have a tent?" Luce asks.

I roll my eyes. "My dad's is broken. Rhett's bringing his."

"You're sharing a tent with him?" Atlas asks, sitting up straight.

That's the part of all of this that he has a problem with?

"No, he can sleep outside."

"Should you take something? A weapon? Grab a knife or pepper spray," Luce says.

"I'm covered, don't worry."

"Good. Let us know what happens," Jesse says. "And if you need help."

If I need help with . . .

Oh my god. If I need help with body disposal.

Well, I won't, because I know what I'm doing. I have everything planned, my bag still in my closet and ready to go.

• • •

I arrive at the creek early, wanting to be the first one here. Somehow that feels like having the upper hand, and I can do with feeling like I'm not totally at Rhett's mercy.

It's a small victory.

My backpack with warm clothes, a flashlight, and a sleeping bag weighs heavy on my shoulders. I packed a hammer from my dad's toolbox. A knife is too intentional. Not that a hammer to the body is friendly, but it feels less brutal.

It's darker tonight, thick clouds still hiding the sky. I know once we go into the forest, it's going to be pitch-black.

And the only person I'll have with me is a guy I don't trust.

Rhett walks over, backpack on his shoulders, grinning like he's a predator about to play with its prey. I'm in no mood for any of his crap, so he's going to be disappointed if he thinks he can push me around today.

"So tell me what changed your mind," he says.

"You're the one who keeps saying we don't have a choice. Now, where are we going to set up camp?" I ask, and start walking up the mountain, wasting no time.

He doesn't mention my impatience. Instead he follows and asks, "When was the last time you saw a bear out here?"

"I think we should pitch the tent up there," I say, pointing up the mountain. "The higher the better." Where we used to camp. It'll be the perfect place to hide things I never want found.

"Because Garrett and Truett were out here last month and saw one closer to town than usual."

"We'll be able to camouflage the tent with shrubs up there too."

Rhett stops and sighs sharply. "You are so frustrating."

"I'm sorry?"

"You know what I'm talking about!"

I stop and turn to him. "You're having your own conversation too. I'm trying to figure out where we should sleep so we can get this over with."

"And I'm trying to figure out if we're safe out here."

"Then why are we here? Wait, no. I get why you gave me this dare, but why are *you* here?"

"You're right, we'll set up at the top," he says, turning back around and hiking the steepest part of the hill.

All right, that was weird. "Rhett, what's going on?"

Does he think that this is a way to get closer to me?

"Why didn't you give Ruthie this dare? You could have had a nice romantic evening in the woods."

"Shut up, Marley," he replies, monotone and bored.

"Not happening."

I want to push and push until he cracks. We need to know if he's the one who sent the message, if he's the one who knows what happened.

"Come on, Rhett. We have hours until morning. Why don't we get it all out."

"Get what out? You're doing a dare."

"But *why*?"

"Senior pranks."

I jog to catch up with him. "Yes, I know it's senior pranks. You've never joined in, so why now?"

"I like the woods. I like camping."

I snort. "You're so full of it. Do you think you sound credible?"

"I really don't care what you believe."

I roll my eyes. "All right, keep your secrets. Not that they're secret."

He doesn't bite. Instead he throws his bag down and huffs. "This'll do."

We're not quite at the top, but I'm not going to argue. It's useless at this point. I have bigger things to worry about.

There's about an hour left until we're plunged into darkness. There's just enough space between trees for us to be able to see around us.

"What do you want me to do?" I ask.

Rhett does a double take and lifts his brow. "Are you willingly cooperating?"

"Don't get used to it." I point to the sky. "It'll be dark soon, and we need to set up."

"Where are you going to sleep?" he asks.

"Don't even try, Rhett."

I was actually going to ask him that, because I have no desire to share a tent with him, but again, it's going to be a waste of energy. I have a limited amount of time with him, thankfully.

He unzips the bag. "We're going to need wood."

"You're lighting a fire? Do you expect us to sing camp songs and share s'mores?"

He laughs. "I don't share s'mores."

"What's happening?"

He laughs again. "Don't worry, we won't tell anyone we got along for two minutes." Straightening, he throws a flashlight to me, which I catch. "Look, let's call a truce for the duration of the dare. It's going to be a long night if not."

"O-okay."

Away from everyone else, I can see more of the old him, the one I was friends with.

It won't last.

"Don't go far but get as much dry wood as you can. We'll need rocks and a clear patch of ground, so we don't set the forest alight."

"Sure thing, Eagle Scout."

"You know the top-ranking Scout?"

I shrug. "My cousin's just joined and talks about nothing else. Back soon."

"Danny has? Nice. But you do know 'back soon' is a bad thing to say in the middle of the woods."

Yeah, well, I don't think there's anything scarier out here than me. Someone who helped cover up a murder.

I leave him to pitch the tent and walk off course, needing to be fast. The ground here is undisturbed and far enough away from any routes to make it the perfect place. This spot is already out of the way.

The ground is a little damp and covered in slimy green moss, but I burn the bag of evidence and bury the ashes, then manage to gather enough wood to keep a small fire going for a couple of hours.

The tent is up when I get back. Rhett's cleared a circle on the ground and outlined it with a small wall of rocks.

"That looks good," I say, dumping the wood down beside him. A couple of branches hit his leg, but he says nothing.

"What took you so long? I was about to come searching. Hold on, did you just give me a compliment? Wow."

I roll my eyes. "Now, now, we called a truce. It took a while to find enough dry wood."

He nods, accepting the lie, and takes the wood to make a fire. It's still warm out, but we're completely shaded here, so the temperature will drop pretty quickly soon.

"Can I ask you something?" I say, sitting down and watching him strike a match.

"That's rhetorical, right? You're going to ask regardless."

"True."

He sighs, prodding the small fire. "Go on, then."

"What happened in eighth grade?"

"If you can't remember any of it, I fear for your SAT results."

"None of your friends are around to laugh at your dumb jokes, so you might as well be honest."

"Nothing happened."

"You're full of crap, Rhett. What are you scared of?"

"All right. Let me ask you something first."

"Shoot. I'm not a scaredy-cat."

"Why do you care?"

I whack him. He winces, rubbing the spot where my knuckles

just made contact. That felt kinda good. "Because we were friends and then *nothing.* No explanation. You just stopped talking to me one day. You're no Einstein, but even you must see how that's confusing and hurtful."

He dips his chin, and it's the first time I've seen him look even remotely remorseful. "I don't know. People change, I guess."

"Overnight?"

"Yeah, Marley. Overnight. No explanation and no warning."

I look over at him and he's still staring at the ground, but I feel his eyes roll.

At what point do I ask him outright if he's the one sending me messages? I want to get this over with so I can find out what it'll cost to keep him quiet, but I'm actually terrified of having that conversation.

He already has loads of money, so I don't think he'll take a bribe. Also, I only have about four hundred dollars.

"Why are you here?" I ask, not quite ready to be so direct.

"The bear. I'm not totally heartless."

"Your brother's dare. I know my way around these woods, unlike Bryany and Elizabeth. I won't get lost."

He knows this because we spent half of middle school in the woods hiking and camping with my dad. Before he became too cool for me.

"Just seems like I should be here."

"That's not a real answer."

"I never said I'd give you one."

Do you know?

I clench my hands into fists, frustration building inside me like

I'm a pressure cooker. How much longer before I burst? A part of me hopes he knows, and he'll tell someone. That way I won't have to look over my shoulder for the rest of my life. Otherwise we'll never be able to relax, not really.

Just look at all those old cold cases getting solved, like, twenty years later thanks to new technology. What's to say that once we're out of college and settled into our perfect lives this won't come back to bite us?

Atlas and I could be sitting on the porch while our children play, and the cops could show up.

We'll never know what's coming.

That's our future.

I'm not sure what's worse, that or prison.

"Rhett, please."

I don't know what I'm asking. For him to tell me why he wanted to come. For him to tell me what he knows.

"What's the deal with you and Ruthie?" he asks.

"Ruthie?" All right, that I didn't expect. "What do you mean? She hates me and I think she's a shallow, hateful witch."

He nods, smirking, trying to act casual, but I can see the tension around his eyes. He's fishing for information, and I have absolutely no clue what that could be. I've never spent any time with Ruthie on purpose.

Does he think I hate her because I'm jealous?

"That's it?" he prods.

"Why are you asking me this?"

"She's . . . always talking about you, how to mess with you. By the way, don't leave your drink at prom. Laxatives."

"She was going to spike my drink?"

"Her final revenge."

"Revenge for what? That evil little jerk."

I'm tempted to put laxatives in *her* drink and see how she likes it. Who plans that?

He full-on laughs and nudges my arm. "Forget her, just watch yourself around her, okay?"

"Yeah, thanks. Is that why you're here? Because that didn't need to be a camp thing. You have my phone number."

He shrugs. "I guess I figured we should camp one last time. You know, before you go off to California. With Atlas still?"

"Yeah, I'm with Atlas. Why did you say it like that?"

"Like what?"

"Like you don't believe it."

"Don't see him as the California type."

"There's a type?"

"Yep, and he's not it. It's too sunny."

Atlas does prefer fall and winter, but that doesn't mean he wants to be somewhere with that climate for college.

"He can do four years of hotter weather," I say. "We'll pick where we want to be after."

"Right, because you'll still be together."

"Why are you being an asshole?"

"I'm not."

"It's going to be a long night if you keep doing this."

"Fine," he says, standing. "I brought buns and hot dogs. I'll make dinner."

"We need to keep the fire under control," I say.

"Yeah, don't want the woods to go up like Arthur's."

I side-eye him, adding another few sticks. "That's not funny."

"I'm not laughing," he says seriously. "Think George will be okay?"

"I hope so. Mom's keeping me updated, but there's been no change yet."

"Ruthie's convinced there's a killer in town."

"What?"

"Well, maybe not a killer, because George isn't dead. You don't think Arthur burned his house down, and that's why he's staying away?"

My jaw nearly hits the floor. "With his grandson inside?"

"Maybe he thought George was out. On a cozy date with you."

I'm not reacting to that, because it's ridiculous. "You need a hobby to keep that overactive imagination occupied."

"Whatever, the cops will figure it out soon enough."

I don't move as he pulls a pan and small cooler from his backpack. That's not because I'm unwilling to help, but because of everything he's said. I can't make sense of it, and I can't figure out if his words have a hidden meaning.

But he does know something.

19

Friday, June 2

The next morning, after arriving home at five a.m.—an hour before my parents got home—I was able to shower and pretend I had a normal night in.

I jump in my car to go to school. Rhett and I slept after eating hot dogs and making small talk. I can't say he's absolutely not the person messaging me, but after last night, I don't think he is.

I do know he was weird about Ruthie and Atlas. But he's weird about a lot of stuff.

All he's done is confuse me more, because there's something going on with Atlas, beyond him distancing himself from me.

I drive over the bridge with my window down and the warm breeze drifting in. The sound of water rushing underneath makes me smile. I love hearing the river, but I haven't been in it since Arthur. Sounds the same, but I don't think it'll feel like it used to.

As I reach the top of the bridge, I gasp. Across the river, on the bank, close to where we left Arthur, is a swarm of cops.

They've found him.

One of the cops looks up and makes eye contact. White dots dance in front of my face. I jolt backward in my seat and slam my foot on the brakes. The car swerves before it stops, grazing a sign pole. The sound of metal making me grit my teeth.

Oh god.

I look out the window, and sure enough the cop is watching me. Shit. What will he think of this?

Stay calm. It's okay.

Taking a breath, I pray that the cop will be too distracted to bother with me. I'm wrong. He starts to walk my way, treading carefully on the high riverbank before it drops.

Oh god, it's *Sam.* My dad's friend. Of all the cops who could've seen me.

I clear my throat, preparing myself to have to talk to him.

It's fine. You're fine.

I glance behind Sam, to the white tent that he disappears behind. Could Arthur's body have washed up there? It's not like we weighted him down.

They just threw him in and assumed he was too far from town or any hiking routes to be found.

We thought the tide would take him.

I need to get to school and find Atlas.

"Hey!" Sam shouts, waving his hand to get my attention.

I cut the engine and open the door.

From down there Sam can't reach me, unless he wants to go back into the forest to then join the road again. Unlikely, given what's currently happening.

"Marley? Are you okay? I heard a crash," he says as I move to the edge of the bridge.

I look over the railing, clenching my trembling, sweaty hands together. "Yeah, I'm okay, Sam. I'm fine. It was just a scrape."

"Are you sure? Do you want me to come up there?"

No, go away.

"Oh no, I-I'm fine, really. The pole is still standing."

"I'm not concerned about the pole. Your dad would want me to make sure you're okay."

He's not going to let this go.

"I'm fine, I promise," I say.

"What happened?" he asks, using his hand to block the sun from his eyes.

I look down at him. "Just a lack of concentration," I say, pointing to the tent. "I'm so sorry. Look, there's no damage to the sign and only a little scratch on my hood."

"You're not in shock?"

"No. Feel like a total idiot, though. First time I've ever hit anything." God, I wish that was true. "It's just, I saw you guys and the tent. What's going on?"

"I can't say just yet."

I want to ask if it's in connection to Arthur's disappearance, but I don't want them to think that I'm inserting myself in the investigation or looking for information. At the same time, it's been a week, and isn't that what someone would ask?

"It's not Mrs. Hokanson wandering off again, I passed her walking her dog," I say, waving my hand toward the police presence and death tent behind him. "Why the tent?" My hand flies to my heart. "Oh my god, Arthur! George told me he's missing."

"I really can't say, and I'm guessing you should be getting to school."

There was no hesitation in his reply, and from what I can tell, he's not suspicious. He's relaxed, as if we're discussing my favorite class at school, something he usually asks as a way to make polite conversation.

"Sam, is Arthur . . . Is he okay?"

"Have a good day, Marley," he replies. "Get your dad to look at the bumper, even if it doesn't look like there's any damage."

"All right," I reply. "You have a good day too, Sam."

I give him a wave and get back into my car. He's already walking away when I start the engine. Shoving the car into drive, I avoid the sign again and get back on the road, leaving scrapes of blue paint behind on the pole.

As I make a right to take the route to school, I spot Rhett sitting in his car in a turnout on the edge of the forest.

Rhett watches me as I pass, and I feel his eyes burning holes in the side of my head.

How much of that did he see?

And why the hell is he just sitting there?

I pull into the school parking lot and run from my car to Atlas's. He's leaning against the door, chatting with Leon, but when he sees me, he slaps Leon on the back and leaves him behind as if he senses imminent danger.

"What's wrong?" he asks.

"Found," I pant, shocked by how out of breath I am. Though I think it has everything to do with the fact that our victim has just been discovered and not my sudden exertion.

"Found what?"

"Arthur's been found."

Atlas's jaw falls, and he stumbles another step closer to me, reaching out like he wants me to hold him up because he's hanging on by a thread.

"Who? How?" His voice is gravelly and his skin paling. "Marley, what did you hear?"

I shake my head. "Nothing. I *saw* it. Cops everywhere on the riverbank when I was coming over the bridge."

For some reason I don't tell him about the crash. He already thinks I'm going to crumble and send us all to jail.

"What the hell. How do you know it's Arthur? The river was flowing. He could be long gone by now."

How many bodies does he think are in there?

"I'm *really* sure. There was a tent up and dozens of cops. I asked Sam if Mrs. Hokanson had wandered off again. Then made it seem like I'd just remembered something, said George was asking about Arthur because he hasn't come home."

He nods. "Good. That's good. You made it sound like you were speculating."

"That was the plan. But what do we do now? It's not normal for people to be found in rivers. There will be an investigation."

I'm absolutely petrified of this leading back to us. To lose so much because of an accident. But I know, with absolute certainty, that it's what we deserve.

Still, I can feel myself being reeled in by the chance at a normal, successful life. One without courts and prison and public shame. One where my parents don't have to scrub *murderer* off their door or move away.

"We were careful. Jesse's car is clean. No one touched him without gloves. We stay calm and wait for this to blow over," Atlas says. He stretches his back, squaring his shoulders as if to make himself bigger. There's no amount of artificial growing he can do to make this right.

"O-okay."

"You good, Marley?" His face is ashen, like he's fighting real hard to hold his breakfast down.

"I'm not the one who looks like they're about to pass out."

"I'm fine. We should get to class. We need to keep everything normal," he replies, staring holes into me.

"I was sick one day, Atlas. I've been here since."

He lifts his palms. "I'm not criticizing, but it's more important than ever for us to keep it together. Come to me if you're struggling."

But in public, hold it in and pretend.

"I get it."

"I mean it."

"I said I get it, Atlas. Bell's about to go." I turn and walk away from him, now irritated as well as terrified and drowning in guilt.

He doesn't try to talk to me as I head inside, but I hear his footsteps right behind me. I bet he's watching me like a hawk, ready to pounce in case I throw the doors open and announce what we've done.

My first class is with Luce, thankfully not Atlas or Jesse.

Unfortunately, also with Rhett.

I'm still on edge about the forest night and can't be 100 percent certain he's not the one who messaged me and was trying to throw me off.

This is one huge nightmare that I would give anything to wake up from. Apparently not my freedom, though.

I make a right, shoving my way into the classroom. Atlas's sigh is the last thing I hear before the door shuts and blocks him out. I've been in love with Atlas for years, at least two before we actually got together. We've fought and gotten on each other's nerves . . . but this situation is the first time he's doubted me.

It's not just me who would face serious consequences, so for him to believe I would mess this up and tear apart his life too is like a kick to the gut.

Then there's Jesse and Luce. I've been best friends with Luce for years. She knows everything about me. I thought I knew everything about her.

I take a seat on the plastic chair next to Luce and turn to her. The teacher isn't here yet, and the rest of the class is chatting loudly. A couple of guys from the football team are throwing a ball to each other. Rhett is right at the back, whispering something into Ruthie's ear. She's going to catch something if she keeps letting him get that close.

"What?" Luce asks, taking one look at my face.

So I guess I don't look normal.

"The cops found Arthur in the river."

Her eyes widen like in a cartoon. "Oh shit! Are you serious? Marley, what the hell? What are we going to do?"

"Shhh," I hush, and pull her closer. "We do nothing. The guys are sure we're in the clear. Nothing was left at the scene, and we used gloves to . . . move him."

"This is the start of it, isn't it? We're going to have to lie and lie and lie."

"Why would anyone question us?"

"We did the dare, Marley," she whispers back, her breathing heavy.

"Yeah, but not on that stretch of road. For all anyone knows, we took a right at the crossroads and went back home."

Which we did, after we'd disposed of Arthur's body.

"God, this is . . . What is it? There are no words," she says. "What we've done is . . ."

"No words?" I say, and she nods.

She's right. There are no words in the English language strong enough to describe the horror we have committed. The weight of it is almost as heavy as knowing we are going to spend the rest of our lives covering it up.

"Are you ready for another dare?" Rhett asks, sitting on our desk.

Luce and I sit up, and I shove his arm. "Go to hell, Rhett."

My palms sweat as I watch him, looking for any micro-expressions that could tell me if he heard us talking. He just looks suitably smug, as always.

"Ah, baby, your words hurt."

"Your words are hurting your girlfriend," Luce says. "She's not at all happy that you're constantly trying to flirt with Marley."

I don't know which one of us wants to punch her more, but Rhett and I have the same look of annoyance.

Her comment works, though. Rhett stands. "You're insane, Luce. Both of you be ready tonight."

The news of Arthur being found obviously hasn't hit town yet. It would be all anyone could talk about if it had.

"Rhett, I cannot stress this enough, leave us alone and find another obsession," Luce says, waving her hand to dismiss him.

Her bravery has me smiling. Very few people stand up to Rhett. It's always glorious to watch when someone does. His face reddens and he clenches his hands into fists, knuckles turning white with the effort he's using to hold back.

He's never hit a girl, and I don't think he would, but he does not like being challenged, especially in front of others.

I wish she would stand up to Jesse more.

"You need to watch yourself, Luce. You're on very thin ice here."

He walks away, back to Ruthie, who's staring straight through me.

"What the hell did he mean by that? 'On thin ice'?" I say.

Luce shakes her head, the color draining from her face. "Don't go there. You said he didn't mention anything about it in the forest."

"He didn't, not really, but that doesn't mean he doesn't know."

She grabs my wrist, and that's when Mr. Jackson walks into the room with a DVD in his hand.

There's a collective cheer as he inserts the disc.

I'm glad it's not something I'm going to have to focus on. When he flicks off the light and sits at his desk, his head in his laptop, I take out my phone.

Marley:

What dare?

Rhett:

I thought you were done?

I want to be, but his little water-related warning has me right on edge again. Someone knows what we've done, and I have to figure out who. It's even more important now that Arthur has been found.

Marley:

Are you giving me one or not?

Rhett:

I think I'm going to give us one since we had so much fun in the forest.

Marley:

What about Luce?

Rhett:

She can sit it out.

I don't like this at all. He wants to get me alone again, and he's probably the one who knows.

Marley:

When and where?

Rhett:

I'll let u know

I push my phone into my shorts pocket and then press against the knot in my stomach.

"What?" Luce whispers.

I shake my head, forcing myself to look at the screen. "Nothing."

Maybe nothing. Rhett definitely knows more than he's saying; I'm just not sure it's about Arthur.

20

I only take three steps outside the classroom before I notice the whispers.

The next thing I notice is Atlas jogging toward me.

He shakes his head. "It didn't take longer than one period for the news to get out," he says, keeping his voice low.

"I'm going to meet up with Jesse, I bet he's freaking out," Luce mutters. More like *she's* freaking out and hoping he'll be able to calm her down.

I watch her leave until she disappears into the crowded hallway.

"Have you seen Jesse?" I ask when she's out of earshot.

He shrugs. "Not since first thing this morning."

"Does he know?"

"There's no way he doesn't. It's all over school. No one even cares about the chickens on the quad."

"What?"

"A few guys from the team and I grabbed five from Theo's

neighbor's, since it nearly made Fuller's head explode last time. It doesn't matter now."

"You pulled another prank?"

His eye twitches. "Come on, Marley, we need to be normal. How does it look if we suddenly stop? Besides, you went camping with Rhett freaking Wilder."

My jaw drops. "Are you *kidding* me? I didn't do that by choice. We thought he might be the one messaging me!"

He rakes his hands through his hair and huffs. "I know. But you're all over the place, acting on every suspicion, no matter how tiny it is."

"Why are you putting all of this on me? I'm not the only one who was suspicious of George and now Rhett. I'm the one trying to figure it out and save us all."

"All right. I'm sorry, okay." He looks up and down the hallway. "Let's not argue."

I can tell there's more he wants to say but he's holding back. Well, same.

"What's the gossip about the . . . discovery?"

"There's a lot. We know officially that a body has been found. Doesn't stop people from making up a whole load of crap. Everyone knows George has been looking for Arthur. With the fire, there's talk of a serial killer . . . and guess who the main suspect is? Or rather the main suspects are."

I roll my eyes. "The Wilders."

He nods.

We need all eyes to be on anyone but us. Doesn't mean I don't hate it. "*We* did this, Atlas."

"Nothing's going to happen to them, unfortunately."

"Nothing *should* happen to them. Not about Arthur, anyway." I take a deep breath. One lie has escalated. One victim has become two.

"Not here, Marley. You can't do this." He takes my hand and pulls me along. I barely take anything in. All I can think about is George lying in that hospital with no clue that he has no family left. When he wakes up, he'll learn that his grandad is dead.

Atlas pushes me into an empty classroom and closes the door behind us.

"I'm fine. We need to get to class."

"We have a minute," he says, looking through the square of glass in the door. "Everyone is too busy gossiping to worry about being late. I need to know that you're going to be okay."

"Are you going to be okay?"

He shrugs. "I don't have a choice. Push it to the back of your mind."

"That works?"

Because so far, I've had a zero percent success rate with that.

"It makes it bearable." He shoves his hands into his thick hair again. He's anxious. "We don't have a choice," he repeats, and I'm not sure it's me he's telling this time.

I bet I could get Atlas on my side if I decided to go to the cops. I'm not sure about Luce.

"It's going to be so much worse if the cops figure out what happened. You know that, right?"

"Marley, I can't hear that right now. We need to get everyone together again."

"Why? So Jesse can give us the usual speech about how our lives will be over? I go back and forth a lot. If we speak up, it'll affect every part of our lives going forward, our families' lives too. But how do we live with this?"

"I think you should fake an illness again."

"What? You told me to act normal."

"Yeah, and you can't. If you're going to fall apart, you need to do it at home."

I take a step back, his words physically painful. "Atlas . . ."

"Hey, I'm sorry. I don't mean to be a jackass. Hey, stop moving away from me." He steps closer and grabs my wrist. "Don't look at me like that. I'm protecting you. I get it, babe, I know you're struggling too. Do you need to go home?"

"There's nothing like covering up a murder to show all the different sides of the people you thought you knew."

Dropping my hand, he lifts a brow, his jaw set. "That's not fair. You're acting like this only affects you."

Am I? Maybe. . . . I don't know. They just seem to be dealing with this a little too well, as if we hit a bird and dumped it.

"And you guys are acting like it doesn't affect you at all."

"Wow." He takes a step back, shaking his head. "That's awesome. I tell you what, come find me when you've taken your head out of your ass."

I'm about to tell him to stay and talk, since he's the one who dragged me in here, but he spins around and leaves, throwing the door open so hard that it bangs on the table behind it.

We're only a fraction into the forever that we're going to have to keep this secret for, and it's already destroying us.

Atlas doesn't want to be anywhere near me right now. We seem to end every conversation with an argument, and now I'm doubting if he would stand with me if I wanted to speak up.

Can I destroy my parents and friends to clear my conscience?

I leave the classroom to a totally empty hallway. Damn it.

I jog to the locker room and slip inside the door without anyone seeing. My locker is by Luce's. She's already getting changed into her gym clothes.

"Hey," I say, gritting my teeth as my hand slips on the locker handle.

"Are you okay?"

"Just had a fight with Atlas, but I'm fine."

She looks over her shoulder and back to me. "Crazy about the body, isn't it? In our town."

I turn slowly to face her head-on. That's when I notice everyone else. We're in a packed room, and almost every other conversation I hear is the same.

It must be Arthur. Did he jump? George obviously wants to inherit the house now. Maybe he fell.

"Yeah," I say, my voice croaking. "It's awful."

She pulls her T-shirt over her head. "Everyone thinks it's Arthur."

"Of course it's Arthur."

Luce and I both turn toward the source of the statement. Ruthie.

She narrows her eyes at me, now having the attention of all the girls. "Come on, as if any of you are still questioning it. Arthur goes missing, and a week later a body turns up. It's obvious, isn't it?"

That last part is for me. Her hostility and bullying tactics make me want to flirt with Rhett. I'd never actually do it, because I hate him more than her, but I can picture her face and it's glorious.

I smile through the nausea. "If only we could all be as clever as you."

She rolls her eyes and walks off with her friends.

"I won't miss her," Luce says.

"Same."

• • •

After school I sit in the kitchen with my mom, watching her as she makes homemade pizzas.

I steal a strip of bell pepper and munch on it while she rolls out dough and checks her phone beside her.

"Waiting for something?"

"Huh? Oh, Dad's meeting Sam for a drink after his shift. He said he'd let me know if there are any developments. A body found." She shakes her head.

"Everyone is saying it's Arthur."

"Unfortunately, I think they're right. He's been missing for, what? A week now?"

Eight days, to be precise.

"Yeah," I say, the pepper getting lodged in my throat. I cough and she looks up. "I'm fine. Have you heard how George is?"

I've been dying to ask but too scared, despite that being a general thing you'd ask.

"I popped in to check on him before I left. No change. But his doctor is confident. George is young and healthy. Sam and Melinda are coming to dinner. We'll hopefully know more then."

"Do you think it'll take that long to identify the body? I mean, everyone in town knows who Arthur is."

"Oh, they will know already, but there's a proper procedure. Typically, the family is notified first . . . but I guess that isn't possible in this case. Julie in admin has been trying to locate someone."

"You think he might have other family?"

"Arthur never said, but it's possible. Julie's going to keep trying. We're all hoping George wakes up soon."

Not everyone is. Jesse wants him dead, and he was missing from school for the rest of the day. That makes me massively nervous.

"You don't need to worry about this stuff, though, honey."

"So you don't think there's a serial killer on the loose?"

She laughs. "Goodness, is that really what people are saying? No, I don't. We don't know the cause of the fire yet. There was an accelerant, but Arthur had cans of gas lying around. With the heat we've had, you can see how accidents happen."

"And what about him turning up in the river?" I ask.

"I'll admit, it's difficult to believe that he fell, because he probably knows the mountain better than anyone, but he could've been distracted."

I nod, unable to ignore the horrible thoughts in my head.

We might just get away with this.

21

Atlas and I huddle by my window, listening to Sam and Melinda chatting in my garden with my parents.

I went on a quick snack-and-drink run in case we wanted to avoid our guests for the rest of the night. I'm not sure I can stand Sam asking how I am and if my car is fixed. My dad buffed the scrape out as best he could. It's barely noticeable.

I can't talk about *why* I crashed in the first place . . . and I don't want Atlas to know.

It only takes them ten minutes to get on the subject.

I press my palm to my chest, willing my heart to not burst through it.

We're about to get an update on the case.

Atlas looks from them to me and back again. He arrived before they did so we could get upstairs and not have to speak to them. I don't think either of us is ready to speak about Arthur in front of a cop.

He takes my hand, and I can almost pretend it's like old times.

But his grip is limp. The affection is fake. He doesn't want to be this close. To be honest, I don't right now either.

I'm not going to tell him that everything is okay, because it's not. Even if we're never caught, it won't be okay.

My hand is heavy in his, both of us trying to follow the investigation without asking questions and raising suspicion. When Mom mentioned Sam coming over for dinner, I knew this was our chance.

Neither of us told the others, because they would have wanted to come too. I don't want Jesse in my room, and he's still MIA anyway. Luce has barely said two words to me, so I don't really feel like hanging with her.

Besides, I seem to catch a lot of attitude for still believing we should do the right thing. I can't now, though. Not since Jesse set Arthur's house on fire. What else is he capable of?

Sam usually keeps out the details of his cases when he discusses them. There's no way for him to talk about this without us all knowing it's Arthur, though.

Nothing like this happens here. The cops are usually dealing with vandalism and the odd shoplifter. Rhett and his brothers would keep them busy, but their dad makes any misdemeanors disappear.

"What's happening at the station, then?" Dad asks. "We're all waiting on this autopsy."

Sam shrugs. "Injuries in line with a fall, as we assumed. There was one weird thing, though. The official report isn't in, but the tox screen showed he had a high level of oxycodone in his system. Not enough to kill him, but it'd make him drowsy. But it's strange—we don't know where it came from. He doesn't have a prescription for it."

My mouth falls open.

"What does that mean?" Atlas asks.

"It's a strong painkiller. My dad had it a few years ago after having his appendix out. Highly addictive, so he only took it for a couple of days."

"Gosh, poor Arthur," Mom says. "Where do you think it came from?"

Sam shrugs. "The grandson didn't mention anything about it when he reported him missing, and he said he hadn't seen anyone around the house. He did say that Arthur had trouble getting up, thought it was maybe the onset of arthritis, but he wouldn't see a doctor."

"So you think he was getting the medication from elsewhere?"

"It's too easy to get hold of. A lot of kids use it for a high." Sam shakes his head. "Idiots. Wrecks lives."

"Do you think Arthur was addicted?" Dad asks.

"Hard to tell. Would explain the high dose—you need more and more as the addiction takes hold . . . but Arthur?"

I listen to them with my heart thumping wildly.

"Marley," Atlas whispers. "We're going to be fine. He was off his head. Probably why he walked into the road."

"I never saw him walk stiffly," I say.

"You heard what Sam said. Can't you see, this is a good thing. We're in the clear. I'm messaging Jesse. Don't worry, I'll keep it discreet."

Don't worry? I didn't think he was about to outline our crime over text and give the cops a slam-dunk case.

I can't deny that this massively helps us out. The drowsiness from the pills would account for why he went over a bridge . . . but Arthur buying those from someone on the sly. I'm not sure.

As I watch Sam and notice the frown on his face, I'm thinking that he's not quite convinced either.

"Do you think that's it? Case closed?" I ask.

Distracted with his phone, Atlas shrugs.

I want to shake him. I'm so freaking envious of his ability to move on from something and not have it constantly in his head.

When he's done, he looks up, and the smile he gives me transports me back to pre-Arthur. "Jesse's psyched. See, all we had to do was wait it out and keep our cool." He reaches out and takes my hand. "We're going to have the best summer and figure out this long-distance thing. We can see each other on weekends."

"Right, because it's all done now."

"I'm not saying that. Don't mistake my relief for coldness. I still feel goddam awful for what we did. I'll never forgive myself, and I deserve that, but everything we've done since hitting him is to have a life and be better people."

Would better people cover it up or confess? I don't speak the thought aloud, because it'll only cause another argument. We haven't been in the best place recently, both of us snappy and taking our bad moods out on each other.

I squeeze his hand and tell a lie. "The best summer."

"I should head off anyway," he says, checking his watch.

"You need to be somewhere?"

He looks up like a deer caught in headlights. "Just my dad wanting family time again."

That's a lie. I can tell by the way his dark eyes dart away and his body tenses.

"Right, I'll see you later, then."

Nodding, he stands and brushes his hand over my shoulder. "Later, babe."

No kiss. He walks out of my room, and my heart sinks.

Everything is changing.

Why are they all being weird and pulling back from me? This has changed us all, but they're still friends. What would make them ditch only me?

I stand and pace my room, trying to figure out whatever is happening here. But there's tumbleweed in my head, rolling around looking for a freaking clue.

I walk to my desk and pull out a drawer, hoping I have some candy stashed in there. Sugar will help, right?

I run my fingers over a couple of Tootsie Rolls and a gummy shaped like a SpongeBob Krabby Patty.

Hold on. . . .

I dig around in my little jewelry dish.

My pin badge is missing.

The same one as Luce's. It was definitely here. I remember putting it away after I told her I wouldn't wear it. Hers is stuck in Arthur's floor vent, and now mine is missing.

My hand flies to my throat, where I feel bile hit the back of my tongue. There's only one reason someone would take this.

If the badge is found while they're tearing down Arthur's, it will look like *I've* been in the house.

• • •

Monday, June 5

After another welcome quiet and rainy weekend, I arrive at school early, ready to meet Luce. She's in the parking lot when I pull up, leaning against her car and studying her reflection in a pocket mirror. I want to grill her about the badge, but I have to be smart about this.

If I confront her, they'll all know I'm figuring out their plan.

Which, I'm thinking, is to make it look like I was the only one in Arthur's house that night. It'll be my fingerprints on the watch. I have to get Rhett to scrub it . . . somehow.

I'm going to play nice until I know exactly what their plan is.

I've been stewing on it all weekend and plotting, trying to figure this thing out and plan for all scenarios. I managed to go see George too, and it only made me more determined.

"Hey," she says as I get out. "Jesse filled me in about the autopsy."

"Yeah, it's great," I say, feeling sick. I can barely meet her eye, but she smiles as if she hasn't been rooting around in my room and stealing from me. "Sam didn't mention taking it further, so I think we're good."

"You don't sound convinced, babe."

Ugh. *Babe.* How fake is she being?

Okay, as fake as me.

"It's just bugging me. Arthur and painkillers."

She purses her lips. "All right, I admit it's weird as hell, but why else would he have that in his system?"

"He wouldn't, I guess."

"Look at the facts and not what's going on in your mind. If he was in a lot of pain, he'd take something, and I Googled them last night, and they're, like, wicked addictive. It's not like he was taking them to party."

A small bubble of laughter pops from my mouth before I can stop it. That was an interesting image. "Yeah, you're right. Where were you all weekend? This is becoming a habit."

"I was busy. My parents were home.

"Oh, look who's here," she says, scowling as Rhett pulls in. Ruthie sits on the passenger side, smirking at us as he drives by.

"I don't like those smug expressions she keeps giving us."

Luce links her arm through mine, and it takes every ounce of self-control not to bat her away. "Soon we won't have to see them ever again. Ignore her, she's just hateful because her boyfriend has a thing for you."

We walk into the hall, where seniors are gathered, some of them kneeling on the floor. "Right," I reply, watching her closely. She looks like my best friend . . . but I don't feel like Luce is anymore.

"What's going on?" Luce asks as we continue into the hall.

I leap back as I spot what they're gathered around. "Rhett, stop this!"

He laughs, looking up from the fire extinguishers he's holding. There are five of them, and each reads FOAM on the canister.

"Shut up, Marley," Ruthie snaps.

Ellie and Dayshawn each pick one up. Then Jonah, Freya, and Mikey follow suit.

This is the kind of stunt that colleges aren't going to appreciate.

If there's an actual fire and someone has stolen the extinguishers, a lot of people are going to get into some serious trouble.

"You have two minutes before Ruthie pulls the alarm," he tells them. "Split up and cover as much of these corridors as you can. Let's foam this place up!"

Okay, I admit it kind of sounds fun. No one can be killed by doing that. But isn't it a de-escalation? Jesse had to drive without lights at night.

They dart off, each taking a different door or splitting if they used the same one.

Rhett turns to me. "Lighten up, this is going to be awesome. Ruthie, you'd better be counting. Ed, you know what to do next."

Ed nods, his pale, spotty face even redder than before. "Yes, boss," he says, and runs for the exit at the back of the room.

I raise a brow and Rhett laughs. "I didn't even tell him to call me that."

"And what are you doing for this dare?" I ask.

Luce tries to pull me away, but I have never backed down from Rhett. I think that's the weird obsession he has with me. That and maybe, or I hope, guilt over how he threw our friendship away.

"I've given it."

"Yeah? And why don't you play? I think maybe it's because you're a coward."

"Shut up, Marley!" Ruthie snaps, holding her phone up because I'm assuming counting to 120 is too taxing for her.

"If you're bored of this, you can tap out," he says, stepping closer.

"Why, so you can make something up about me and ruin my life like your loser brother did to Henrietta?"

His eyes narrow and he takes a deep breath.

"I'm not scared of you, Rhett, and I sure as hell don't worship you like your groupie over there."

He lifts a brow but makes no attempt to stand up for Ruthie. I bet he won't even remember her name in three months' time.

"Is that right?" he asks.

"That's two minutes," Ruthie says, running to the wall.

She smashes the box next to the window, and a shrill alarm wails above us.

I shake my head. "Come on, Luce. Time to evacuate."

In the corridor a teacher is ushering people to the nearest exit. "Walk calmly to the meeting point. You all know what to do by now."

Mr. Goldman dashes past, jaw wide and holding his kippah to his head. They'll assume this is the real thing because no drill has been planned. Or at least they'll have to act as if it is. It's not like that thing hasn't been set off on purpose before.

I'm half-tempted to stop and let them know what's going on, but I'm not going to do that. Luce laughs as we turn the corner and see the walls and ceiling are covered in foam.

All right, maybe the teachers won't assume this is real.

We walk faster, the fire exit just up ahead. I laugh, sidestepping a blob of foam that falls to the floor.

"Everyone out!" the principal bellows. "And I need names!"

The school has CCTV, so it won't make a difference if no one comes forward. I idly wonder if they'll be able to walk at graduation after this.

Luce and I walk outside, following the crowd to the meeting point. I stand with my class and look for Atlas.

He pushes past a couple of people and rakes his hands through his hair. He's wearing his football uniform because the seniors were playing each other today. Kind of like a final fun practice.

"Marley," he says, reaching for me. "There's a fire on the quad. Know whose dare it was?"

"What? Rhett dared those five to use the fire extinguishers in the halls, then Ruthie pulled the alarm. There was no fire."

The five extinguisher-happy renegades are standing together with their heads hanging. Two teachers are yelling at them, the now empty extinguishers on the grass.

"I just walked past it. There's *definitely* a fire."

"Ed. That's what Rhett was telling him to do."

"Ed did that?" Atlas asks.

I shrug. "He got a dare."

"At least Rhett seems to be leaving us alone now."

He's not leaving me alone; apparently I have another dare coming up. Though I don't feel afraid of it anymore. Perhaps I should be, but a lot has changed, and things can't get any worse.

Atlas believes Arthur's death is sorted out, and Rhett's moved on too. Maybe Atlas will start being normal with me again . . . and maybe he'll tell me his secret. The one he didn't want to admit to before the dares started, the one I think Rhett might know about.

"They're really letting them have it," Atlas says, craning his neck to watch the teachers discipline the fire five. No sign of Ed, so maybe they don't know about his involvement yet.

I look around the field and notice Jesse with his hands shoved in his pockets. He's not looking at the drama in front of us, he's staring right at me.

22

Once the small fire has been extinguished, we're allowed back into the building. The whole thing lasted about an hour from start to finish. Fuller has officially banned all pranks, but there are only a few days left of school anyway, and no one cares about getting into trouble now.

Fuller is the least of my worries. I don't even care if I'm not allowed to walk at graduation.

The longer this goes on, the less I care about anything.

I follow the crowd out toward my final class of the day, but I don't get far before I'm shoved into an empty classroom. Spinning around, I face the person who grabbed me. I expect to see Rhett, but it's Jesse standing in front of me.

"What are you doing?" I ask, my heart thudding so fast I'm instantly lightheaded.

"What are *you* doing?"

His eyes are wild, as if he's been taking something, but I know him better than that. I'm terrified, but this change in him isn't due to any substance.

He's a killer.

"I-I'm not doing anything."

"You're lying. You're going to open your big mouth."

"No, I'm not. I don't want this to get out either, Jesse. My future is on the line too."

He squares his shoulders and breathes noisily through his nose. I want to take a step back, but I'm afraid to move. "Don't screw this up."

"I'm not going to, Jesse. Come on, we're friends. We all want the same thing here," I say, trying to pacify him. I just want out. "I won't tell anyone."

"Damn right you won't. I'm getting the hell out of here in a month."

He shouldn't be anywhere but prison. Arthur is dead. George is only just hanging on.

"We're all out of here. We just need to hold it together and stick together."

I'm flat-out lying now. I don't want to be around him at all. He scares the hell out of me.

"I think we're past that, Marley."

"Why?"

"Why?" he snaps. "Because you can't leave this alone. God, you've been talking to George and Rhett. You're getting messages."

"I'm trying to act normal. I always talk to George when he's in town. How would it look if I suddenly stopped when his grandad goes missing?"

His eyes narrow again, but he knows I'm right. My friends are blaming me when all I've done is help them cover this up even though I feel so damn awful and guilty.

Surely we all feel that?

As I look into Jesse's eyes, though, I can tell that he doesn't.

Has he always lacked empathy and been so detached?

"We're on the same side, Jesse," I say, my stomach in knots because I don't know if he's buying it. He's been absent from my life for days. I don't know what he's been up to or what he's thinking. "We should go, or this will look weird."

He steps to the side, blocking the door, and holds the handle. "Keep it together."

I'm not the one spiraling out of control.

As soon as he's out the door, I rush to the window, looking through the small square of glass until I see him disappear around the corner.

When I'm satisfied that he's gone, I rush out and sprint to my last class.

Sitting down in the corner of the room, I watch as Mr. Goldman clears his throat, not seeming to care about my tardiness.

I listen to him as he begins to rattle on about morals and character, telling us how personal success is just as important as professional achievement. We should do our best in college and be our best selves everywhere.

His words are sandpaper on my skin.

My breaths are short and shallow, making me feel dizzy. If I had to stand up, I'd probably hit the floor.

My friends are setting me up.

It doesn't help that I can feel Rhett's eyes on me. My vision blurs, I can feel the walls closing in, crushing into me. Anxiety digs its claws into my stomach so tightly I don't think I'll ever get it out.

"I—I don't feel well," I say, interrupting Mr. Goldman's sermon.

"Do you need to go to the nurse?" he asks.

I nod and place my clammy palms on the table as I stand, testing my ability to keep upright. The world tilts but I manage to walk out the door.

"Marley, wait up!"

I groan at hearing Rhett's voice, only having made it a few steps out of the room.

"Leave me alone." I walk straight past the nurse's office and out the side door. I don't care that my car is in the lot; I just need to walk, to get lost in the mountains for a while.

Rhett doesn't listen. I hear his footsteps behind me. He could easily catch up, I'm not running, but he's choosing to stay back.

"Please, go back," I say.

"Not happening," he replies. "You're clearly not okay."

"Why do you care?" I snap, stepping into the sparse tree line behind school. It'll take a few minutes of uphill hiking before I reach the forest.

"You know I care," he says.

"Funny you only say that when no one else is around. Stop acting like I still mean something to you and leave me alone."

He catches up to me then, grabbing my wrist to stop me.

I wrench from his grip and throw my arms in the air, not wanting him anywhere near me. I can feel the cracks deepening, and I just need to be alone. "Get off! What the hell do you want?"

He steps closer, and I suck in a breath to calm my frayed nerves.

"What do you want?" I ask again, but even I can tell my voice doesn't hold the usual contempt.

He opens and closes his mouth as if he's going to speak but isn't sure what to say. Then he takes a deep breath. "Okay, I need to ask you something."

"What?"

"Do you know what happened to Arthur?" His voice is low, and it's the first time I've ever heard him sound afraid.

I lick my dry lips and try to keep my face straight, while inside I feel like I'm dying. "He fell from the bridge," I say, giving him the cops' working theory.

I want to tell someone so bad, even him. I just want someone else to know, to help, to take the load off, because it's too heavy, and I don't have anyone. To open the wound and let some of the infection out.

He shakes his head and takes one step closer, now very much invading my personal space. It almost makes my legs buckle. "Why did you leave school?"

"I don't feel well."

"Where are you going?"

"Up the mountain. No one will know where I am."

"I will."

"Yeah, well, I never thought you'd follow me. I need to sit down," I say, placing my hand over the thumping in my chest, close to passing out.

This is too much.

Rhett takes my hand and pulls me a few steps deeper into the forest, where we won't be seen, to a fallen tree. We're still ages from our spot, but I don't think I'll make it.

He sits beside me, stretching his legs out in front of him. Tilting his head, he looks up through the lush trees to the sky. Only slivers of blue can be seen through the leaves.

"You should go, Rhett. I'm just having a bad day and need some space."

"Ruthie's made a few snide comments about Jesse's dare. She hasn't said anything direct, but she's implying that you guys hit Arthur."

My gasp takes me by surprise, not at all inconspicuous.

Oh god, it's her sending the messages. I close my eyes as a wave of nausea threatens to take me out.

I hear Rhett move. "You've gone gray, Marley. Are you . . . no." The next thing I hear is something between a groan and cry of shock.

I squeeze my eyelids together tighter as if I could make myself disappear.

"It's true," he says, his tone hollow.

"Stop," I whisper, folding in on myself and tucking my head into my knees. "Stop. Please."

"Tell me what happened."

Why isn't he running away?

"You don't know what you're talking about. Please leave me alone."

"I'm here and not at the station, Marley. Doesn't that tell you something?"

"Go. Please."

"I'm not going anywhere. Will you look at me?" He tugs my arm and I almost fall into him. "Tell me what happened."

"Why don't you just ask Ruthie?"

"I don't care about her! God, how can you not see what's right in front of you?" he snaps, scowling at me. With a sigh that feels like it cuts him, he lets go of my wrist. "Tell me what happened that night, Marley. Look at you, this is killing you."

"It was the stupid dare, Rhett! The stupid dare that we just *had* to do. Jesse was driving, it was so dark, and he was going too fast." I sit taller, my mind painting vivid images of what happened. "Luce, Atlas, and I were in the truck. Arthur came out of nowhere, walked into the road just past a bend. Jesse had no chance of stopping. He was just . . . there."

"Keep going," Rhett says.

"At first, we thought it might be a deer or some other animal. But I knew it was too big. We stopped and looked around. Found Arthur. He was already . . . gone when we got to him." I sob.

"Please keep going. What did you do next?" he asks softly, sounding so much like my old friend that I almost cry harder.

I lower my head and wipe the tears from my face. "Jesse had gloves, a box of tools. You know, stuff to fix his car if it broke down."

Rhett nods, encouraging me to continue.

"We put the gloves on, and Jesse and Atlas put him in the . . . bed. It was like he was nothing, lying there. Then . . . we dumped him."

"I feel like you're skipping over a lot of information. I don't want just the facts, Marley. You were involved in a murder. You dumped a body. Stop giving me bullet points."

"Oh, that's not good enough? What do you want to hear, then? How it's eating me alive? How I can't stop thinking about it every second of every day?" I stand, throwing my hands in the air and shouting, "How I wish I could go back in time and call the cops? I never should have agreed to do what we did. I see him every time I blink, and I would do *anything* to make this right." I choke on a sob. "I need to make this right, Rhett. I need to."

He leaps to his feet and wraps his arms around my back, holding me so tight I think he might be able to keep me from splitting apart. "Hey, shhh, it's okay."

I struggle in his grip for a heartbeat, but then I feel my body give way like I don't have one ounce of energy left, no more fight. I'm just done.

Rhett's arms tighten, stopping me from hitting the ground, and I feel my body shake against his. I'm such a mess. "I've got you. It's going to be okay."

"It's not," I cry into his T-shirt. "It's not."

He holds me until I take the weight of my legs again. Then he pulls back, keeping my arms in his grip. I don't know if that's to prevent me from collapsing or running away.

"How does Ruthie know?" he asks.

That wasn't the question I expected.

"I have no clue. None of us have said anything, and we especially wouldn't to her. I can only guess that she saw us. It was late and dark, but that road is the one she'd use between the creek and her house. But her first message didn't come until the day of the rainstorm. When did she leave the creek that night?"

"Before me, but I didn't pay much attention. Her message?"

I run my hands through my hair, not caring anymore that I'm telling him all this. He can go to the cops. He can tell the world. I just want to stop pretending.

"She's been messaging me. I mean, I think it's her. We thought it was George first. Then I thought it was you. It's why I agreed to camp with you."

He lifts a brow.

"Now I think maybe it's Ruthie. Maybe she's targeting me because . . ." *Because she thinks you like me.* "Um, we don't get along."

He laughs but it's cut short. "Yeah, that's the reason. What happened to George?"

I shrug. "They won't tell me exactly, but I do know that it was Jesse who set the fire. He's been so different. Mean, controlling. He believes I'm going to crack. I mean, look at me. He's not wrong."

"He's an asshole."

"They started being weird with me almost right away, leaving me out of things, conversations. Even Atlas," I say, my heart breaking as I admit that aloud. "I don't know what's going on, and it's so scary."

"This is so messed up."

"It's like they've just decided they don't like me anymore. . . . They're planning something without me."

Hearing my words tears my heart to shreds. We were all supposed to have each other's backs.

"What could they be planning?"

"I don't know, but I'm sure Jesse is responsible for Arthur's house burning down."

Rhett frowns. "Do you think he would hurt you?"

"I didn't use to, but after George, it wouldn't surprise me. He's already freezing me out, right? That's what he's doing?"

"Possibly." He scratches his head. "All right, we need to figure this out. Leave Ruthie to me."

"What?"

"I can get her to shut up. Don't worry about her, you need to focus on what your *friends* are up to."

I shake my head, grabbing his arm. "Rhett, you don't know what you're saying."

"Actually, I do."

"No, you really don't. I can't let you help me cover this up. You don't want any part of this."

"That's not your choice to make. This is going to ruin the rest of your life."

I shake my head. "*I* can't cover this up anymore."

"You didn't hit him, and you didn't dump him."

"I helped dig the grave!"

His face falls. "Dig the grave? Marley, he was found in the river."

I bite my lip and shake my head again. "We buried him first. In the forest, way off trail. But the first message told us the grave was sinking when we had all that rain. So . . . we moved him. Dug him up and dumped him in the river, let the current take him. Only he didn't get as far as we hoped."

Rhett's face pales.

"So, you see why I can't keep this in for the rest of my life."

"Jesus, Marley," he whispers.

"That's who I am."

"No, that's what you've done." He pinches the bridge of his nose. "Is there anything else?"

"That's not enough?"

"It's more than enough. You're still not throwing your future away."

"I think it'll come out. Luce and I have the same handmade pin badge, bought it from this lady at the spring fair. It's a little book that says, 'Reading is a superpower.' The night we stole that stupid watch, she dropped it down a floor vent and couldn't get it back."

"I'm not following."

"*Mine* has gone missing. I noticed yesterday. They've all been to my house since. Atlas last night."

Rhett frowns as he tries to follow my train of thought.

"I'm the one who's losing it. They've been terrified that I'll speak up and we'll all go down. Rhett, I think they're panicking now that Arthur's been found, and they're setting me up to take the fall."

23

Rhett rakes his fingers through his hair, messing it up. "What's to say it's not Ruthie who snuck in and stole that badge? I knew there was something going on with her. She's been more obsessed with you than usual, muttering cryptic messages about canceling you or some shit."

"I want to believe it's Ruthie so bad, but it doesn't make sense for her to take it or to know that Luce's is missing."

He nods. "We need to find out what's going on."

I wipe my eyes. "You shouldn't get involved. This isn't your problem. In fact, you should stay as far away from me as you can. If or when this gets out, being near me could ruin things for you too."

He shrugs like it's no big deal. "I'm in, Marley."

"You're insane."

"Probably."

"Why?" I whisper.

"You know why."

I shake my head. "Rhett . . ." Before I can argue my point and get him the hell away, he takes a final step toward me, and his lips meet mine.

I should push him away. This is *Rhett* after all, but instead I pull him closer.

What the hell are you doing?

His hand tangles in my hair, and it's enough to wake me up from my nightmare.

"Bad idea," I say, ending the kiss far later than I should.

He drops his hands to his sides. "Not from where I'm standing."

"You just found out that I covered up a murder, Rhett!"

"I like you. A lot. Never said it was rational."

I *so* can't deal with this right now. "What am I going to do?"

"I'm assuming you mean about your friends and the douche. First, we need to figure out what they're doing . . . and steal that badge back from whichever one of them has it."

"My guess would be Atlas."

He smiles. "I'm really going to enjoy rooting through his room."

"You're not going to do anything. He's half ghosting me, but we're technically still together, so I can show up at his place."

Rhett's eyes don't leave mine. I can tell what he's thinking. I just let him kiss me when Atlas and I haven't broken up. "Wow."

"Okay, there's no time for any love-triangle, teen-drama bullshit. This isn't *Riverdale*."

"Moving on," he says, smirking. "All right, you snoop in his room. Wouldn't he give the pin to Luce, though? They're planning on pretending that it's hers, right?"

"I'll be looking there too, but you're probably right. He'd want to get it to her as soon as he could. If that's what they're doing. Still could be Ruthie."

Please be Ruthie.

He groans. "Fine, I'll search her room, look for a little book badge or a phone."

How the hell did I get here? Where the only person I trust is Rhett Wilder.

"If you'd have told me two weeks ago that I'd be relying on you, I would've laughed in your face."

"You're welcome," he says dryly.

"Sorry, that was bitchy."

"Are you good now?"

"Not even a little bit. I still want to confess, Rhett, but I don't want them to get away without taking responsibly too. I'm doing this so they won't have any incriminating evidence solely against me. Don't even try to talk me out of it. Okay?"

He salutes. "Yes, ma'am."

"Promise me."

"I've got your back, Marley, okay? Let's go, because I want to get out of Ruthie's before her mom comes home."

"All right."

We walk back to the parking lot at school, almost tripping a few times because it rained last night and turned the mossy ground into a Slip 'N Slide.

"Call me when you leave Atlas's," he says, opening my door for me. "And, Marley?"

"Yeah?"

"Ask him about college."

"What?"

"Just do it, yeah? Speak soon."

"Wait, no!" I grab his wrist and yank him back. "You can't say that and walk away. Rhett, at the moment, you're the only one being honest with me. I want to hear it from you before he lies. Please."

"All right," he says. "I saw a list of colleges seniors are attending in the fall. Atlas is going to be in Ohio, not California."

"What?" I breathe.

"I'm sorry he's a coward."

"Oh my god. When was he going to tell me? I'm such an idiot."

He's spent the last six months planning our future, one he knew he wasn't going to be a part of. This is why we've been drifting. He's been letting us.

"You okay?"

My heart hurts, but beyond that I'm *furious* and petrified.

"I will be," I say, looking at Rhett like a whole different person is standing in front of me. "Hey, thank you, Rhett."

"Can I have that in writing?"

"Why ruin this moment?"

He laughs and raises his hand. "Sorry. Hurry up and be careful."

"Same."

I get in my car, and before I can reach for the handle, he closes the door. Anger simmers in my stomach at being such a fool. Why couldn't Atlas just tell me that he wanted to study somewhere else?

How far would he have let this go?

I start the engine but wait a second, watching Rhett get into his car. He leaves first, heading in the direction of Ruthie's house. As

I drive to Atlas's, I replay the conversation I've just had with Rhett over in my head.

His reaction to my friends' behavior has only strengthened my concerns that I'm being set up. There is no other reason for my badge to be taken. Why would Ruthie bother with that? She knows what happened, so it only makes sense for her to turn us all in or blackmail us. She might hate me the most, but I can't see her caring if my friends go down too.

I *really* don't want it to be my friends, but I think at this point I have to accept that they don't care about me. We're not as close as I thought. Did they even have a second thought about dropping me? The way Rhett did.

It burns to have it happen again, and it's so much worse this time.

I'm not sure how I'm going to handle Atlas yet, but I'll figure that out once I'm there. I want him to grow up and tell me the truth.

I just hope Rhett finds evidence that Ruthie is the one messaging me.

I park in Atlas's driveway and head to the front door. His parents probably aren't home yet, but they park in the garage, so I can't tell.

Atlas opens up as I'm approaching the door.

"Marley." He looks over my shoulder down the street. What's he looking for? Is he expecting someone, or does he just not want to be seen with me? "What're you doing here?"

"What am I doing here?" I lift a brow, my stomach tightening. "Can I come in so we can talk?"

"Yeah, in my room, my dad's home," he says, leading the way upstairs. He closes the door behind us and turns to me.

"Care to tell me why you're ignoring me?" I ask, cutting to the chase because I cannot stand all the mind games. I want to open with the college thing, but that feels very final. I'm holding on to him by a thread. One I know I should cut myself.

He folds his arms and then releases them. "I'm not. Things are . . . difficult. I just need some space to deal with everything. You've needed that too."

"You don't seem to need space from Jesse or Luce."

"They're not my girlfriend. There's no pressure there."

What a load of crap. "Why do you feel pressure with me? Pressure to do what?"

Sighing, he sits down on his bed. "I don't mean to be distant. I'm struggling to take care of you as well as me."

"I don't need you to take care of me—I'm not three. We can be there for each other. I just need you to be honest."

He lifts his eyes to meet mine. "You've been falling apart, and I've been trying to hold you together. It got to be too much."

Atlas has never been deceptive, or at least, I didn't think of him that way before Arthur and the college bombshell, so I don't know if he's telling the truth. I don't know if he's involved in setting me up, or whatever they're doing, but he was the last one in my room before I noticed the badge gone.

"Pushing me away is your way of taking care of yourself?"

"Just for a minute. I can't help you if I'm this broken."

"Why didn't you tell me that?" I ask, sitting next to him on the bed.

He smiles sadly and takes my hand in his. "Because I wasn't ready to see the disappointment in your eyes. I didn't want you to feel like I don't care, and believe me, I understand that stepping back and not talking to you has done that."

I search his face for any chink in the armor and don't find one. "I'm sorry I made you feel that way."

"It's not your fault. It's the situation. I don't know how to move past this."

This sounds like a breakup speech. At least he's finally owning his feelings. At this point I just want him to do it. I want a clean break from all of them.

"Do you want to call it quits?" I ask, hoping he'll tell me about college. He was the one to suggest we go to colleges in the same state because he didn't think long-distance would work.

He shakes his head. "I don't know. No. Maybe. I still love you, but this will always be between us. No matter what happens from now on. I don't want to hurt you."

I'm so confused. He looks and sounds like the Atlas I know, but there's a tightening in my heart that's stopping me from believing him. I can't tell if it's intuition or paranoia. Doesn't matter, I guess. He's leaving.

I wring my hands. "Why would staying together hurt me?"

He glances at me sideways and pops his lips. "School's almost over. Things are going to change. Maybe, after what happened here, we both need a fresh start."

"This is rather sudden considering you were the one who planned our semi-long-distance relationship. You worked out schedules until Christmas so we could still regularly see each other. You talked me down when I got worked up about us growing apart. 'A six-hour drive isn't that bad.'"

"It's not that I don't want it to work. But how can we keep coming back to each other and not bring any of *this* with us?"

I narrow my eyes. "You're using this as an excuse. God, Atlas, just *tell me the truth.* Don't I at least deserve that much?"

He scrubs his hand over his face. "Okay. . . . Okay. Marley, I'm not going to California."

There it is. The first truthful thing he's said to me in a while.

"I'm going to Ohio State."

I nod as pain rips through my chest. It's so much worse hearing it from him. "Since when?"

"Since March. I'm sorry I didn't tell you sooner."

"I feel like you're using Arthur as an excuse."

"I'm not."

"But you've known for months! Why not tell me earlier? I'd understand if Ohio is where you'd rather be, but you've spent all this time lying to me. What was the point of all your planning if you never intended to follow through?"

"I didn't want to hurt you. We've been together for years."

"When were you going to tell me? The day I drove to your college and was told you'd never gone there?"

"No," he sighs, running his hand over his jaw. "I'm not sure. I was trying to find the right time."

"When you accepted your offer to Ohio, *that* was the right time."

"I'm sorry," he says again.

"Where do we go from here? Things are weird with everyone."

I don't want to tell him about the badge because I don't trust him.

"They're worried about you."

"Jesse's being horrible."

"He's scared."

"I'm scared too."

"You're making things worse."

I grit my teeth, the heartache lessening. "You don't even want to see if we can put this behind us and move forward?" I ask, moving toward his desk. It's littered with candy wrappers and half-empty water bottles. A photo of us in a frame sits beside his laptop. We have our arms around each other, smiling at the camera. It was only taken a few months ago, but it feels like years have passed since we looked happy like that.

In a little over a week, our relationship has fallen apart.

We deserve it, to be fair.

I run my hand over the photo and turn around, leaning on the desk.

"I can't stop thinking about him, Marley. It's there *all the time.* I thought it'd get better, that I'd figure out how to live with it, but I can't. I'm going to leave sooner. Spend the summer near campus, get ready for college."

"You're leaving now," I whisper.

"I'm so sorry," he says for the third time.

"I guess we found that thing we couldn't get through together, huh."

He dips his chin, and I wonder if he's thinking about how much he's changed too. We were supposed to grow together. Gone is the guy who used to tell me it was us against the world.

Now it's him against me.

"Don't make this any harder, please."

I ball my hands and scowl. "Are you for real? I'm not the one doing anything."

"It's all you talk about. I can't keep going back and forth about the Arthur thing. I just want to forget it, and if I have any chance at doing that, I need to never talk about it again."

The Arthur *thing*.

That's what our part in ending his life has been reduced to.

"You're blaming *the Arthur thing* on me, and that's not fair. I'm so done, Atlas. I'm getting my hoodie. If you find anything else of mine, just drop it off. I'll box your stuff up," I tell him, opening the door behind me.

"Don't be like that."

"Like what? You've just told me we're over and you're leaving soon. How am I supposed to be?" I yank my hoodie off a hanger and spin around.

"Were you even going to tell me or just send me a text from Ohio?"

"Don't." He stands and makes his way toward me, stopping a few feet away. "I'm sorry. I hate this. I never wanted it to end like this . . . or at all. You must see that it'll be easier this way, though, right?"

Actually, yeah. This past week hasn't only changed him. I've seen Jesse's and Luce's true colors too. And my own.

We'll forever be the people we've morphed into.

There's no going back.

"You still could've done this properly. You're making me hate you."

He steps back, taking a sharp breath. "Marley . . ."

"Let's leave it there, Atlas, okay? No need to keep talking. We're done and you're going. Have a nice life."

I storm past him and run down the stairs.

He doesn't try to follow.

24

I drive home slowly, knowing that if I drag it out a little longer, my dad will be at work and my mom will be in bed after a long day shift, and I won't have to pretend that I'm okay. I'm so tired of pretending, I feel like I might fall apart.

While I drive, I tell Siri to call Rhett.

I really am a different person now.

"Hey," he says, his voice light, as if he was looking forward to my call.

"Well, that was a disaster," I tell him. "But it was pretty much what I expected."

"What happened?"

"Where are you?"

"Driving back from Ruthie's. Has she always been that annoying? Anyway, where are you?"

"I'm driving home too. Can you meet me down the trail near the creek? I don't want to talk about this on the phone."

"Sure, I'm a minute from there."

"Same. I think I see you," I reply, noticing a car weaving around the hill, the same stretch of road where we hit Arthur. I haven't used it since.

Rhett stays on the line, though neither of us says anything else. I watch his car grow larger until we both pull onto the dirt road, the one that leads to a flattened patch of grass as near to the creek as a car can get. It's sort of a makeshift parking lot.

We don't go that far, though, both just pulling off the road enough to not be seen by anyone passing by.

I get out as he walks over to my car.

"Well?" he asks, holding his arms out to the sides.

"Couldn't tell a hundred percent if he's in on it, didn't mention the badge, but he did defend them and told me I'm the problem."

"He's a douche. Nothing at Ruthie's, couldn't find another phone, but she'd probably hide it well. What did Atlas say?"

"Oh, just that we've grown apart, we're over, and he's moving to Ohio after graduation rather than at the end of the summer. He's known he wasn't coming to California for months. At least he finally told me."

"Right," he replies, scratching the back of his neck. "Um, I'm sorry."

I laugh, surprising myself that I can find anything amusing right now. "You're sorry?"

"I mean, not really. That's what you say, though, right?"

"I guess." I lean back against my car. "He wasn't bothered when I went in his room, so if it was him who took the badge, I don't think he has it now. He'd want to give it to Luce straightaway."

Rhett moves closer, leaning next to me. "So the working theory now is that Luce and Jesse are setting you up. Maybe Atlas too. Ruthie is behind the messages."

"Uh-huh. We're no closer to knowing."

I'm just down one boyfriend. Which I'm not sure I'm that cut up about anymore. He's not exactly worth crying over, since I don't think he gives a damn about me.

"Are you all right?"

"Yeah," I mutter, pouting. Everything's falling apart so fast I can barely keep up.

"You don't look okay."

"Kick a girl while she's down, why don't ya."

"That's not what I meant."

"What am I going to do now?"

"We're going to steal the badge from Luce," he replies, grinning like a cartoon villain. "All right, I know I'm not one of your crew or your asshole boyfriend—"

I cut in with "*Ex*-boyfriend."

"You dodged a bullet. I'm not one of them, but I am here."

"Atlas was supposed to be here."

"That dude is sacrificing you for his own benefit. I'm here, Marley, and I'm willing to sacrifice everything to help you. Seriously, if it gets out that I know, college is over."

I shake my head, taking his hand. "I will never tell anyone you knew. I promise, Rhett. I'll protect you."

He squeezes my hand, and it feels kind of strange. "How do you want to handle Luce?"

"Pass."

"Wouldn't a breakup be the very thing you'd go to your best friend for?" he asks, lifting a brow.

"Duh! Why didn't I think of that?"

"Probably the thought of being set up for murder. Does things to your mind."

Straight to the point. "Right. That. Okay, I'll go to Luce's now, cry on her shoulder, and snoop around her room."

"What do you want me to do?"

"Nothing. The less you're involved, the better. You should go home, I'll call you later." Having a purpose and a plan is keeping me going. It's . . . exciting.

He shoves his hand into his hair and exhales sharply. "The less I'm involved. You wouldn't be in this situation at all if it wasn't for me. I'm involved. I'll do anything to keep you safe, so don't push me out."

"You're an idiot."

"Get used to it."

"We'll argue about this later. Right now, I need to build a solid case against them. All of them."

Rhett's brow rises. "You're sure?"

"One hundred percent. I'm going to Luce's. After, we can figure out what to do. There's evidence in Luce's uncle's shed in her yard. The shovels that were used for . . . you know. We need to get them before they think of it."

"If they haven't already moved them," he says.

"Rhett?"

"Go to Luce's and keep her busy. I'll get the shovels. No arguments. We don't have much time because they're already planning."

"There are tons in there. It's the two with blue handles. They'll be very clean."

He nods. "All right. You go ahead. I'll park up the road so she doesn't see."

"Hop her back fence, you shouldn't be seen that way," I say as I walk back to my car.

We get back in our cars, and Rhett follows me and then cuts down the back street behind Luce's house.

I park out front and knock on her door, not bothering to call ahead.

She opens the door a minute later.

"Hey, what's up?" she says, flashing me a smile that's as fake as a pair of Jordans from Wish.

"Can I come in? Atlas and I just broke up."

Her brows lift high up her forehead. A little too high, as if she's rehearsed this surprised expression.

"Yeah, come in. What happened?"

I shrug. "He said things have changed and he's leaving for school right after graduation. Apparently, the long-distance thing won't work now. It's an excuse. Arthur changed everything. I just wish he'd admit it, you know? I'd rather hear the truth, no matter how much it might suck."

She closes the door behind me and then gives me an awkward hug. Her arms are stiff; it's not her usual bone-crushing embrace. I've lost her too. "Are you okay?" she asks.

"Not really."

"I'm sorry. Let me grab us a soda and we'll talk."

"Yeah, I'll meet you in your room."

Her fingers circle my wrist as I turn away. I look back and she grimaces. "Sorry, it's just that my room is a *serious* mess. We're talking stuff everywhere. I've started the pre-college clear out. Can't believe I've kept so many clothes that I haven't worn in years. Go through to the game room, and I'll be there in a sec."

Luce's game room has a huge sofa, a PlayStation, and a pool table. It's a place we've hung out in for years. It's where Atlas first admitted that he liked me.

He can go to hell.

I walk away from Luce, knowing that I need to get in her room because she's never cared before about how messy it was.

It'll only take her seconds to grab sodas, though, so I need to think of another way of getting in there. Her bedroom is downstairs, two doors away from the game room. I just have to think of a way to distract her for a few minutes.

I can't believe we're doing this.

No, I can't believe we have to do this.

Somewhere outside, Rhett is breaking into her uncle's shed. I just hope he gets the right shovels. I'm not sure what I'm going to do with them yet, but I'm not giving my ex-friends the opportunity to have potentially vital evidence.

Luce walks into the room as I'm sitting down. She hands me a soda and asks, "What happened with Atlas?"

Like you don't know.

I plaster on a miserable expression. I don't feel sad, I feel *angry.* It seeps from every pore on my skin and burns deep inside me. I want to make them all pay for what they're trying to do to me. Especially Atlas. He should've had my back, but he's feeding me to the wolves.

"He's going to college in Ohio."

I watch her microexpressions and want to snort as she widens her eyes in a way that's faker than her hug.

"What? Since when?"

"The whole time, but he was too much of a coward to tell me until now."

She shakes her head. "Wow. I'm sorry, Marley. You two don't think you can make long-distance work?"

At this point, I'd rather date a troll.

"Not now. He said that I've changed, but honestly, it's him. I'm the one trying to figure out who's messaging me, even going camping with Rhett. Obviously, that means I'm the one to worry about."

I load as much sarcasm into my tone as I can, so she knows how crappy their treatment of me is. She wasn't exactly all for getting rid of Arthur's body either, *and* she almost threw up over the crime scene. It's totally unfair that I'm the one being set up.

But they're right about one thing. I am the one they need to worry about.

I tap the edge of the soda can as my mind spins, trying to think of a way to distract her, when a loud crash comes from the garden.

Luce gasps and my eyes widen.

Rhett. God, why is he so clumsy?

"No one's home," Luce says, leaping up and running from the room.

Someone's on edge because they have evidence in their garden. I should follow her and make sure that Rhett's okay, but this is my chance.

I sprint to her room and throw the door open. How long do I have? Thirty seconds? Less?

Her cluttered room is full of artwork, most of it hers, abstract stuff that I can never make sense of, but it always looks good. I run to her shelves and scan the little jewelry dishes and clear plastic tubs. Then I move to her desk, pulling drawers open with clumsy hands.

I find the badge quickly because I know all of her hiding places.

In her little skull-shaped jewelry dish is my badge. If this is how she hides things, she should fear the cops finding her clothes from that night.

I snatch it up, heart in my throat as I hear the back door slam. With the badge stuffed in my shorts pocket, I close her door gently behind me and dash into the game room.

When she gets back, I'm looking out the window, my face pressed against the glass as I pretend to watch the backyard.

"No one's there," she says.

I spin around, pretending that I didn't hear her. "God, you scared me. What was it?"

"My mom's flowerpots fell from the potting table." She rolls her eyes. "They were stacked high."

Quick thinking on Rhett's part to knock those over.

"You panicked a bit. Everything okay?"

She shrugs. "Just a bit on edge, you know? I'll relax once Jesse moves the shovels."

I flash a smile as fake as hers. "Glad it was just the pots, then. I'm going to go, Luce."

"Already?"

"Yeah, I'm not great company right now."

"Will you be okay? I know you and Atlas have been a thing since forever."

Well, forever is over.

"It'll be weird for a while, but it is for the best. He's not the same person he used to be and not in a good way. I don't trust him."

She nods. "I get that. He didn't tell you about college for months."

That's not the main reason, but I smile anyway, letting her believe that she's right.

"See you later," I say.

She follows me out of the game room and watches as I leave, not something she has ever done before. How could she side with them?

I can't wait to take her down.

I slam her front door a little harder than necessary, but I'm pissed.

Rhett is waiting for me half a block down the road. I get into his car and take my badge out of my pocket. "Got it."

He smirks. "Nice one. Shovels are in the trunk. What are we doing with them?"

"I'm not a hundred percent sure, but I know we need to make sure Jesse doesn't get away with this. For Arthur *and* George."

"So plant the shovels at Jesse's house, hope Luce's badge is eventually found in the wreck of Arthur's, drop my ex-friends' hairs in the back of Jesse's truck."

"Yeah, but how are we going to get the cops to look there?"

"We're going to help them out, but I don't know how to do that without incriminating you too. Everyone at the creek knows you were in the car during the dare."

"I don't care about that, Rhett. I deserve whatever punishment is coming my way. I just want to make sure I'm not the only one who goes down for this."

"Let me think about it, all right? There must be a way."

I'm about to tell him not to bother when my phone dings.

Mom:

George is awake. Thought you'd want to know.

I release a breath that I didn't realize I was holding. "George is awake. I think he's going to be okay," I say.

Rhett side-eyes me. "Do you think Jesse will try to finish him off?"

"I wouldn't be surprised. He might be worried George saw him. I need to keep an eye on Jesse."

"How?" he asks.

"I need to get some tracking devices."

"I have a couple of AirTags. We can plant one in his truck at the same time we hide the shovels on his property."

My brows rise. "Nice."

Maybe we could've left the shovels where they were so Luce's involvement would never be questioned, but I want evidence against them all.

My phone dings again.

Unknown:

poor u for losing ur bf.

I read the text again and watch it disappear.

"What?" Rhett asks.

"Message said 'poor you for losing your boyfriend.' How would Ruthie know that Atlas and I broke up?"

"How would anyone know?" he asks.

"Hold on. . . ." I check my location-sharing app. "Well, this might explain it. Atlas is at the creek and probably telling everyone he's single."

"You need to delete that! He's been able to see where you are the whole time!"

I tilt my head to the side. "I'm not stupid, I turned my location off over the weekend. He's just not thinking, and hopefully he won't."

"You have anyone else on there?"

"Only my parents. Hence why I need trackers."

"What if Jesse gets a ride with someone? We wouldn't be able to see that."

"I don't know who he would trust now. It's a possibility, but knowing how paranoid he's getting, I think he'll drive himself. How are we going to get their hairs for Jesse's truck?"

"I was thinking we check their gym lockers. I've watched them brush their hair after gym, and I assume Luce will have one."

"Good idea. Yeah, she does. We need to do that tomorrow."

Lockers need to be cleared out by the end of the week, so we have to move fast.

I take a long breath as my heart leaps. "I feel like this is about to go off, and I don't have much time to protect myself."

"Let's take your car home and I'll pick you up. Less suspicious if we're not in a convoy."

I nod and open his door. "Yeah, okay."

He drives off as I walk to my car. He's totally right. We still have a couple of things to do, and we're more likely to be seen if our cars are driving around together. His windows are tinted, so we'll be more inconspicuous.

He follows me to my house, then I hop in his car, and we head to his.

Rhett pulls over outside his massive house, heads in to grab his spare AirTags, and heads straight back out.

He's left the car running, and we speed off toward Jesse's. I'm exhausted, mentally and physically. All this cruising around and having to think about what to do next to protect myself has drained almost every ounce of my energy.

"I need to visit George," I say, stifling a yawn. "How long do you think it'll take to get out that he's awake?"

"In this town?" he asks, his question rhetorical because we know it'll be all over by now.

"Right. What do I do tomorrow?" I ask.

"You turn up at school like normal. I mean, you wouldn't want to miss the big quiz, would you? Ms. Mabel's been working on it for weeks."

I roll my eyes. "Can't wait. I don't know what to do, though, where I fit in now. Atlas is an asshole and my friends are as fake as Fuller laughing at the pranks."

Rhett doesn't say anything else, and I wonder if that's because he feels guilty for being the one who started all of this. I shouldn't be in the car with him right now, really.

We've gotten halfway there when my phone dings.

Unknown:

https://news.rocky.creek.com/rocky-creek-resident-arthur-nelson-murdered-1928652

I stare at the link, reading the headline from our local news station, and click right before it disappears.

"What is it?" Rhett asks.

"I—I think you need to pull over."

"Why, what's going on?" he presses.

The phone wobbles in my hand and falls to my lap. "It's a link to a news article. Headline reads, 'Rocky Creek Resident Arthur Nelson Murdered.'"

"Shit!" Rhett says, swerving to the side and slamming on his brakes so we don't overshoot the turnout. "Sent by Ruthie?"

"Must be," I whisper.

"All right, new plan. I'm going to swing back and take you home. We can plant the evidence later, but I think Jesse will be hypervigilant if he's just gotten this news too."

"When he's at school," I say, my voice as rough as sandpaper. "He's very big on keeping up appearances, so he won't skip a day, especially now that we're near the end. We can use that, right?"

"Yeah, we'll do it during school. We have third period without the others."

"We'll need to be back for fourth, I have that with Luce and Jesse."

"What does the article say?"

I shake my head and hand the phone over, unable to read what I've done in black and white. It's too freaking much.

Rhett looks at me and back to the phone. "It says that after the full autopsy, the cops think his injuries were unlikely to be sustained in a fall from the bridge. No water in his lungs either."

I take a sharp breath.

"What else?"

"Investigation is ongoing, but his death is being treated as suspicious, particularly since his house was burned down and his grandson is in the hospital. Marley, are you okay? You're not looking so hot."

"I'm scared. I've spent the last week wishing we could just tell the truth, and now I'm petrified it's going to come out."

He reaches across and takes my hand in his. "We're going to fix this."

"Arthur's dead. Nothing can fix this."

"You know what I mean. You're not going down for something Jesse has done."

"Don't pretend that I'm innocent, Rhett. I could've spoken up at any point."

"Why didn't you?"

"Shock at first. Jesse made me believe that my parents' lives would be ruined too. He's not wrong. But then he burned Arthur's house to the ground with George inside, and I was too scared to speak up. He'll do anything to protect himself."

"You need to be really careful. I need you to let me see where you are, you know, in case he comes for you. There's another." He holds up a tag.

It's not like I haven't thought the same things before, but hearing it out loud sends a chill down my spine.

"O-okay," I tell him, shoving it in my pocket.

At least if Jesse tries anything, Rhett will know where I am.

"All right. Do not let any of them into your house."

"Wasn't planning to. I think I might get a call, though, now that the cops are treating Arthur's death as suspicious. At least I'll be able to record the phone call."

"Whoa, bad idea. If anyone gets hold of that, you'll be incriminated."

I nod and open the door. "I'll see you tomorrow."

"Lock your doors."

Rhett waits until I get inside before driving off. I lock up and turn the alarm on, being quiet so I don't disturb my mom.

My phone rings ten minutes later as I'm climbing into bed, the front-door-camera app freezing.

"Hi, Luce," I say.

"Hold on, I'm getting Atlas and Jesse on too."

I roll my eyes at the sound of her voice and their names. I'd rather never see or speak to them ever again, but it's not like I have a choice.

Besides, I'm supposed to still like them at this point.

"I'm here," Atlas says.

A second later Jesse's on the line. "This doesn't change anything. We keep quiet. All of us!"

No pleasantries.

"We keep attending school and pretending everything's fine," he continues. "There are only a few days left anyway."

"We still have all summer," Luce says. "How are we going to hang out around town knowing the cops are hunting Arthur's killer?"

Atlas snorts. "You guys can do what you want, but I'm leaving after graduation."

"Maybe we should go too, Luce. We can tell our parents that we want to get set up, earn some money in Philly before school starts," Jesse says.

Jesse and Luce don't seem to have fallen apart.

"Yeah," she replies. "Maybe that's a good idea. We were going to go in mid-July anyway, so we'd only be, what, a month early?"

"What are you doing, Marley?" Jesse asks.

This is my test. If I tell him I'm staying until August like I'd always planned, he'll worry that I'll have a whole summer to break.

"I've already had a look at a couple places to stay in LA," I lie. "I'm getting out. We all need a fresh start."

I hear his exhale down the line. "Good. I'll check up on you in LA."

"Why?"

"Make sure you're settled."

"How kind of you," I reply, clenching my fists.

Atlas doesn't intervene. Not that I expected he would anymore.

"I was thinking about Rhett and Ruthie being extra weird with Marley," Luce says. "I mean, if it's not George, it could be one of them, right?"

"Now that I'm thinking about it, the messages don't read like Rhett," I say, my heart skipping at the thought of involving him even more. He's already taking huge risks for me. "But I don't know why Ruthie would bother."

"Because she hates you," Luce says.

"Then wouldn't she go to the cops?"

"Not necessarily," Jesse says. "She would love holding this over us."

"Let's just make sure first," I say.

"Hey, what if we're asked about the dare?" Luce asks. "What do we say to the cops?"

"We tell them we did it and then went home. There's footage of you getting back," Jesse says.

"Yeah, at, like, three in the freaking morning," Luce says.

"It's only my house," I say. "Atlas dropped me off, so it looks like we went home to his between the dare and me getting back."

I mean, it's flimsy, but it's all we have.

"Right," Atlas finally says. "We went back to mine, watched a movie, and lost track of time. *Hunger Games.*"

"Put it on Netflix now and then a few other things so it'll be in your recently watched," I tell him.

"Good idea," he replies.

Maybe I'm convincing them that I can be trusted. I need that, just long enough for them all to relax. I tap the badge that I now have back with me and lie down.

"We've got this," I tell them.

25

Tuesday, June 6

Mom and Dad are up for breakfast, both drinking black coffee because they've been working so hard and not getting enough sleep. But they both have the next two days off, so I have to be more careful about what time I'm getting home.

I force another bite of pancake down. It's usually one of my favorite breakfasts, and I need to eat it to prove nothing's wrong.

Mom turns the radio down, the latest information about Arthur now over.

She shakes her head. "I wonder what happened to him."

"I spoke to Sam last night; he thinks it could've been a hit and run," Dad says. "Either the driver dumped him after killing him, or he was hit on the bridge and was knocked over. Either way, it's awful."

"Poor Arthur."

"Do you think George is up for visitors?" I ask. "He could probably use a friend right now."

Mom smiles. "He's not awake for long, but I'm sure he'll appreciate a visit. After school, though—you don't want to miss these last few days."

I absolutely *do* want to miss them. I'd love to run away to California right now and leave all of this behind.

"I'll go this afternoon," I tell her. "Does he know about Arthur?"

"Last I saw him, no. He's in and out, still in a very bad way."

"What, do you mean he still might die?"

"It's a possibility."

"But he woke up."

Dad squeezes my arm. "I wish that meant he was in the clear."

"Has he spoken?" I ask.

"Apparently he asked where he was before falling back to sleep. Keep faith, Marley, it's positive that he's woken up," Mom replies.

Except that doesn't mean he won't die. What total crap is that?

I need him to be okay.

"What will happen with Arthur now?"

"Sam said they'll wait to see what happens with George. If he pulls through, he'll be able to organize the funeral," Dad replies.

"And if he doesn't?"

"He will still be laid to rest. Sam's got someone searching for his lawyer."

I nod, relieved that he will be buried or cremated properly. No grave in the woods and no river.

"I hope they find whoever did that to him," Mom says, shaking her head.

Dad shrugs. "There's not a lot to go off, only that they believe he was hit by a car."

"Could it have been an accident?" Mom asks. "If he was hit on the bridge, the driver might've assumed it was an animal. If it was at night, of course. It's awfully dark in that area of town. I've hit deer I haven't seen until they were under my wheel."

A chunk of pancake gets lodged in my throat, and I only just manage to swallow it before I choke.

"I don't think they're ruling anything out. I suppose it's a possibility, but you would check what you hit, surely."

She shrugs. "Not everyone does. Marley, you better get going."

I push the plate away. "I'll brush my teeth and head out."

• • •

When I got to school, my anxiety was buzzing. No matter how many times I give myself a pep talk, I can't stop from wanting to throw up. The badge is in my pocket because I can't trust my friends not to steal it again, along with Rhett's tracker.

It feels really weird without Atlas. I hate that, because I'm so angry with him and whatever he might be up to. But it does. We've spent every day since the start of high school together, becoming friends right away, before he asked me out. The end-of-year schedule has me doing more activities with him. We've never been in so many classes together. It feels like a punishment now. One I'm sure I deserve.

Now he's pretending that I don't exist. He hasn't glanced my way once, and we've been in class for twenty minutes.

I'm at the back of the room, watching him chat with Theo. Unless seats were assigned, he always came straight to me.

I hate that it hurts, but I'm glad that the raw, unfiltered anger is stronger.

Rhett walks in, and the turned-nose look he gives Atlas manages to make me smile. It's something I wish I could do, but I don't want to be that girl. I don't want Atlas to think that I'm still hung up on him. I'm giving him space until I can figure out how involved he is with the others' plan.

In another game of musical chairs, Rhett walks straight to me and drops down in the next seat. Of all the stupid things he could've done.

"What're you doing?" I ask, hyperaware of Atlas's gaze and shocked expression.

"Sitting down, ready for class. Ms. Mabel's quiz."

"You're sitting next to me."

"We're so winning this quiz," he mutters, smirking.

"This isn't funny, Rhett. We don't sit together."

He shrugs like this is no big deal. To him I guess it isn't. He couldn't care less that people are looking and whispering. Atlas has turned around, but his shoulders are hunched and he's doing something on his phone. Reporting to Jesse and Luce, maybe.

"Last few days, Marley. Stop caring what people think. You're not going to see most of them again."

"I don't think I'll see any of them again."

"Drama is next period."

It's not, but I get his point.

Ms. Mabel hands out pages to each group of two and goes to her desk. She's smiling as if this has been her best idea yet. "I'll collect them once you're done, and we'll see who the winners are."

Rhett looks down and pushes the papers away.

"Have you seen Ruthie?" I ask.

"No, but I'm not exactly looking for her. We need to find that phone."

I glance around the room. There are maybe four groups doing the quiz. Ms. Mabel doesn't seem to care that the rest of us aren't. She just needs to keep us in the classroom until the end of the lesson anyway.

"I was kind of thinking you could do that while I'm in gym. I know her locker number."

A smile spreads across his face. "You're on."

"Can you try not to enjoy this so much? It's not a game."

"I'm not psyched for the serious part of it. I like this part."

"Plotting."

"We usually do that against each other." He nudges my arm, something Atlas doesn't miss as he takes another not-so-subtle look over here. "I like being on the same team."

"I think you're the only one who's on my team."

"We can take 'em."

"Don't really want to." My head hurts at the thought of messing with my friends, but I have to protect myself.

What if I've made a mistake. Trusting Rhett could be my biggest one. Second to Arthur, obviously.

"The asshole can't stop looking at you," he whispers.

"I know. He'll find you sitting here suspicious. I don't like it, Rhett. Do you think he knows I'm onto them?"

"Because I'm sitting next to you?"

"Yes! I don't think you understand how paranoid doing what we did makes you. We now question everything and everyone. Trust nothing. He'll be asking himself why I'm talking to you, especially now, after the dare. He'll know what they're trying to do to me and wonder if I'm getting you on my side and what that could mean."

"Like, I'm providing you with an alibi for that night?"

"Can't see that standing up, but yeah, maybe. It'll be a thought, I'm certain of it. He'll also wonder if it's revenge, but everything goes back to that night. I want you to give me another dare in the group. Make it look like that's why you sat here."

"No."

"You have to, and you have to make it a good one. If they start to worry that I'm figuring it out, it could push them to act sooner . . . with whatever they have planned, and I need more time."

"Marley, I don't want to give you another dare."

"Something big that hasn't been done before."

"No."

"Has to be something I will hate."

"Have you thought about George?" he asks.

"Every minute," I whisper.

"No, I mean, have you considered that he might be involved?"

"Where did that come from? Are you just trying to change the subject?"

"No, listen. I think I overheard Ruthie on the phone with George."

"What?"

"I didn't really take it in because I was pissed at her for calling me her boyfriend. She definitely muttered George's name."

"It could be another George or her talking about George to someone else."

He tilts his head. "Maybe, but it could be something."

"I don't know what to do with that."

"You should talk to him. See if he knows something."

"Oh, come on. Arthur was his uncle. If he knows, then I wouldn't be sitting here right now," I whisper.

Rhett and I both jump when Carina screams in the middle of class. Her eyes are wide, and she holds her phone up, staring at whatever on the screen has caused that reaction.

"Miss Perry, do you mind telling us why—"

"Ruthie's dead!"

26

My eyes immediately search for Atlas. He does the same, looking over to me with an identical expression of shock.

"D-d-dead?" Ms. Mabel splutters. "How do you know that?"

With a trembling hand, Carina turns the screen around. "She was found on the ground outside her house, her bedroom window wide open," Carina says, tears spilling down her cheeks. "I need to leave."

"Of course," Ms. Mabel says. "If any of Ruthie's friends, or any of you, need to talk, please let me know."

The classroom explodes with conversations all about the same thing. I watch as everyone gets their phones. Rhett does the same.

I look over at him, and my stomach drops. "Rhett . . ."

He cuts me a look. "Don't even ask me. You know I didn't do anything to her."

"She wouldn't do that to herself," I say. "Would she?"

"No. She has a place at her dream college. *Had.* God, she had a place." He takes a deep breath.

"I'm sorry," I say. "Are you okay?"

"I . . . No. . . . I can't believe she's gone. I mean, I'm all right, but it's a shock. We weren't together, you know, it was just . . ."

"I get it. Do you want to leave?"

"I'm going to have to. Her parents are cool, and I need to check in."

"Yeah, of course."

He grabs his bag. "Rhett, someone did this to her. Did you see anyone else last night?"

"No," he replies. "But it's not like I was there late or for long."

"What does it say about her online?"

He holds his phone up again. "'The body of eighteen-year-old Ruthie Marx was found outside her home in the early hours of Tuesday morning. Police are treating the death as unexplained.'"

Unexplained because she wouldn't have jumped. An accident is a stretch. Why would she be leaning out there?

"I'll be back after lunch, and we can go through Luce's and Ruthie's lockers."

"Don't worry about that today."

"Feels like we're running out of time, Marley. I don't have a choice."

"Yeah," I whisper, avoiding his eyes. His ex, or whatever she was, has just been found dead, and we're still talking about how to help me out.

What the hell has Jesse done now?

I glance over at Atlas and wonder if he knows, if he was part of it, or if he was only told that Jesse had sorted it out. How far are they willing to go to cover up what we did? With Ruthie out of the way and them setting me up—allegedly—they could potentially walk free.

No one else knows. Except that Rhett does . . . and Atlas is becoming suspicious of him all over again.

If Jesse is behind Ruthie's death, what's to stop him from trying the same with Rhett?

I mean, Rhett's family's money might. They'd use their wealth as a weapon to find Rhett's killer.

Atlas stands and moves past the table. Ms. Mabel is talking to a few students who've gathered around her desk. She doesn't care that we're all up and moving around.

He takes Rhett's seat. "Ruthie's dead," he mutters as if I don't know.

Yeah, did you do it?

"What do you want, Atlas?"

"Don't be like that. We need to discuss this."

"Why?"

"Come on," he whispers, leaning in. "You don't think this has something to do with us? Or Rhett freaking Wilder?"

"Why would it have anything to do with us?"

What I really want to ask is why Rhett would be involved, but I'm supposed to hate him. I don't want Atlas to know that I've thawed to the middle Wilder.

"Sh-sh-she knew," he splutters, as if he can't believe I'd ask something so stupid. My question was more rhetorical than anything, but I also want him to acknowledge that Jesse has totally lost it. He's helping to protect the wrong person, because Jesse would sell every one of us out to save himself.

"We don't know that."

"You still think it might be Rhett sending the messages? He and Ruthie could've been in on it. You looked pretty cozy with him."

I turn my nose up. "Are you joking? He was being his usual arrogant self, telling me he'll give me another dare if he wants to."

"What?"

"I can't wait to get the hell out of here and never see anyone from this town again."

"Wow."

I huff. "Like you don't feel the same. You broke up with me because you do."

"So we're both going after graduation?"

"I haven't made solid plans yet, but there's no way I'm staying for the whole summer."

If I could leave now, I would. This town used to be safe. It was home, a place I would always return to. Now it's tainted with death and horror. I don't want to be here for a second longer than I have to.

He nods, frowning, and I wish I could read his mind. Something is going on in there. He's calculated, thinking several steps ahead. I'm late to the scheming party, never believing that I would have to protect myself from my friends.

I guess we were doomed from the second we all agreed to cover up what we'd done.

"That's probably a good idea. You should leave, Marley. Straight after graduation." He stands, throwing his bag over his shoulder. "I can't sit in here any longer."

I watch him walk out of the room without a backward glance. I'm already forgotten.

Whatever.

Ms. Mabel opens her mouth but decides against challenging him. She was the one who said we could go if we wanted.

His words are etched into my mind the way our initials are carved into the wall of the girls' bathroom.

You should leave, Marley. Straight after graduation.

Whatever they have planned is happening right after graduation. That's on Saturday, so I don't have much time left to counter whatever they're doing.

After the quiz, I had gym, and then it was crafts instead of English. I couldn't focus on any of it.

When the bell rings, I walk, dazed and angry, to the lunch hall. There are other people I could sit with, but I'm not good company, so I grab a wrap and head outside. I want to leave and go home, but I need to be here for when Rhett gets back.

I also need to speak to Luce to see what she thinks about Ruthie's death. She hasn't "broken up" with me yet, so I have no problem hunting her down.

I walk across the quad and around the side of the school. The large field is buzzing with action. People walking from group to group, all of them talking about Ruthie. As I walk, I hear a few theories. After Arthur too, there's a murderer on the loose.

They're not wrong.

His injuries from the crash might have presented the same as a fall from that bridge, and perhaps dropping him helped cover up what really happened, but that theory can only last so long now that Ruthie is dead.

I wonder what the cops think. You couldn't get two more

different victims. An old man, a recluse who barely speaks to anyone. Then a teen girl who demanded attention wherever she went.

There's no relation, no way their lives cross over.

I won't let that happen.

Luce comes into view as I pass a crowd of freshmen, looking at her phone and laughing at something. Kind of insensitive, but she might not know about Ruthie.

"Hi," I say, reaching where she's sitting under a tree.

She startles and tucks her phone away. "Oh, hi, Marley."

I sit down. "You good?"

"Ruthie's dead, so no," Luce replies. "Are you okay?"

So she does know.

"Not really."

"No, I mean, like, emotionally and all that," she replies, watching me as if she's looking at a bomb.

"I'm not following. What do you mean by that?" I ask.

She shuffles awkwardly and picks at a blade of grass. "You've been really weird recently, Marley. We're worried and, to be honest, a little scared."

"Scared of what? And you surely understand why I haven't been myself!"

"You pushing everyone away is a concern. You're snappy and don't seem to want to hang out with us anymore."

"What I don't want to do is pretend when we're all alone together! And you're the ones who have been weird with me, stopping talking when I approach. Is it too much to ask that we support each other?"

Luce shakes her head. "This is what I'm talking about. Why do you constantly want to discuss murder and death?"

What the hell is happening here? She's being beyond weird, and I can't figure out where this is coming from.

"I don't want to, but I can't ignore it. You're asking me to take this to my grave, and I will, but I can't pretend that it never happened."

She pinches the bridge of her nose. "The rest of us don't want to talk. We agreed to move on."

"It's not even over," I breathe.

"Babe, I am here for you."

"Am I the only one getting mixed signals? You're here for me, but you want me to be silent. Luce, come on, this must be killing you too. You want to be a nurse! Jesse doesn't seem to be struggling at all."

"Hey. You don't know what he's going through," she says, her back straightening and eyes shooting daggers at me.

"I'm not saying he's happy about this, Luce, but he's—"

"Just stop. I don't want to hear what you have to say about him." She gets to her feet, grabbing her phone and backpack as she goes. "Keep your head down until graduation and stop talking about Jesse."

I clench my fist and watch her walk away from me.

There's no going back.

They're the ones going down.

27

I slip inside the locker room, hiding behind rows of lockers until I'm sure the coast is clear. My back scrapes the peeling maroon team-color paint on the walls.

As I walk around the corner, something catches my eye and I jump.

Rhett, leaning against the far lockers, smirks.

"Not funny."

"Sure. Present for you," he says, handing me a sandwich bag.

I take it and smile at the two hairs inside. "Best gift I've ever received."

"Which locker is Ruthie's?" he asks. "And Luce's?"

I walk past him and point to Ruthie's locker. "Do you know her code?"

"My birthday."

"Are you serious?"

He shrugs. "She was obsessed with me."

"Right."

"You remember my birthday," he says as I open the locker.

"We were friends for years and I'm not an idiot."

"Smells better in the girls' locker room," he says as I rifle through Ruthie's things. It doesn't feel good now that she's dead, but I can't afford to let a little thing like human decency get in the way right now.

"I can imagine."

"It's like old sweaty socks in there, and you never get used to the smell."

"Great. I'll check Luce's for her brush. You find that phone," I tell him, and move across the room.

"Yes, boss."

I open Luce's locker and start looking. One thing that's still on my mind a lot is the pain meds found in Arthur's tox report.

Something flashes across my mind as I spot a sling piled at the bottom of Luce's locker, from an injury at Christmas.

George's shoulder.

I've seen him rubbing it a few times. George told me Arthur was having mobility issues, and he never came back to me about getting my parents to visit.

The day the house burned down, I thought it might be George sending the messages because he walked past my house.

My mouth falls open as I move things out of the way in Luce's locker. George wasn't coming to see me that day. . . . He was visiting Malcolm at the end of the cul-de-sac to buy pain meds.

It was George who was taking the pills and slipped Arthur some.

"How's it going?" Rhett calls.

"Oh, still looking."

"Same. She has so much crap in here. It's supposed to just be gym stuff."

George encouraged Arthur to sell the house, but he wouldn't... so he dosed him and let him wander off. Plenty of places he could get hurt with the sheer drops and winding roads.

That was risky because it wasn't guaranteed to work, but maybe that wasn't the first time. The night of the accident, George was out at the end of the property. Maybe he was waiting until late before he sent Arthur out. Maybe that's why he was surprised to see me.

I don't know. But I need to.

I have to get into George's room and find those pills. The house is still standing. An actual miracle. But no one's been inside yet because the authorities are waiting for it to be deemed safe to enter.

Moving a hoodie, I find Luce's hairbrush and pull a strand out. I drop it in the bag, leaving out the part that I touched. I squeeze the hair between my index finger and thumb on the outside of the bag and snap off the part I've touched.

"Got a hair," I say.

"Couple more places to look for the phone."

I close the locker, my mind still on what I need to do with George. Step one would be finding proof to support my theory.

If I'm right, I can use this.

"Got it," Rhett says, holding up the phone. "You're the only contact. What a surprise there...."

"Oh my god, thank you!" I say, spinning around and taking it from him. I shove it in my back pocket. "I'm going to go check in with George."

"Why?"

"Because I haven't since he woke up, and I said I would. I don't want to give my mom an excuse to ask questions."

"So we're splitting up again."

"I'll see you this afternoon. Just do something normal for a while, and we'll meet later."

He nods. "Call me."

We split ways. I'm not at all comfortable telling him what I suspect, because I don't fully trust him, even now. He's proving himself, but he's ditched me before, so what's to stop him doing that again?

At one point I trusted Atlas, Luce, and Jesse too.

I go to my car, keeping myself out of view. This afternoon's classes are the only ones I won't have with any of my ex-friends. No usual schedule. We're being split between different movies and group games.

They won't know I'm gone. I'll be back before the end of school, pretending that I watched *Avengers: Endgame.* I've seen it, so I can answer questions if Jesse asks. I don't think he's smart enough to see what I'm doing. He believes I'm too scared of him.

Their worry is that I'll break and go to the cops. They have no idea.

I pull up near the creek and park in a turnout. The sky looks as angry as I am. Thick, dark clouds steal the light. It'll probably pour soon.

I walk through the edge of the trees, keeping a little bit of cover in case anyone drives past. The plan is to access the house the same way we did when we broke in to get the watch.

Moving past the trees with Arthur's house directly in front of me, I keep low and out of view of the road. I'm facing the back door.

Crouching down, I run awkwardly and slip through the open back door, ducking between the tape.

I look around at the black, singed wood in the kitchen. Half of the cabinets are missing; the ones farthest from the door are still intact, though covered in soot. The fire department did a good job of putting the fire out, but I can't see this being repaired.

I walk into the hallway and grimace at the charred staircase. It was a miracle that George got out.

Well, it's now or never.

I place my foot on the step, and it creaks beneath me, moving more than it did the first time I came up here.

Groaning, I take another step. *Please don't fall through these.*

I take the next few steps slower, gently placing my weight, breathing shallowly, as if I'll be lighter without so much air in my lungs. Or maybe it'd work the other way around.

Nothing in this house looked solid before the fire.

I reach the top and tiptoe toward the room George was in the other night. His door is wide open, everything damaged from the smoke but otherwise still in place.

I pull my hand into my sleeve and use my covered hand to open a drawer in his desk. The room is bare, but he only visits once a year, so I didn't expect a lot of stuff.

The thick smell of smoke hangs heavily in the air. Embers sit all over the floor, leaving my footprints. I have generic Converse, so I think I can wash these and it'll be fine.

I close the empty drawer and move to the closet. In the corner, just like where I hid my stuff that I needed to ditch, is a gym bag. I unzip the top and shake my head. A bottle of oxycodone is lying at the bottom.

George *was* drugging his grandad.

Who the hell does that to their grandpa?

I pad back over the smoke-damaged floor and am at the top of the stairs when I get a call.

Rhett.

"Hey," I say.

"Marley, we have another problem," he says.

"What?" I ask, pocketing the small bottle of pills, needing somewhere else to put these things. I'm full of evidence, but I don't want to carry a bag, or it'll be obvious where I'm hiding things.

"There's a lot of talk about Ruthie being involved in Arthur's death. The new rumor is that someone killed her because of it."

"Who do they think did it?"

"No one's offering a decent explanation for that . . . but apparently the cops are interviewing students. That means we'll both be questioned, me especially, I guess."

As Ruthie's not-quite boyfriend, the cops will definitely want to talk to him.

"Are you nervous about that?" I ask, descending the stairs slowly so he doesn't hear.

"No, it was always coming. What are you going to say?"

I carefully reach the bottom, sighing a breath of relief that I didn't fall. "Nothing right now. You can't mention Jesse."

"Wasn't planning to."

My heart thuds and my hand itches to touch the small tube in my pocket. "I'm going to the hospital. I'll check in after."

"Okay, speak later."

He hangs up, and I sneak out of the house, heading for my car and the hospital.

28

After doubling back because I had another light bulb moment and needed to run a couple of errands near home, I pull up at the hospital and make my way to George's room.

So much is making sense now, those puzzle pieces beginning to make a picture.

He's lying in bed when I walk in. His eyes, now open and alert, flick to me.

"Hi, George."

He winces, trying to sit up. "Marley, what're you doing here?"

"Came to see how you are," I reply, stepping closer. I perch on the edge of his bed. "You doing okay?"

He shrugs. "My throat is killing me, and I don't think I'll ever get the smell of smoke out of my hair, but I'm alive."

"What do you know about the fire . . . and everything?"

Surely, he's been told about his grandad. He would ask if he's been found, right?

"I don't remember the fire. The cops have been in, but it's all a blur. I think I remember waking up and realizing there was smoke, but nothing after that. Cops aren't certain it was arson, because my grandad had cans of gas all over the yard, but they're thinking it might be."

"George, what have you been told about your grandad?"

He turns his head, flinching. "I know he's gone."

"I'm so sorry," I say, trying to figure out if he's acting right now. Why wouldn't Arthur be the first thing he mentioned when I asked how he was?

"Thanks," he mutters. "I don't really want to talk about it, if that's cool."

"Actually, no, it's not cool. Because I know that the strong pain meds you've been popping for your shoulder were found in Arthur during the postmortem."

His whole body tenses, but he doesn't look back over.

I'm right.

"Don't panic, no one else knows, and I have the evidence. Saw you out near my house, thought you might be coming to see me, but you were buying from Malcolm, weren't you?"

"You don't know what you're talking about."

"Oh, I do. How many times did you drug him and encourage him to go for a walk?"

Very slowly, he tilts his head and faces me again. "Enough to have seen some things."

So he does know. My heart races. It was definitely Ruthie behind the messages, I have her phone on me, but George saw too.

"Do you know Ruthie well?"

He scoffs. "I ran into her that night. She tried to contact me a few times after. I had a feeling she saw too, but I couldn't be sure. Anyway, I didn't want any part of it. The less involved I got, the better. Where do we go from here?"

"I'm going to keep these pills and your secret so you can inherit Arthur's estate. In return, you're going to help me."

"How?"

I sit on the bed, smile, and then tell someone my full plan.

George's brows rise as I finish.

"I can see you've thought this through."

"It's all I've thought about."

"No one can ever know about the pills, Marley."

"They won't. Did you have blood work?"

"Yeah, but they only tested for oxygen and carbon monoxide levels. I've read my chart. Or what I could make sense of. No mention of anything else."

"Good. Then you're in the clear. Any other questions?"

He laughs, then coughs, holding his chest. "No, I think I'm good."

"Okay. Here's my old phone, but wait for me to contact you first."

"All right," he says, taking the phone and slipping it under his stack of pillows.

He knows I need to keep his secret and he needs to keep mine. If not, we're both in jail.

I leave the hospital, putting some space between me and George, which is necessary because I don't feel as bad as I thought I would. . . . I feel like an absolute boss.

No need to dwell on that right now.

It's hot as hell out, muggy in a way that only a cool shower will fix. I'll feel gross until then. Jogging to my car, I check my phone and see a new pic on Insta from Atlas. It's him, Luce, and Jesse on the field.

They're wearing the clothes they had on today, so he's obviously not struggling with what they're doing or breaking up with me.

I grit my teeth and call Rhett.

"How did it go with George?" he asks, picking up nearly immediately.

"All good. Just needed to show my face."

"You on your way to Jesse's?" he asks.

"Yeah, look, I need you to go back to school instead. Get Atlas's tennis shoes from his locker. I don't think he's emptied it out yet."

"What for?"

"Meet me after where we park to hike to our spot. I'll explain everything then."

"All right. Be careful."

"You too."

I get in the car and crank the air up, enjoying the icy blast against my clammy skin. Now I need to go plant some things in Jesse's truck. He's making it kind of freaking obvious by getting Luce to bring him to school most of the time.

Still, his idiocy works for me; it's easier to plant things in his truck when he's not around. I glance at the backpack on my passenger seat, slowly filling with everything I need to prove my friends' guilt and my innocence.

I pull up on Jesse's road, far enough back that I can't be seen by his immediate neighbors. Then I dart between the bushes his dad is letting grow wildly out of control. Jesse's truck is nicely hidden in his carport.

It's close enough to his house, to his bedroom window, that I think this will work. The backpack weighs on my shoulders, digging into my skin. I slide it to the ground and open the zipper.

Malcolm lent me this, and it better work.

I pull the little device out and press the button. At first nothing, but a second later I hear the pop of Jesse's truck unlocking. Malcolm's definitely behind a spate of car break-ins, then.

Pushing my sleeve down, I cover my hand and open the door of Jesse's closed truck bed. I put the device away and take out a little bag and open it. Inside are hairs from Jesse, Atlas, and Luce. Hers is long and wound around in a coil.

Without touching them, I gently shake the bag, dropping the first hair at the very back of the bed, the second one up on the side, and Luce's closest to the door. It'll look like the boys climbed inside to get Arthur in. Or that's what I'm hoping anyway.

I put the bag away and cover my hand again to close the bed.

This wouldn't be the first time Jesse has left his truck unlocked, so hopefully he'll just think he was careless again.

Slinging my bag over my back, I walk back toward the bush. That's when I hear footsteps crunching on the ground.

I think my heart skips, like, ten beats. I stumble sideways, shoving myself into the overgrowth just in time.

Atlas and Jesse walk toward his front door.

They laugh, jostle each other, and Atlas says, "We should ditch the rest of the week. It's boring as hell."

"We need to keep things normal, man. You've already messed with that by breaking up with Marley early."

Early. When was he planning on doing it? What a coward.

They're almost at his front door now. I want them to slow down so I can hear more.

"Couldn't wait. Things were getting weird."

"She was getting weird."

Jesse fiddles with the key in the door.

Atlas shoots him a look, and I think he's about to defend me. "I get why she's finding it hard, but she's a massive risk."

Not so much.

Jesse snorts. "Won't be a problem—"

The door slams shut, and I'm cut off from what they were going to say. I probably don't want to hear it anyway.

Jesse is so wrong, though. I *will* be a problem.

29

Rhett throws his hands up as I get out of my car in the turnout, Atlas's tennis shoes pointing toward the sky.

"What's going on? Why do you want these?"

"Why are you touching them with your hand?"

Frowning, he drops the shoes, way too late.

"What the hell is happening?"

I use my sleeve again, making a mental note to keep some gloves in my car, and pick the shoes up. "Did you only touch the backs of these?"

"Yeah, why? Marley, explain."

"We'll scrub your prints. We're going to press these into the ground near the burial site. It's rained heavily since we were there last. We need to be careful, walk on moss, not mud."

"Won't these wash away too?"

"No rain forecast for the next week, but that's not a guarantee."

"So why are we here?"

"Because it's only a matter of time before the dare comes up and the cops start connecting the dots. I have to do everything I can, right?"

He nods. "Yeah, okay."

"Are you good? You don't need to do this, Rhett."

"Will you stop saying that? I told you I'm in, and I mean it."

"Having someone else know scares me," I admit, and start walking. He follows like I thought he would, because he's really serious about seeing this through. I wish he wouldn't be.

"Have I not proved myself, Marley?"

"Yes." I'm not sure. I don't think I'll ever be able to totally trust anyone again. "Of course you've proved yourself. I'm so grateful, but paranoia is part of me now."

"I'm on your side," he says.

"I know you are."

Rhett knows the woods as well as I do, so there are no irritating questions about which way we're going, how much longer it'll take, and if we're getting lost.

He's not as chatty as usual, but that works for me because I'm so drained.

"Rhett?" I say when we're only a few minutes away from the burial site.

"Mmm?"

"How am I going to live with myself knowing I've done all of this?"

I'm enjoying this planning and using my brain to outsmart my friends rather than pass exams, but I don't enjoy that I'm having to do it because of a dead man.

"It was an accident, Marley. And your so-called friends are the ones pushing you to do all of this. They're going down if this gets out, and you're going to college. Do something good. I know you will."

"And what about you?"

He shrugs. "I'm already doomed, right?"

"No, that's not right. You don't have to turn into your parents. Over there, that's the spot. Keep to the moss," I say.

"My feet are sinking into the ground," he says.

"The ground is softer near the . . . grave. Wait here and I'll do it."

"I can help."

"We can't afford for your shoe prints to be found here."

"What about yours?"

"I'll be careful," I say, walking ahead.

"You're shutting me out."

"I have no time for jealous drama right now, Rhett."

I keep my steps light and placed on thick patches of moss, avoiding the mud like the plague.

Crouching down, I press one of Atlas's shoes mostly in the moss, overlapping in the mud so the edge of the tread is in the mud, lightly because it has been raining. There are trees above me, the leaves packed so densely they could have protected the print, keeping a shallow tread to lead the cops back to Atlas.

His fancy, limited-edition sneakers that he spent hundreds of dollars on are about to get him in more trouble than his mom thinking he's irresponsible for splurging on such expensive shoes.

He's relieved that our relationship is over. I'm going to make him wish it never happened at all.

"Are you done?" Rhett calls.

"Yep, we can go," I tell him, retracing my steps. The trodden moss rises behind me, concealing each of my prints as if the universe is on my side too.

Rhett takes the shoes from me, using his sleeves the way I was. "I'll put these back in his locker, but do you think he's noticed?"

"No, I just saw him and Jesse skipping school. They got back to Jesse's house as I was leaving, didn't see me. Atlas wouldn't have been so chill if he knew they were missing."

As we're walking back to our cars, my phone dings.

Luce:

r u home?

I snort. "I think Luce has noticed that I stole my badge back."

"What did she say?"

"Just asked if I'm home. I'm going to ignore her."

"What are you doing now?"

"I'm going to go home and shower. I'd come with you back to school, but I can't take the risk of running into Luce and Jesse if they're back at school."

"Yeah, I've got this," he says, raising Atlas's shoes in his hand. "And I'll hide the shovels at Jesse's on my way back if he's gone."

"Thank you, Rhett."

He smiles. "Anytime."

We part ways, and I drive home, dropping off the keyless-entry device to Malcolm before I go into my house. I lock up and pull the blinds in case Luce decides to skip class and stop by.

I take a shower and change into comfy clothes before going downstairs and sitting facing the window. I can only just about see out through the tiny gaps I left in the slats, but that's the way I want it. I need to be able to see others before they see me.

It's mom who gets home first from shopping with her friends, and now I have to pretend even harder. Dad's golfing, so he'll likely be gone for ages still.

She kicks off her shoes and closes the front door. "Are you okay? You're home early. Are you feeling ill or just a little overwhelmed about leaving school?" she asks.

I shrug. "Early day, no one wanted to stay after what happened to Ruthie," I say, knowing she's aware of the schedule change at school and won't question me. "I can't wait for college, though."

She flops down on the sofa and kicks her legs up on the coffee table at the same time there's a knock on the front door.

I jolt, almost snapping my neck as I look up so fast.

Mom frowns and mutters, "Sam. What's he doing here?"

Outside, I can see the police car parked.

My insides clench, stomach churning as she opens the door.

"Sam, is everything okay?" Mom asks, and I can tell by the tone in her voice that she's worrying something might be wrong with Dad.

There's a pained expression on Sam's face. "Hi, Claire. I'm sorry, but I need to ask Marley some questions . . . down at the station."

30

I sit opposite Sam and another cop, Officer Ricky. She has a harsh pointed face and a sharp bob.

Sam's the opposite with his soft smile.

They've gone through my rights and told me I'm here because they've had an accusation.

It's game time.

"I'm sorry, who's accusing my daughter of *murder*? Tell me this is a joke," Mom demands.

"I can't say, but Marley is not under arrest here. These are just questions," Officer Ricky says.

Sam sits forward, his forearms on the table, fingers locked together. "Look, this person claims that you hit Arthur Nelson on the bridge and pushed his body over."

"What?" I say, widening my eyes. "What the hell?"

"Ridiculous," Mom mutters beside me.

"This person claims the damage to your car was due to the

accident, and they only kept quiet because you threatened them and have since broken into their house," Officer Ricky says.

So "they" is Luce.

But it couldn't be more perfect, because there's something my friends don't know about the damage on my car. I didn't realize they'd even noticed it. God, this is so perfect.

I frown. "I'm sorry, this is a total waste of time. Sam, you *literally* watched me hit that pole on the bridge."

"I know, and that's why this is just a chat. But we'd like to get to the bottom of why this person is accusing you. I'm sure you appreciate how serious this is."

I curl my hands together and chew on my lip, making myself appear nervous.

"I don't know who would do this. I mean, senior pranks have been going on, and you know they're kinda escalating."

Sam scratches the stubble on his chin. "Do you think this is a prank? Because I have two dead people, one of them eighteen years old."

"Ruthie," I whisper. "Are they connected? Because everyone at school is saying there's a killer in town."

"We can't speculate." Sam moves a fraction closer. "But, Marley, is everything okay?"

I shrug, blinking back tears that I'm not sure I can make shed, so I have to be careful. "Someone's just made up that I *killed* a person, so not really."

Mom pats my arm. "Sam, can you just tell us who's making up such awful stories about my daughter?"

He's already said that they can't. I want to roll my eyes at my mom's stupidity.

"I'm sorry."

"But you know it's a lie, right? You saw me. I don't know what happened to Arthur, but it was nothing to do with me."

Sam nods. "As I said, I'm just trying to get to the bottom of why someone might accuse you."

"I—I think it might've been my friends."

Mom gasps. "Marley! No. You have good friends."

"We're not talking much anymore."

"What happened with your friends?" Sam asks. If he's irritated by my mom's comments, he doesn't let it show.

Neither do I.

If I'm going to get through this, I have to keep my cool.

"Well, there was this thing that happened that I didn't agree with. A dare." I wring my hands together. "We had to let ourselves into Arthur's house and take a watch."

"Marley!" Mom gasps.

"I know! It was stupid, and I didn't want to."

"I think you'd better start from the beginning," Officer Ricky says.

"They'll be . . . mad that I told you. We took a watch to prove that we'd done it, but we took it back. Well, Jesse did."

Sam leans forward again. "Slow down, Marley. Start with the dare."

I blow out a breath. "Okay. It was dumb, *incredibly* dumb, but we got this senior dare to break into Arthur's and take a gold watch."

"From Rhett Wilder?" Officer Ricky asks.

I nod. "Yeah. We had to show him and then take it back. It was horrible."

"Who broke into his house?" Sam asks.

"Me, Atlas, Jesse, and Luce. The door was unlocked, we just let ourselves in. Went up to his bedroom and took a watch. Luce dropped her pin badge down a vent in his floor and freaked out. After showing Rhett the watch, Jesse said he'd take it back."

Officer Ricky tilts her head. "Why did only Jesse return the watch?"

"Well, I wasn't going back in there, was I? Totally hated it, wasn't the rush that the others thought it would be, at least not for me. Luce wasn't going back after thinking her badge would be found and she'd be arrested. I told Rhett that he had to keep me out of crap like that. I got involved in some stuff at school like moving Fuller's office, putting chickens on the field, and planting glitter balloons, but that was it."

"Okay, and when did your friendships begin breaking down?" Officer Ricky asks.

"After that, we hung out still, but it was different. I always felt like they didn't want me around. I'd catch them whispering and stop when they noticed me. I think we'd been growing apart a bit for a little while, but I didn't really see it until recently. They still wanted to do the dumb stuff. You heard about the fire at school, right? Well, I wanted no part of it." A tear rolls down my cheek. "I want to go to college!"

Sam nods. "Okay, so what dares have you turned down?"

I shrug and then bite my lip before saying, "Setting off fire extinguishers. There was talk about switching out senior staff cars in the middle of the night, but I don't think that happened."

"Right," Sam says, glancing at Officer Ricky. He knows I'm worried and hiding something. Good. "I think that one would have been reported."

Beside me, I can feel Mom's anger.

"Is that it, Marley? Because you look scared. If someone has done something and you know about it, you need to come forward," Officer Ricky says, reading exactly what I want her to from my mannerisms.

"Nothing," I say, a little too fast. "I don't know what happened with Arthur."

"Or George. There have been fire-related dares, and you're now telling me you broke into Arthur's house," Sam says.

"Not that night, I swear. Arthur was home when we took the watch. The dares have been to set off alarms and extinguishers, not set fire to someone's house."

"You haven't heard anything about the fire at Arthur's?"

"No, and George is my friend. About the only one right now too. I would tell you if I had."

"What about Atlas, honey?" Mom asks.

"He broke up with me. He's going to Ohio State and didn't tell me until yesterday."

"What?" Mom says, her voice higher each time she speaks.

"Sorry I didn't tell you," I say. "But I didn't want to talk about it."

"I can't believe any of this."

"They're acting different. I keep telling myself that I'm better off without them if this is how they're going to treat me . . . but it hurts."

Mom opens her mouth to say something else, but Sam gets there faster, trying to keep this "informal chat" on track.

"Marley, how well did you know Ruthie Marx?"

"Not well. We've had classes together for four years, but we've never hung out. I don't think she likes me much." I frown. "Liked, I guess."

"Why do you say that?"

"Well, to be fair, we were never on each other's radar until she started seeing Rhett. Sam, you know Rhett and I used to be close in middle school. I don't think Ruthie liked that we had a past, despite me and Rhett not even talking since before we started high school. She had a few arguments with Luce. Jesse and Atlas too, when Rhett got QB over them; she sure stood up for her man. Why are you asking me that? Is it true that there's a killer in town?"

"Let's not get ahead of ourselves," Officer Ricky says.

"I'm not, but Arthur and Ruthie are dead. George almost was."

"We're investigating a number of possibilities."

"That's not a no. Are we safe?"

Sam raises his palms and smiles. "Breathe, Marley. There is nothing to suggest that anyone else is in danger."

I can see him connecting dots in his head. My friends shutting me out, their behavior changes, the dares. If he just gets there a little quicker, I can build on this, weaving my clues and evidence in as I go. Maybe they'll find the footprint before it rains again.

"Marley, do you think your friends are capable of hurting Ruthie?"

"What?" I splutter, like it's the most outrageous thing I've ever heard. "No. No, they couldn't. . . . They . . ."

"Are you sure?" Officer Ricky asks. "Because you don't seem it."

"I spent four years of my life with them. I can't even think about that."

Sam and Officer Ricky exchange a look, and I know things are about to get very real for my ex-friends very fast.

31

I leave the station with my mom and can see she's about to explode with questions. But she believes me, and so does Sam. I'm not totally sure about Officer Ricky, but I think she's on my side. She certainly seemed suspicious of my friends.

Mom drives us home, firing questions off one after the other.

I repeat everything I said with Sam and Officer Ricky, not wanting to give her too much yet because she'll only turn around and demand I tell the rest.

It's not time yet. The information has to trickle out when I need it to.

She lets me go to my room when we get in, and she goes to make dinner.

The first thing I do is call Rhett and fill him in.

"So, you're not saying anything about the car dare yet?"

"No, that'll get out soon enough now that the cops are asking around. I need it to seem like I'm too scared to say anything. I'll crack later."

"What do I do? They asked me about Ruthie, but it was a quick chat. I think my parents intimidated them a bit." He chuckles. "What do I say about the dare?"

"When the time comes, just say that you did set Jesse's dare."

"And you didn't want to do it but went along. I'll tell them that Jesse said he could drop you off on the way."

"Thanks, Rhett."

"I've got your back."

"Same."

"Which one of them do you think it was who dropped you in it?"

I turn my nose up. "Luce. She texted me asking if I was home. I thought it was weird because she hasn't spoken to me for ages unless I initiated it. I just don't know why now. Why risk saying anything at all?"

"They must feel confident that they can make you take the fall."

"That makes me nervous, but we've done enough."

"Are you certain?"

"I've thought of everything. How was the gossip after I left school?"

He chuckles. "I'm sure you can imagine."

"I haven't been online yet."

"Steer clear. I'm working on it."

"You have enough influence to stop people from writing crap on my page."

"You know it."

I can't see how that's possible, but I do appreciate the thought. No one is going to care much about what Rhett says or does anymore. High school is over.

After a rather awkward dinner with my parents, both grilling me on the situation with my friends and threatening to call their parents, I'm finally allowed to go to bed. It's only when I'm safely under the covers that I check online, heading straight for the articles about today rather than what my peers are saying.

I honestly couldn't care less what they think anyway. Not now.

> *Eighteen-year-old Marley Croft was picked up at home by a patrol car and two officers in line with the murder of Arthur Nelson, who was found on June 2. The teen was later released without charge. A source reports that Miss Croft is the first person of interest related to Mr. Nelson. The question remains if his death is linked to the murder of Ruthie Marx, who was found on the morning of June 6.*

Okay, that wasn't too bad. Another site is reporting something similar, both stating that I'm not facing charges and was released after answering some questions.

It's definitely only a matter of time before someone squeals about the dare. I would prefer it to be sooner so I can put the second part of my plan into action and really get this thing going, but I can work with whatever.

• • •

Friday, June 9

My parents left for work at five a.m. after ordering me to stay home for a couple of days. There's a media storm going off. I know that my friends have been questioned, but arrests take time.

I hope the cops hurry up and collect evidence.

They're just giving them time to build their own case.

My parents will be checking in on their breaks and watching the doorbell to see if I've left. It's a senior ditch day, so I have a long weekend.

It's super easy to go around the back and avoid the camera. I use it when I want them to think I'm home.

I turn on the TV and watch the local news station with a loaded bowl of Fruity Pebbles. It doesn't take long to hear Ruthie's and Arthur's names, but so far, mine is kept out of it since it was just questions.

There is some speculation that Ruthie's family wanted to buy Arthur's land. But that doesn't account for why she was murdered, does it? George is the only Nelson left, and he wasn't in any position to push anyone out of windows.

It's embarrassing to listen to residents' thoughtless theories.

I don't want Ruthie's family or Rhett's to go down for this. It *has* to be Jesse. He's the one who started all this. He's the one who stole my boyfriend and best friend.

I hate all of them now, but that's so not the point.

Atlas:

u ok?

What the hell do I say to that? My texts might be monitored, so I need to be careful. Has he not been questioned?

Marley:

everything is fine. I promise.

Atlas:

you sure? You were at the station!

We were too

They were and now they're out. That must mean Sam hasn't told them it was me dropping them in it. What game is he playing? I need to calm down. It hasn't been that long.

Patience.

Marley:

it's fine. Pls tell Jesse I took care of it.

Atlas:

he's pretty stressed about it

Marley:

I know we're not together but pls help me out. I swear it's fine now. Tell Jesse that.

Atlas:

I will

Rolling my eyes, I put my phone down and shovel another heaping spoonful of cereal in my mouth. Atlas is such an idiot. How have I never realized that before? I must've been blinded by the pretty face.

I do want to contact Luce and see if I can break her, but I know that wouldn't be smart. I have to keep my distance from them all, make it seem like I'm scared of them.

I check back on my texts again and have nothing inconspicuous the night of the accident, just the "love u" text from Atlas. Not unusual.

Jesse's messages started a few days after. My timeline is good and will support the being-with-George-until-the-early-hours story.

Rhett and I need to keep our distance now. We've already been seen together too much at school. I won't be able to pretend that he was being his usual moody self if we're seen outside of school too.

This part is the worst, sitting here and hoping things happen the way I need them to. I want to push things along so it's over and I'm in the clear. That's the mistake that so many people make. I won't be following that path. I can be patient.

By midday I'm going out of my mind, so I let myself out the back door and pull my baseball cap down over my eyes as I walk toward Arthur's house.

I debated going back to see George, but I don't know how that will look, since I'm about to use him as my alibi, but we've been calling using my old phone. My ex-friends are going to heavily deny that they dropped me off, if they eventually admit to the truth and try to take me down with them.

I stop and step back into the trees as I spot forensics and a cop car outside Arthur's. Placing my hand over my badge, attached to my T-shirt, I smile. They're looking for Luce's. They must be.

Walking on, I head through the forest and past the creek. No one is here today, which is weird, particularly now that there's a lot of gossip. They must all be somewhere else, spreading their theories. I haven't bothered checking because I'm not interested in the narrative that I killed Arthur.

My phone rings as I approach the middle of the forest. Rhett.

"Hi."

"Marley, Jesse is near you! I'm on my way, but you need to watch out."

"What?" I hiss.

"It's going off with the cops."

I spin around. "I can't see him," I mutter.

"You will soon." I hear his car door slam. "His car is parked on the edge of the forest. Listen, Martha went to the cops about the dare. I don't know what Jesse knows, but it's convenient timing, right? I saw Atlas flying down the road."

"Where was he going?" I ask, picking up my pace and watching over my shoulder. I don't hear footsteps, but the ground is no longer as crunchy as it was.

"I'm not certain, but he was going in the direction of Jesse's house."

"You think Atlas knows what's going on?"

"I'd say so. Where are you going?"

"I'm going into town."

Just need to get there before Jesse catches up to me. I'm confident that I can outsmart him; I'm not confident that I can outpower him.

"You're cutting across, so you'll come out by the grocery store?"

"Yeah."

I'm so freaking relieved that Rhett knows the mountain as well as I do.

"I'll be waiting there."

"Where is he?" I ask, my heart hammering as I break into a jog. My feet stamp clumsily as I try to focus on listening to Rhett and listening for Jesse while getting out of this forest alive.

If Jesse catches up to me, I don't know what he will do.

Actually, I do know, and that scares the crap out of me.

He's coming for me.

My stomach squeezes in anticipation. I can't see him, but I can feel that he's close. I fumble with my phone, ending the call, knowing it'll slow me down, but I don't think I can outrun him for long anyway.

I can see the edge of the forest ahead, the daylight breaking through the leaves. Panting, I push myself until my quads burn and my lungs feel like they've been punctured.

I dodge a tree, slowing for a second to dart between two so I avoid the dip in the ground. I don't make it past the tree because Jesse's hand grips my hair and I'm yanked backward.

Screaming, I land heavily on the ground, the air getting knocked from my lungs. My phone drops to the ground, and I cough and claw at his hand.

"Don't even think about it!" he spits, dropping his knees into my thighs.

"Get off me!" I shout, scratching at the exposed skin on his forearms. If he's going to kill me, he's going to leave a lot of DNA behind.

"What have you done?" he growls. "What have you done?"

I try to kick my legs to throw him off balance, but he doesn't budge, his knees digging into my muscles so hard that I start to lose feeling in them.

"Jesse, get the hell off me!"

"You think you're so smart. What are you going to do now, huh? I've got you." He leans forward, and his knees dig harder into my thighs. I grit my teeth to stop myself from screaming out in pain. I'm not giving him the satisfaction.

His forearm presses against my collarbone. "You're setting us up."

"You're insane. Get off me!"

"The cops are at my fucking house! Why is that?"

The pain in my legs intensifies to the point I think I might throw up. "Martha told them about the dare. Jesse, move!"

I shove his chest and finally manage to throw him off just enough to get some relief for my legs. His knees slide to the side, still pinning me to the damp ground, but at least the pain decreases.

I wiggle my toes, trying to get the feeling back into my legs.

"Tell me what you did," he spits.

Hurry up, Rhett.

Shaking my head, I say, "Let's talk about what you've done. The cops had me at the station, Jesse! Which one of you did that? Why would you lie about me?"

He narrows his eyes. "You're the one who wanted to squeal."

"You're not making any sense. Let me go! I wouldn't have said anything, I swear."

"Stop lying!" he spits. "We couldn't because you took that goddam badge. Why?" he growls.

"What the hell are you talking about? Help!" I scream.

"No one's here, so scream all you like."

"I told you I'd keep quiet. You're hurting me! Jesse, get off. Please, I'll do whatever you want." I suck in a ragged breath. "Don't kill me."

"Shut up! Just shut up, Marley. You're ruining everything."

"I haven't been anything. Please let me go. Where are the others? Do they know you're doing this? God, did you kill Ruthie?"

"Shut up!"

I scream and twist again, frantically trying to get away, but he's far too strong.

"Hey, get off her!"

Jesse's jaw drops, and he looks up just as Rhett tackles him, throwing all his weight into Jesse's chest. They both thump to the ground beside me. Rhett throws a punch, connecting with a sickening thud to Jesse's cheek.

"No!" I shout. "Rhett, don't! Let's go!" I search the ground and find my phone. Shoving it into my pocket, I test my balance by getting to my feet. My legs tremble, but I stay upright. "Rhett!"

He lands another punch, this one to the side of Jesse's head, and his eye almost instantly begins to swell.

"Rhett, I need to get out of here."

He looks up at that, letting go of Jesse's shirt with the hand that was holding him down.

"Did he hurt you?" he asks as Jesse rolls onto his side, groaning.

"I-I'm going to be fine. I can stand. We need to go before he gets back up, Rhett, he's dangerous. You don't know what he's capable of."

Rhett frowns but I tug him hard. He follows, and together we run out of the forest.

"What did he do?" Rhett asks as we reach his car.

I get in and slam the door, my hands trembling from the adrenaline.

"Marley?" he prompts, starting the engine.

"Um . . . he pulled me down by my hair, knelt on my legs so I couldn't move. God, that hurt so bad, I wasn't sure if I'd be able to run if I got away from him." I fiddle with my phone. "Rhett, he was insane. He knows what I've been doing. I don't think he knows you were helping me, though. We should try to keep it that way."

"I just showed up and punched him in the face, Marley. I think he's going to know."

Damn it, he's right.

"We can say you were hiking and heard me scream. We really should try to keep you out of this."

He nods. "I mean, we can try, but I don't think it's going to work. Take a look up ahead."

"Oh crap."

In my driveway is my mom's car . . . and a police cruiser.

32

Rhett made a quick getaway because we need to keep him out of this. He stopped before we reached my house, and no one saw him.

Now I'm back in a freaking interview room with my rather-angry mother beside me.

Sam smiles, trying to put me at ease. "Marley, we know about the dare that Jesse Reece accepted from Rhett Wilder. We know that you, Lucia Sanchez, and Atlas Ford were also present."

I dip my chin. "I—I wasn't," I say.

"We have a source saying you went with the group to Jesse's truck."

"Yeah, that's true, but I didn't go with them. Not far anyway. Luce and I were both scared and wanted Jesse to pull out of the dare. Atlas was up for it and wouldn't listen. It was stupid and dangerous. They said we could get out. I did. Luce stayed."

"You got out?"

"Yeah, when we reached the main road. I saw George walking, and they dropped me off with him so I wouldn't have to walk back alone at night."

"George Nelson?"

"Yes."

"What happened when you left with George?"

I shrug. "We went to his house for a while. I lost track of time and got home at, like, three in the morning. You can check the doorbell."

Mom's eyes burn into the side of my head. I actually think I'd be in less trouble with the cops if they knew the whole truth.

"What were you doing at his house for that length of time?"

I feel my cheeks heat, and I know it's not because of what I'm about to say, because it's a lie, but rather saying something like this in front of my mom. "We . . . you know. Were together."

"Marley," Mom gasps.

"I didn't plan it. We were talking and then it just happened."

"What happened next, Marley?" Officer Ricky asks.

I look at her. "What do you mean?"

"Well, up to this point you were still talking to your friends, correct?"

"Correct."

"You've previously told us that the relationship with your friends has broken down."

I thread my hands together and stare at the table. "We grew apart."

"When was this? After that night?"

I sink back in my seat just enough to not look like I'm being theatrical.

"Marley, we need to know what happened that night," Sam presses.

"I—I don't know. I wasn't there."

He lifts his brow. “Perhaps not, but something has you frightened.”

“I can’t,” I whisper.

“Who are you scared of?” Mom asks. “Marley, you need to tell the police everything. No one can hurt you.”

I raise my eyes and stare at her. “Are you kidding? Arthur and Ruthie were murdered! George is in the hospital.”

“Oh, honey, is that why you were so worried about him? Because you two . . .”

“Yes, Mom,” I say, turning away from her as if I’m embarrassed.

“Marley, if you know who killed Arthur and Ruthie, you must tell us,” Sam says. “We can protect you.”

“Well, I’m not *certain.*”

“Marley.”

“They changed after that night. When I saw them at school, they were weird, having private conversations. Luce looked . . . haunted and didn’t want to talk, just stuck right by Jesse. I mean, they’re pretty much always together, but this was weird because she would happily spend time with me too. Jesse was angry, had a scowl on his face and snapped at me a few times. I knew something was wrong.” I take a long breath. “And then Arthur was found, and it came out that it wasn’t an accident. I had a suspicion then, because Luce was driving Jesse around more and that never happens. Um, then when it was reported approximately how long he’d been dead . . . the timeline fit.”

“Did you question them about it?” Officer Ricky asks.

“I asked if something happened, because they were all acting out of character. Jesse started getting mad, told me to stay out of it because I was always *sticking my nose* in his business, which isn't true. So, then I kind of knew. He didn't leave me alone after that. I have so many messages from him, you can look. He was constantly checking in on me."

"I can't believe this," Mom whispers.

Officer Ricky leans forward a fraction. "Did Jesse or any of your friends admit to what happened?"

"No," I reply. "So I'm not *sure,* but I . . . I think it was them."

Sam nods. "What about Ruthie?"

I shrug. "I have no clue about Ruthie. She wasn't with us in the truck, and I didn't see her when I got out. When she died, I wondered if she'd watched to check that they'd done the dare. I mean, there wasn't a watch to bring back to prove it. But I'd just be guessing."

"Why would Ruthie be the one checking?" Sam asks.

"I don't know if she did, but she and Rhett were kind of an unofficial thing. She was weird after that night too. Well, sort of."

Officer Ricky raises her brows. "What does that mean exactly?"

"We were never friends with her. She didn't change, but she was more . . . I don't know. She watched them more, hung around a little longer. I didn't think it was strange until she died. Ruthie wouldn't have jumped out of that window. I didn't really know her that well, but she had a scholarship to a great college and couldn't wait to move out of state."

"Do you think your friends are capable of murder?" Sam asks.

"I didn't. I never would have believed that, and I don't want to, even now that we're not on good terms. I've slept over at their houses and trusted them with my fears and secrets." I shake my head. "I want this to be a misunderstanding so bad, but I can feel that it's not, and that terrifies me. I don't know what to do. I don't . . ." I take a breath and place my hand over my heart.

"Shhh, it's okay," Mom says, rubbing my back.

"It's not okay, Mom."

"Marley, is that blood on your fingernails?" Sam asks.

I almost smile but catch it in time. Curling my fingers into my palm, I nod. "Yes."

"Whose is it?" he asks.

"Jesse's," I whisper.

He and Officer Ricky look at each other. "Why?"

"I went for a walk. I stayed in for as long as I could, but I was going crazy. Sorry, Mom. I kept to the forest because I didn't think I'd see anyone else. Thought I'd be safe just for thirty minutes."

"What did he do?" he presses.

"I was walking through the forest on my way back home when I heard footsteps. I couldn't see anyone, but it spooked me because it was definitely not an animal. I've been camping and hiking with my dad enough times to know the difference between animal and human steps."

I've also been camping when Sam's been with us, so this is all true. It'll help build my credibility.

"I got a call from Rhett. He said he'd seen me go into the woods, and then he saw Jesse nearby. He watched him change direction and come after me. Jesse grabbed me from behind. He was screaming about cops at his house. I hung up with Rhett because I knew I had to record. I thought Jesse had come to . . ." I sniff and wipe a tear. An actual tear that I manage to conjure from nothing. "Um. Yeah, I thought he was going to hurt me, so I recorded the attack."

"I'm going to need that, Marley."

I nod, taking the phone from my pocket, opening the app, and handing it to Sam.

He plays the now-edited version. The one that ends right before Rhett arrived.

33

Saturday, June 10

I scroll social media, ignoring my own page for now. News of Jesse's arrest has spread like wildfire.

The relief I feel that he won't get away with this vibrates through my body. He's killed accidentally and on purpose. And he's going to pay for it.

I'm trying to find out if Atlas and Luce are still in custody, but there haven't been any more sightings of them. There's a relay of information coming through, like on the night Leon drove the ducks to school.

Now I'm going out of my mind because I only know where Jesse is. I could get Dad to call Sam and ask, play the fear card, but I don't want to involve them just yet.

This afternoon is graduation, and we're waiting to hear if I'll be able to walk. I'm not bothered either way at this point, but it wouldn't look good if I didn't. I think Fuller might be over pranks and the class of 2023, so he's pushing back.

Mom and Dad have both taken the day off work, so I'm struggling to find a way to get out of the house.

I half watch the rain pelting against my window and half my phone screen. It wasn't supposed to rain yet, so I don't think the footprint will hold up if they find out about the first burial site, but I think I have enough anyway.

Something catches my eye as I scroll. Atlas. He's climbing onto the roof below my window. The way he used to sneak in and out if my parents were home. Why can't the cops just charge him already?

I'm tempted to scream, it wouldn't look good for him, but I want to hear what more he has to say. I set my phone to record, now super mindful that he might've done the same, and open my window.

"You need to get out of here, Atlas," I say. "I'm giving you one warning because of who we used to be."

"Cut the crap! What the hell are you trying to do?" he snaps.

"Back off. My parents are home."

He rolls his eyes, water pouring down his face, plastering his hair against his forehead. "The cops are everywhere, searching my house! What the hell is wrong with you?"

"Back off, Atlas. I mean it. Leave me alone. All I want is for you guys to leave me alone."

His scowl transforms his face, eyes wild and unpredictable.

He reminds me of Jesse.

I know how to deal with Jesse.

"You have to stop this. We're going to go down!"

"You did it."

"Stop it! You know what *we* did."

"Mom! Dad!" I scream.

Atlas's eyes widen. He looks over his shoulder and back to me like he doesn't recognize who I am. Well, same. They've changed me, turned me into someone who doesn't trust another soul, who constantly must protect themselves.

Over the sound of the rain, I can hear footsteps thundering up the stairs.

Atlas wobbles, almost losing his balance before he shuffles to the edge of the roof. He swings his legs over the edge and takes one last look at me. Eyes wide, mouth slightly parted. He knows that I've won.

Dad bursts through the door. "What's wrong?"

"Atlas was on the roof."

Dad runs over in time to see Atlas sprint across the yard. "I'm calling Sam," he says, taking his phone from his jeans pocket. "Close that window."

"What were you thinking opening it?" Mom says, placing her hand on my shoulder. I didn't realize she'd come in, but she would hardly wait downstairs for Dad to fill her in.

I turn to her while Dad makes the call.

"I—I don't know. Atlas wouldn't hurt me, and I wanted to know why he was here."

"We have no idea what he's capable of, Marley. I cannot believe you were so reckless."

"I'm sorry. I just have questions, Mom. We were together for three years."

"That person is gone. You need to stay away from him."

"I will," I promise. "Have you heard about graduation?"

"You're allowed to walk, but I don't know if it's a good idea."

"What?" I say. "This is so unfair."

Dad hangs up. "Calm down, Marley. We're just trying to look out for you."

"Fuller is the last person who would want me at school right now. You know he hates drama, so if he's saying I can, it means that he knows I'm innocent."

"Marley . . ."

"No, Dad. I don't want to miss graduation because of something my old friends did. Come on, this isn't something I can miss. Please."

He sighs, relenting. "Fine. But we're not hanging around to be the center of gossip."

"Okay. We can leave straightaway. I just want to walk and get my diploma."

"You'd better get dressed," Mom says, her voice tight, as if she wants to fight Dad because she's not totally on board.

It will appear like I'm hiding something if I miss graduation. I need everyone to believe me and not them.

I spend the next hour showering and getting ready. I curl my hair, apply makeup, and change into a black dress and matching heels. It's an outfit that I could also wear to a funeral.

Mom and Dad take me to school and go to find seats in the auditorium. I walk the halls, taking everything in one last time. I'm not supposed to be here, but hanging out with my classmates doesn't sound fun anymore.

"I knew you'd be hiding."

I spin around and come face-to-face with Rhett for the first time since he tackled Jesse off me yesterday.

"Am I the center of gossip?" I ask.

"The rest of them more so. There's a massive photo of Ruthie up, and people are angry."

"Rightly," I say.

"Agreed. The cops had me at the station yesterday, that's what I was doing before I came to find you."

"You okay?"

He nods. "Everything's good, Marley. Jesse and the rest of them are going down for what they did to Ruthie and Arthur."

"And George. He could've been killed."

"Yeah, and George. Have you heard from him?"

I have, but Rhett doesn't need to know that. "No, but my mom said he was being discharged. I'll have to find out where he's going. It's not like he can stay at Arthur's."

Rhett shrugs. "Forget him, he'll figure it out."

Forget him. Something that seems so easy for Rhett to do. Once he's finished with a person, he drops them. I feel a bolt of sympathy for George and a burning anger for the girl who once cried herself to sleep because her friend ghosted her.

"You should get back before your parents find us. I assume your dad won't be happy that you're talking to me."

He scratches his jaw, wincing, and I know I'm right. Doesn't matter that perfect Rhett Wilder is the reason we're all in this mess. He can't do anything wrong in the eyes of his parents, and if he does, it disappears.

"I'll see you in there, yeah?"

"Yeah, go," I say, and try to smile.

I watch Rhett retreat and then check my phone, rereading a

message I received just before he came in. It says to meet in the guys' locker room. I have about five minutes before I need to be with my classmates to walk.

I push the door to the gym open and immediately gag. It's so gross when you first walk in, the smell of sweaty feet wafting through the room. I'm about to go into a much smellier place, though.

Opening the next door almost makes me vomit for real. How the hell are boys this stinky? I turn my nose up and call, "Hello?"

I move deeper into the room and walk around the corner. "You here?"

A thud from the door closing behind me makes me jolt. I spin around, my heart in my throat.

Jesse smirks. "Now, why would you be so jumpy?"

"What the hell are you doing here?"

"Don't you mean what the hell are *we* doing here?"

I frown. "What?"

With a roll of his eyes, he taps the locked door beside him, and I hear another set of footsteps.

Luce moves into view, and they both look like they want to kill me.

34

My heart stalls. They're not who I was expecting.

"You can't be here," I say.

How are they here?

"You think we're going to let bail conditions get in the way of this?" Jesse spits. "You've set us up! We're facing charges for two murders! Cops are crawling around, searching our houses! My goddam truck has been taken."

Ha. Good.

"You killed them, Jesse! George almost died too. *You* did that. You're a murderer."

"Shut up!" he bellows.

"You shouldn't be here. You need to go," I say, backing up a step.

Jesse shakes his head slowly, his expression cold and dangerous. Would the others stand and watch while he killed me? Atlas isn't here, but he tried to sneak into my room a couple of hours ago, so he was probably picked up by the cops.

"We don't have long before the goddam cops come back for us, so we had to follow you and do this now."

They followed me into this room. So I wasn't betrayed.

Luce looks quickly between Jesse and me.

"Luce, you can't let him hurt me. We were friends."

Her eyes narrow in the most predictable way. Obviously I don't expect her to play along, but I don't trust anyone. They could be recording this.

"How are you guys out?"

"Bail," Luce says. "Bail, Marley! You think we're friends after this? You're going down too."

"I haven't done anything. You're both insane!"

"Cut the crap!" Jesse shouts again. Someone is going to hear him soon, surely. Why hasn't anyone noticed that they aren't home? There must be conditions to their bail.

"Hurting me is only going to make this worse," I say, taking another step back. They're blocking me in; the door is behind them. "The cops will know it's you. Come on, think about it."

"I don't care. We're not letting you get away with this," Jesse says. "You figured it out, didn't you?"

Yes.

"Figured what out? What are you talking about?"

"Stop pretending you don't know. It's embarrassing," Luce snaps. "You were the weakest link, about to squeal any day, so we had to do something. You figured out what we were up to and formed your own little plan. How, Marley? How did you get them to believe your lies?"

I smirk and move my jacket aside, revealing the pin badge. "You're all crazy. I don't know what you're trying to do, but for once, take responsibility for what you've done and stop blaming everyone else."

"Bitch!" Luce screams.

Jesse growls. "Own up to it or I'll slit your goddam throat right now."

My heart drops as he pulls a knife from his pocket. "Put that away, Jesse. We can talk about this."

I didn't say what he has. Shit. But he said he'd slit my throat, so it's obvious, right? Would that stand up?

"No. Tell the truth right now."

Raising my palms, I reply, "Okay. Please just put the knife down, and I'll do whatever you want."

"That's better. . . . But the knife isn't going anywhere. I have *nothing* to lose now. You made sure of that."

"You do. If you kill me, it's more time. You'd never get out of prison. Think about it. Luce, come on. You don't want to do this."

"Admit to what you did!" he spits.

"All right. All right. Just stay back, please. I did it. I did it all and blamed you. We can go to the cops together."

"She's lying," Luce says. "I can tell, Jesse. We need to get out of here. We won't have long. She's scared enough."

Jesse laughs. "Luce, you really are the stupidest person I have ever met. This was never about scaring her. She's sending us down, and you think I want to waste my final chance to get her alone to make her a bit scared?!"

"What the hell?" she spits, stepping toward him. "Jesse, what are you saying?"

I notice the change in Jesse's eyes a fraction too late. He lunges and sticks the knife into Luce's gut. It slides straight in like he's cutting butter.

I scream, the sound bouncing off the walls and nearly deafening me. She looks up at him, eyes wide and full of hurt. Then she stumbles back, gripping her stomach.

Jesse has nothing to lose. This is his last chance.

To kill us all?

Was this his plan? He can't get hold of Atlas because he's likely at the station now. I can't describe how relieved I am. I hate them all, but I don't want any of them to die.

Luce drops hard to the floor, her knees cracking on the vinyl tiles as she goes down.

"What did you do?" I mutter, watching my best friend's blood pump through her fingers.

Above her is Jesse. Watching. Waiting for his girlfriend to bleed out.

He's sicker than I realized.

I scoot to the side while he's occupied, lost in the imminent death like the Grim Reaper admiring his handiwork.

I sidestep again, breathing as quietly as I can so I don't disturb Jesse. My heart thudding as I go, terrified that he will snap back and realize that I'm about to escape.

A part of me wants to help her. I wanted her in prison, not the morgue, but I have to make sure I can get out.

She sobs as she looks at him, her heart breaking in front of me. I have my phone in my pocket, but how much movement is too much? I'm already moving an inch at a time, keeping my arms by my sides and my head straight.

Jesse has nothing to lose.

I'll call for help, I just need to get a little closer to the door. A few more steps.

Someone must have realized that I'm not in the hall by now. Rhett knows I'm out this way.

I shouldn't be alone right now.

Where is he?

I reach the end of the locker row and have to start moving forward when Luce cries out.

Her raspy breath sends a chill down my spine. Every gasp is a battle she's very quickly losing. She coughs and then her body goes limp, slumping like a rag doll.

My body turns cold.

Luce is dead.

Jesse looks up, his eyes connecting with mine.

He tilts his head, but he's distracted by the sound of sirens wailing close by. Not only sirens, but shouting too.

It's then I notice that Jesse has a tag on his ankle. Maybe they both do. That's what they meant by not having long. He knew the cops would come as soon as they realized they'd left home.

"Jesse, the cops!" I shout, hoping he'll prioritize running over killing me.

This is his endgame.

Run.

His head snaps up, and I gasp. I don't look back to see if he's behind me because that'll only slow me down. Besides, I know he'll follow.

My feet thunder down the hallway. I gulp for air when the oxygen feels like it's burning up around me. Running too fast to slow down for a corner, I slam into a wall. It gives Jesse enough time.

I scream as his arm snakes around me and he pulls me against his chest. I shove myself backward, and the motion almost makes him lose his footing.

"Get off!"

He growls, his fingers digging painfully into my skin as he grabs me and shoves me into the wall. My head bounces off the painted block, dots dancing in front of my face.

Music from the auditorium and sirens outside float through the halls. I drop to the floor and turn over, dazed but still hyperaware that I can't have my back to him. I need to protect myself, to fight until help arrives.

Jesse pins me to the floor the same way he did in the forest, only this time he's more determined.

"You're going to die!" he spits, grappling at my wrists with one hand to pin me down.

I wriggle, pushing his face and the arm with the knife.

"Hey!" someone shouts, the sound echoing, bouncing off the walls as hard as my head did.

Then I hear footsteps. "Get off her!"

Oh, thank god, he's come for me.

I claw at Jesse's face, my nails raking down his skin and leaving a trail of red behind that looks like rivers of blood.

"Bitch!" he shouts, now using both hands to hold the knife.

My eyes widen as I thrash beneath him, the pointed end, covered in Luce's blood, now aiming for my heart.

"Marley!" another voice shouts.

I gasp as Jesse drives his hands down toward me. Twisting, I manage to move my body, using my legs to push him to the side. The metal scraping of the knife on the floor beside me sends a bolt of terror along my spine.

I push again before he manages to correct his balance, and he falls to the side.

"Get away from her!"

I look up, and he's here.

George kicks Jesse's hand hard, the knife scattering across the floor. He picks him up by the scruff of his neck and slams him into the wall.

"Back up! Everyone, back up!"

I scramble to my feet as two cops sprint toward us. Rhett reaches us first, grabbing me and pulling me farther away from where George has Jesse.

One of the cops picks up the knife while the other, Sam, I manage to see through my blurred vision, grabs Jesse's hands.

"Move, George," Sam says.

Once George is out of the way, Sam slaps a pair of handcuffs on Jesse and reads him his rights.

"Luce is dead," I say, sobbing in relief that I am not. "She's in the locker room. Jesse and Luce cornered me in there. He killed her and then he tried to kill me."

"You're safe, Marley." Sam turns to George and Rhett. "Why are you here?"

"I saw her from the auditorium and wanted to check she was okay," Rhett tells him.

"And I came for graduation," George says, moving closer to me. "Heard her screaming and ran. Are you okay?"

I break out of Rhett's embrace and stumble to George. "My head."

"You're bleeding but you'll be okay," he replies, pressing his palm to the wound.

"What are you doing here, Mr. Wilder?" Sam asks.

"I—I knew where Marley was," Rhett replies, and I can feel his gaze on George and me. "Marley, what's going on?"

I bite my lip, waiting.

You're about to find out.

Sam nods, moving to Rhett with his hand on his cuffs. "Mr. Wilder, you're under arrest for the attempted murder of George Nelson."

Rhett's eyes widen.

And this is where I win.

I've taken them all down.

Turning back to George, I smile at his expression.

Sam's partner cuffs Rhett and escorts him along the corridor. "You're okay now," Sam says, and he trails after his partner and Rhett.

"Marley, what the hell is going on?" Rhett shouts over his shoulder. "Marley! Answer me!"

"What did you do?" George asks when they're far enough away to not hear us.

We begin to follow slowly so that Sam doesn't stop. I only have a minute before the gossip starts and my parents come running.

"As if I'm letting him get away with ditching me. No one picks me up and drops me when it suits them. His AirTags were used to track me and Jesse. I told the cops that we took the watch back. Turns out it was Rhett's grandma's, an heirloom, and she gave it to your grandad when they had an affair. Worth a fortune, apparently. If we returned it, how would Rhett have it now?"

George shakes his head, grinning. "He snuck in for it and burned my house down at the same time."

"Bingo. He wanted us to do the dirty work and find out if Arthur still had it first. Of course, I didn't tell Rhett this, and it was still in his house . . . along with a gas canister from your farm, and a couple of pills planted in his car from your bottle. Wiped clean, so don't panic if you touched them. They've always wanted that land, and with Arthur missing, he could finish you off, buy the land, all while blaming the others."

I wish I knew where Arthur's car was, probably in the water somewhere, but I can't bring that up without it looking suspicious. It'll be found eventually, I'm sure. And it's only a matter of time before Luce's badge is found in the house now that the cops are swarming it.

George smiles. "You're the cutest, scariest, and most devious girl I know."

"Thank you."

"So I'm thinking I'm ready for that college transfer. California with my grandad's money?"

I link my arm through his. "I thought you'd never ask."

ACKNOWLEDGMENTS

This has been one of my favorite books to write, and I couldn't have done it without some pretty amazing people.

Ariella and Amber, thank you for being the best representation a girl could ask for.

There are so many people who worked on this book before and after it hit the shelves. Huge thank-you to Wendy, Ali, Kathy, Megan, Jordy, and everyone who helped prepare *The Dare* to be released into the wild.

I would like to thank coffee for getting me through some late nights and early mornings . . . and my husband for making most of it. My children have tried to "help" and it hasn't always gone to plan, but they're cute so it's fine.

To Sam, Vic, and Elle . . . thanks for the sprints and words of encouragement. Also for giving me a GIF kick in the butt when needed.

Readers, bloggers, and vloggers. Thank you all so much for picking up *The Dare.*

HAUNTED BY THE PAST . . .

The Haunting excerpt text copyright © 2023
by Natasha Preston. Cover art by Mark Owen/
Trevillion Images. Flower image © 2023 by scisettialfio/
Getty Images. Petals used under license from
Shutterstock.com. Published by Delacorte Press,
an imprint of Random House Children's Books,
a division of Penguin Random House LLC, New York.

1

SATURDAY, OCTOBER 23

What's the best way to ask your boyfriend how he feels about the one-year anniversary of his father's Halloween murder spree?

Your *ex*-boyfriend, because, oh yeah, you're forbidden to ever see or speak with him again.

Nash never returned to school after five of our classmates were slaughtered by his dad, a man who made me hot chocolate with a mountain of marshmallows whenever I came over.

Jackson Whitmore was two people: the welcoming dad and the cold-blooded killer. It took a long time to merge them.

The memory of what he did is all over town, haunting the residents with constant reminders wherever you look. The memorial statue for his victims sits proudly in the square, in the center of town, visible from every angle—the same location where some of them were found.

I stare at it now. A bronze phoenix with its large wings splayed toward heaven. Five names are engraved underneath the bird. I trace each one with my finger.

Mac Johnson

Caitlin Howard

Kelsie Allen

Brodie Edwards

Jia Yang

There's no getting away from what he did. A reminder is carved into stone.

Jackson's killing spree lasted a week, but it feels like it never ended. The mayor had flowers planted in every inch of soil in the spring. It still smelled like death to me.

Figuring out what to say to Nash has been plaguing me for the past few weeks. Everything I think of sounds totally stupid. Forgetting him has been impossible, and with Halloween coming up, he's on my mind even more than usual.

Still, it's been about five months since we last spoke—on a rainy spring day when we ran into each other outside school. Me leaving late for the day, him going to collect a jacket that had been in the lost and found.

It was a short conversation once we'd asked what the other was doing. Short and *super* awkward. I can still remember the way he tried to avoid eye contact, as if looking at me hurt, and how I felt so guilty for writing him off like the rest of the town.

Dark gray clouds, the same color as my eyes, cover the sky, as likely to rain as I am to cry. I've been finding it increasingly difficult to trap my emotions inside. I'm not supposed to think about Nash. My feelings for him were supposed to disappear along with our contact.

I walk away from the statue and toward Gina's restaurant to

meet Adi for breakfast, still clinging to my phone in case I come up with something good to say. I pass a couple of dressed-up scarecrows, one draped in white like a ghost with smudged black circles for eyes. The other dressed in a tattered black cloak with a distorted face and pointed hood. It's the more sinister one that I have a hard time looking at. You can tell the ghost was made by the elementary school kids. The creepy *thing*, high school.

When I step inside the restaurant, everyone turns their head to watch me. A few people whisper, still not over getting a glimpse of the killer's son's ex.

I feel like a one-woman show.

The one-woman coward show where I ignore my instincts and pretend that I'm fine not talking to Nash anymore.

I duck my head and take a seat at an empty table. Gina's is a country-style restaurant, with red-and-white checkered tablecloths. I scroll on my phone to distract myself from the fact that Nash's name is suddenly on everyone's lips.

My parents were thrilled when I stopped seeing Nash—after forcing me to—and I need them to believe I've given up wanting to. It's much easier if they don't know anything. If I send him a message and my parents find out, they will freak. It will be a freak-out of epic proportions. Their straight-A daughter, headed for a great college, fraternizing—a word my dad *actually* used—with a Whitmore.

It's not something I should even be thinking about.

Everyone in our tight-knit community, including my best friends, thinks it's better if the remaining Whitmores keep to their large property on the outskirts of town.

But what Jackson Whitmore did last year wasn't Nash's—or his sister, Grace's—fault. Not that it matters because apparently everyone here believes they're guilty by association.

It's all bullshit.

I think I might be the only one left who cares about Nash and Grace.

But I'm not allowed to do anything about it and it's slowly eating away at me.

I need to reach out to him, to let him know that he's not alone, but, yeah, I don't know what to say.

Okay, come on. Think of something... As hard as it is for all of us to deal with the anniversary, it must be ten times harder for them. I can only imagine how it must feel to be blamed for something you didn't do.

They lost everything because of what their dad did.

Penny:

i know it's been a while but i still care about you.

Delete.

No, that's absolute crap.

Penny:

How are you and grace doing? I know everyone else blames you but i don't.

Delete.

Penny:

Please don't hate me.

Delete.

I couldn't make these suck more if I tried.

Penny:

Can we meet?

Delete. Delete. Delete.

This shouldn't be so hard! We used to talk about *everything.* We'd send messages, from long essays to full conversations using only GIFs—sometimes no words were needed. I don't think that would be appropriate in this situation. *I'm sorry your dad is a killer but here's a GIF of Tom Hanks waving on a boat.*

Yeah, I don't think so.

So, I end up sending nothing at all. Every time. Which is way worse.

"Penny," my best friend, Adeline, says, sliding into the booth. "Gina has pumpkin-shaped sprinkles on the ice cream sundaes."

I place my cell facedown on the table, ignoring the simmering frustration in my gut. I half feel like I'm waiting on Nash to reply . . . to the nothing I sent.

"You ordered us one, right?" I ask, though I'm not hungry. That seems to be a theme recently.

Can't eat properly because of the big ball of anxiety.

Can't sleep properly because of the big ball of anxiety.

Can't focus well at school or piano practice because . . . well, you get it.

I haven't tried ice cream for breakfast, though.

"Duh," she says, tying her tight red curls on top of her head.

"Sundae eating is getting serious."

"You know it is. I ordered us the doubles." She pauses, taking me in. "What's going on? You look shady and you're playing 'Für Elise' on your cell."

I look down and realize I've been anxiously tapping on the back of my phone. I curl my fingers into my palm. "Everything's fine. I'm just always practicing."

Usually I can convince almost anyone of anything—you've just got to say whatever the lie is with conviction—but my most useful talent does not work on Adi this time. Plus, I haven't played piano in a while.

She raises her brows, her pale green eyes full of suspicion, and leans back against the dark wooden booth. A move that I recognize means she's ready to kick ass.

Adi doesn't have any time for pretending when she knows it's a lie.

"I was thinking about him," I tell her, sighing.

She doesn't need a name to know who I mean. *Him* is pretty much his name now.

Him is Nash.

Her is Grace.

That Man is Jackson.

As if saying their names will release Jackson from federal prison and send him on another spree.

"Don't go there, Pen," she warns.

My heart sinks to my toes. It's not the reaction I was hoping for but it's pretty much the one I expected. Nash is the one thing we will never agree on, the one thing she doesn't have my back on.

"It wasn't his fault."

"I'm with you on that but you probably weren't going to marry your high school boyfriend anyway. You're off to Juilliard and he would rather die than live anywhere near a city. It was never going to work."

That doesn't mean I should write him off. Besides, I don't know if I'll get into Juilliard, not anymore, or if I even want to pursue music professionally. I've let it go in the last year, but I'll save that little confession for another time. My parents won't be too excited.

"What's your costume going to be?" I ask.

"Nice subject change but it wasn't very smooth. I don't know yet. I'll see what Party Town has. You still dressing as a corpse bride?"

"I think so," I reply. I'll never tell her that Nash was supposed to be a corpse groom this year.

We'd been together for a year before last Halloween and had our costumes picked out . . . but we never got to wear them because trick-or-treating was canceled, and his dad was arrested. We were going to be prisoners.

Ironic.

Now the only prisoner is Jackson Whitmore. Nash and Grace, too, if you count being ostracized by the town and isolated in your home. Which I do.

"Penny, try not to think about him." Adi's voice is soft and understanding, but it's easy for her to say that. Nash was her friend, but it didn't take her long to stop checking in with him. Same as our other friends Zayn and Omar.

"I want to text him."

"That's the opposite of not thinking about him."

"I can't just turn my thoughts off. Like you said, it's the anniversary. How must he be feeling?"

She shrugs. "Not your business anymore."

This is getting me nowhere. I wish Adi was on my side with this one. She usually is, but Adi only likes drama that she's not involved in.

We eat our ice cream, her devouring hers and me picking at mine, and then head to Party Town just in time for it to open. The street is heaving with people. Our small town comes alive during any holiday and Halloween is the biggest of the year.

Pumpkins, spiders, ghosts, and bats adorn every shop window and door. Small children are already running around in costume despite it not being Halloween until next weekend. To be fair, they've been at it for the last two weeks.

I remember dressing up the second October began when I was younger.

I loved the lead-up, the costume shopping, and the decorating. Mom and I always got spooky designs painted on our nails. Mine were black with white ghosts. Hers white with pumpkins.

It used to be my favorite holiday.

Adi and I walk past a group of people apple bobbing on the

square, some sort of fundraiser. The mayor is dressed in a Cruella de Vil costume and filling buckets with bright green apples.

It's hard to believe that our town was tainted with horror only a year ago when you see people celebrating. Jackson had always been a bit of a loner, nothing like Nash and Grace, who were popular in school. He owned a scrapyard on his property rather than farming on it, and kept to himself.

He never came into town much, only to get groceries or run errands. My parents never loved me going to Nash's house because they hadn't really met his dad. But he was kind to me, and you can hardly hold it against someone for being a private person.

That is, until they start murdering kids.

Nash said that his dad was happy and had friends who weren't nearby.

I never saw them, and how could he have been happy when he was all alone? But I was always met with a smile and a hot chocolate. He made small talk and encouraged me to go for Juilliard.

We pass the phoenix again and I keep my eyes down this time, not wanting Adi to say anything else about Nash.

Just past the statue is the pretty yellow-brick grocery store with its stack of newspapers outside.

The headline on the front page today reads ANNIVERSARY OF FIRST BRUTAL HALLOWEEN MURDER.

Adi links our arms. "Look, are you okay with the Nash Situation? You know, not seeing him?" she asks, spotting me looking back at the memorial.

My friends all refer to the murders as the Nash Situation. I want to scream that it should be the Jackson Situation, but each time I've brought that up, it didn't end well.

People our age died and that's all that will ever matter.

Nash and Grace are collateral damage.

It *sucks.*

"Why do you care? You told me to forget him thirty minutes ago."

I sound like a whiny five-year-old.

"That's what you *should* do. I'm trying to be a good friend here. I'm sorry I was so abrupt earlier. You can talk to me about him if you need to."

"Why the one-eighty?"

"Because you look sad."

Great, now everyone can tell how I feel with one look. I can't count the number of times I heard whispers of "that one's Nash's girlfriend" since Jackson was arrested.

"Penny?" Adi prods.

"I'm fine."

"Cool, so you can start dating again," she says with a small smile, calling my bluff.

No, thanks.

"Looks pretty quiet in Party Town," I say. "It shouldn't take long to find something."

"Another dodge."

I ignore her and reach for the faded, chipped blue door. Some gargoyle-looking thing hangs on the glass like a wreath.

"It's locked."

Adi peers through the window. "We're right on time. Mrs. Vanderford must be running late."

I lean back against the brick, between the ghosts and skeletons, and wait. "She's probably dealing with Karter's latest stunt."

The shop owner's son, who I unfortunately share three classes with, is a huge bully. He walks around angry, picking fights and telling others what to do. Adi dated him for five minutes when we first started high school, but she soon realized he's a douchebag.

"Girls, I'm coming!" Mrs. Vanderford calls from across the road.

A few more people join us to wait for the store to open. Another girl from school, Mae, her group of friends, and some younger kids.

"So sorry, everyone," she says, panting as she unlocks the door. "Car trouble this morning. Come on in."

We filter into the store and hear her mutter something to herself about the alarm not being on and how her son, Karter, must've forgotten again.

I look over my shoulder to see her shaking her head and ranting about him being irresponsible. Her bad for trusting him, really. I wouldn't trust him to babysit an egg.

Costumes hang from every wall and on racks in between. There's a long section for decorations. Creepy organ music drifts through the store as Mrs. Vanderford slips behind the counter.

Cobwebs hang from the ceiling above me, adorned with black plastic spiders.

Adi leads us deeper into the store and we split up, each of us going to opposite sides of the same rack.

We start in the middle where all the big costumes are. There will be puffy corpse bride dresses along here, I'm sure.

Mae walks past, stopping beside me. "Hi, Penny."

"Hey. What're you here for?"

"We're all going as blood-soaked cheerleaders this year." She rolls her eyes. "Not my idea but it'll be fun."

"Nice. Hey, did you need my environmental science notes?"

"Please! Can I grab them at school Monday?"

"Sure."

She gives me another wave as she heads to her group; one girl is holding up a blue cheerleader costume and the other red.

There's about to be an argument.

I scrunch my nose and call over to Adi on the other side of the rack. "You smell something weird?"

"Probably that," she replies, pointing to Mrs. Vanderford, who's scowling and dumping a takeout box into the trash.

Karter's dinner probably.

"Babe, here's a good one. Mix of black and white," she says, holding it up, but I still can't see a lot of it. We're right in the middle of the aisle that stretches almost the length of the store.

I part the costumes in front of me because it'll be quicker than going around.

As I step forward, my foot kicks something solid.

"Ah. Hold on," I mutter to Adi, and look down.

The first thing that I see is an arm and my brain tries hard to convince me it's a mannequin.

But it's not. I can tell from the red patch of blood seeping through his white shirt.

Screaming, I leap back and slap my hand over my mouth.

"Penny, what the hell!" Adi's voice sounds like she's suddenly miles away.

I back up, almost tripping over myself until I hit the wall and slide to the floor. My eyes fix on the body in front of me. I can't even blink.

Mrs. Vanderford and another employee run toward me, and other shoppers crane their necks to see what the dramatic girl is screaming about.

I gag against my fist as I spot the body's dead eyes staring up at nothing. I recognize him—Noah. Another classmate of ours.

Adi screams and grabs hold of me, pulling my arm up as she tries to get me to stand. "Oh my god! What the . . . Is he *dead*?"

I vaguely hear her words over the ringing in my ears.

Yeah, he's *really* dead. There's blood all over his chest and now I can see that there are a couple darker patches. And the smell. That's what it was, not Karter's takeout.

I think he was stabbed.

"Stop looking, Penny!" Adi scolds, yanking me to my feet. I stand, wobbly, my legs almost unable to support my weight.

"Everyone outside," Mrs. Vanderford says, her voice robotic after the shock. "Come on, outside now. Karen, call . . . call the police."

Adi and I stumble through the store. I walk in a daze as we make it outside and into the crisp fall morning air. I gasp a mouthful of oxygen and my hands tremble in my pockets as I stare at the phoenix in the square, trying to make sense of what I just saw.

"It's happening again," Adi whispers, huddling close to me.

I blink a few times and listen to my pulse thumping in my ears. I'm only semi-aware of my surroundings, the small crowd that's forming outside the store and the whispers of disbelief.

Mae and her friends exit with tear-stained cheeks, no doubt having seen *the body* on their way out.

"Penny!" Adi calls, shaking my arm. "Snap out of it!"

Shaking my head, I turn to her and mutter, "Wh-what?"

"It's happening again. The murders."

"No," I breathe. Straightening my back, I say, "No. Jackson's serving a life sentence in a *federal* prison in Pennsylvania. He's locked up and two states away."

"Yeah . . . but his kids aren't."

I yank my arm out of hers, wishing I could walk away from here, away from her and everyone else. I stare at Adi in disbelief. "Nash isn't behind this."

My lungs resist as I try to suck in enough oxygen. The feeling of being totally helpless is all-consuming.

Adi doesn't respond but she does move away from me and closer to Mae's group, who are now outside with us.

I can't believe that Nash would ever hurt anyone.

This can't be him.

He's *nothing* like his dad.

He wouldn't do that.

I turn around to put as much distance between me and Adi's confusing accusation as possible. That's when I see him. Between the little bookstore and the pharmacy, facing Party Town and staring straight at me.

Nash.

STAY UP ALL NIGHT WITH THESE UNPUTDOWNABLE READS!